TREASON!

Jefferson's grenade exploded in the middle of the machine gun nest, but the firing didn't stop—it merely changed direction. The ground around him began to explode. He leaped to his feet, firing on full automatic, emptying his weapon. The aliens dropped their weapons and ran for safety.

He approached the enemy warehouse with caution. He dove through the opening, rolled to the right, and came up on one knee. There were no soldiers inside. Just huge piles of equipment shipped from Earth. Jefferson didn't believe what he was seeing. It had been delivered to the enemy by their *own* shuttle . . .

JEFFERSON'S WAR
THE GALACTIC SILVER STAR

KEVIN RANDLE

ACE BOOKS, NEW YORK

This book is an Ace original edition,
and has never been previously published.

THE GALACTIC SILVER STAR

An Ace Book / published by arrangement with
the author

PRINTING HISTORY
Ace edition / August 1990

ISBN: 0-441-27242-8

Ace Books are published by The Berkley Publishing Group,
200 Madison Avenue, New York, New York 10016.
The name "ACE" and the "A" logo
are trademarks belonging to Charter Communications, Inc.

PRINTED IN THE UNITED STATES OF AMERICA

10 9 8 7 6 5 4 3 2 1

JEFFERSON'S WAR

THE GALACTIC SILVER STAR

PROLOGUE

DENEB THREE

THE DRAGON TEETH that lined one end of the rain-soaked, fog-shrouded valley looked like something that belonged in the Second World War on old Earth. Directly in front of them were several strands of concertina wiring swinging in the wind generated by the on-going thunderstorm, and behind that, outlined by the flashing of green-gold lightning was a concrete pillbox that could rake the whole approach with machine gun, laser, and mortar fire. On the far side of the valley, just visible through the sheets of dark rain, was an open plain that would allow the tanks to spread out and engulf the majority of the alien infantry, if they could get through.

Second Lieutenant David Steven Jefferson crouched in the thick mud behind one of the dragon teeth and watched as the machine gun probed again. Flashes of orange from the muzzle and then streaks of bright red from the tracers, some of them striking the wet ground and then tumbling skyward. Jefferson didn't move as the rounds came close, splashing him with mud.

"Okay, Lieutenant," yelled Staff Sergeant Richard Mason. He had to raise his voice to be heard over the hammering of the distant gun and the crashing of the thunder that masked the enemy movements. "Okay," he repeated. "You got us into this. How the hell you going to get us out?"

Jefferson nodded because it was a good question. Unfortunately he didn't have a good answer. He had run several ideas through his mind as he lay there, his breath whistling through his clenched teeth, and his fingers digging into the soft mud beside him.

He'd thought of a full frontal assault, or rather as much of one as could be provided by thirty men and women, and then rejected the idea. He'd thought of a suicide attack up the center, using the cover that was available while the rest of the platoon provided covering fire.

The suicide attack seemed like the best idea because it exposed the fewest people to the risk, but he didn't want to assign anyone to the suicide part and he didn't want to go himself. So he crouched there, in a puddle of water, and didn't say anything as the sky opened and the rain washed down in pelting sheets.

"We'd better do something," shouted Mason. "We're not the only ones out here."

Jefferson looked to the rear, where Mason and the first squad were spread out among the dragon teeth and mud. "I don't need you to remind me of my job," snapped Jefferson.

"Yes, sir, Lieutenant, sir."

Jefferson waved a hand and then yelled, "In three minutes I want everyone to open fire with everything we have."

"Won't do any good. The sides are sloped so that bullets bounce off. All we'll do is identify our position for the enemy."

"Just do it," ordered Jefferson.

"Yes sir."

Jefferson twisted around as another burst cut through the night. Angry red tracers lanced through the darkness, striking the water-soaked ground. Dull pops of mortars fell far short, their detonations lost in the flashing lightning and the crashing thunder.

This hadn't been covered in ROTC, thought Jefferson. Small-unit tactics, fire-and-maneuver, and massed assault had been discussed, but not how to take out a single pillbox when electrical storms were playing hell with the electronics, when rain had soaked through the environmental cases of the radios, and the platoon had been given instructions that didn't allow for independent action. Jefferson slipped down, his face inches from the muddy water that was soaking into his uniform, causing him to shiver.

He didn't want to look at the people behind him, waiting for him to decide something. He wasn't all that much older than them. Like him, most of them were young, just out of what would have been high school, if they had been allowed the opportunity to attend high school. Their khaki, brown, and rust-colored uniforms were plastered against their bodies by the rain. Each held a semi-automatic rifle, carried three hand grenades, and one combat dagger. There were two machine guns assigned, a three-point-five-inch rocket launcher, and eight automatic weapons. Second World War weapons for a culture that had barely entered the industrial age. Army rules dictated that they introduce nothing that was too far advanced. Didn't want to give the aliens ideas. Didn't want to mess up their culture and their history.

"Okay," shouted Mason, "we shoot at them. What good does that do us?"

Jefferson squeezed his eyes shut, trying to blank the scene from his mind. When that failed, he turned slightly and hissed, "While the platoon is providing covering fire, I'm going to crawl forward so that I can toss a satchel charge into the firing port."

"Sure you are. And then John Wayne will lead the cavalry over the hill."

"If you have nothing constructive to say," shouted Jefferson, "keep your damned mouth shut."

Mason stood up then, dived forward and landed near Jefferson. He hit with a splash and slid, almost into the concertina. Spinning in the soft mud, he scrambled back, under cover.

"This idea really sucks, Lieutenant," said Mason.

"Okay, smart ass, give me a better one."

Mason stared into the hard eyes of the young lieutenant. Hard, frightened eyes, and realized that the lieutenant had been brought up on John Wayne and Clint Eastwood. They were men who regularly defied military logic and came out of it the hero. There was nothing he could say that would convince Jefferson that he shouldn't crawl out into the wet night with a satchel charge. It was what John Wayne would do and arguing about it would do nothing except make the lieutenant mad.

"No," said Mason. "I don't have a better idea."

Jefferson reached up and grabbed his wet helmet. Water dripped from the front of it. His features were hidden behind the camouflage grease paint he had smeared on his face and the mud that had splattered there.

"Take more than one satchel and get as close as you can."

"Managed to think of that all by myself."

Mason lay there for a moment, the sound of the rain beating down on them and the dragon's teeth. Finally he turned and crawled to the rear, among the men and women of the platoon hidden there, giving them their assignments. He waited, watching, until Jefferson was opposite the depression, but still among the dragon teeth. When the lieutenant was ready, Mason raised his weapon. He opened fire, signaling the others to begin laying down the protective cover.

For nearly a full minute after the shooting began, Jefferson was unable to move, almost unable to breathe. His arms and legs seemed to be frozen to the muddy ground. He kept his face pressed into the mud and his eyes squeezed shut. He pretended that he couldn't hear the firing behind him.

The pillbox answered with a withering fire of multicolored tracers that snapped overhead. When Jefferson finally opened his eyes, he could see the enemy bullets chewing their way through the dragon teeth, chipping away at the concrete and ripping at the mud. The machine gun and rifle fire was periodically punctuated by explosions from mortars placed at the rear of the pillbox.

After what seemed to be seconds to Jefferson, he heard an angry voice behind him.

"What the fuck are you doing? You hit?"

Jefferson kept his head down, using his eyes to survey the area in front of him, watching the spectacular pyrotechnics of combat in the growing twilight. He wanted to answer, but couldn't find his voice.

A moment later he was touched. Still he didn't move until a hand reached under his shoulder and tried to roll him over. Then he hissed, "Leave me alone, you rotten son of a bitch."

"Great. Just fucking great," whispered Mason. "They saddle me with a kid lieutenant who's afraid of everything. Okay, dumbshit, let me have the satchels and I'll go kill the pillbox for you. I'll make you a fucking hero."

Mason crawled forward so that he was parallel with Jefferson. Keeping his head down, he reached for the satchel charge, but Jefferson had a death grip on it. Mason pulled at it, jerked once and then said, "Let go, asshole."

Now Jefferson turned his head so that he could see Mason. The rain had increased and there were occassional flashes of lightning like the strobing of a giant camera. Not the bluish-white of Earth, but a strange, golden-green that danced around the horizon or along the ridges above them, casting everything in an eerie, unnatural glow.

Mason gave a final, mighty tug, and jerked one of the satchels free. "You can stay here if you want. Nobody will know." With that Mason began to crawl off, toward the murky shape of the pillbox. If it hadn't been for the tracers and the lightning, they might have lost sight of it in the gloom created by the heavy rain.

When Mason was gone, Jefferson lay there, cursing himself for being a coward and for letting the sergeant do a job that he should be doing. But even the self-flagellation didn't mean that he could move. He tried to crawl forward a couple of times, but couldn't make his muscles obey. He kept thinking about how easy it would be to move. How simple it should be to ease his right leg forward and follow with his left. In his mind he could see it happening. A slow, steady motion that carried him along the depression, forward to the pillbox. But there seemed to be nothing that would translate that vision into reality. He felt tears of frustration and rage sting his eyes, but didn't care. He just wanted to move, to prove to himself that he wasn't a coward.

Then, as if it had a mind of its own, his left hand reached out and clawed at the muddy ground. He pulled himself after it, thinking that all he had to do was make an effort. Just show Mason that he could move forward if he really wanted to. That he really wasn't a coward.

Magically, his left leg followed and then his right. Suddenly he was in motion, his arms and legs moving in a coordinated effort. He kept going, no longer thinking about the pillbox or the shooting. He was concentrating on moving his body forward with his mind turned off.

And then reality was splattered all over him as a burst from the pillbox tore up the ground in front of him. The mud and water flew, stinging his face and eyes. He stopped moving, ducked, and was momentarily paralyzed.

But he had gotten closer to the pillbox. He could see the dark shape looming in front of him, but it was too far away for him to do anything about it. Besides, Mason was out there somewhere, and Jefferson was afraid that he might somehow kill Mason if he pressed on.

The thought washed over him like a comforting wave. He could do nothing because he no longer knew where Mason was. If he continued on, he might accidentally expose Mason. And he couldn't throw his satchel charge because Mason might be in the way. For the first time in days, Jefferson smiled.

A moment later there was a wild burst of firing. Jefferson carefully tilted his head so that he could see what was happening. Some of the fear that had paralyzed him evaporated, as the machine gun fire stitched through the night.

There was a bright flash that Jefferson thought was lightning, but the crash that followed was not thunder. Bits of concrete were suddenly raining down around him, and he realized that Mason had done it. He had gotten close enough to throw the satchel charge. All the firing was coming from the dragon teeth, and that was tapering as the platoon realized that the aliens' pillbox had blown up.

Jefferson didn't move for a long time. He waited and soon, Mason was back, keeping down because the enemy was still near. He spotted Jefferson and laughed at the mud-covered officer.

"Glad to see that you found some nerve, Lieutenant."

Jefferson got to his knees. "I was coming after you, but I had to be careful. I didn't want to give away your position."

"Sure, Lieutenant. Sure. Well, I appreciate it, anyway. And if I had missed, you would have been able to bring me that other charge."

"That's right."

"Well, great! Let's get back to the others. We've still got to sweep through here to make sure that we've cleared all the enemy."

The single shot caught Mason just below the rim of his helmet and exploded out the back of his head. Jefferson, at first, was confused by the bloodless third eye that had appeared on Mason's forehead. The sergeant was motionless for several seconds and then toppled over.

Jefferson scanned the area wildly, trying to see where the shot had come from. He grabbed his rifle and fired rapidly toward the enemy lines and then into the hills around them. When it was empty, he tossed it away and grabbed Mason by the shoulder, dragging him back, toward his own lines. He was trying to stay down, out of the field of fire and pull Mason through the mud. A sob burst from him.

As he neared his lines, he saw others appear around him and knew immediately that they were his men and women. The aliens, although about human height were extremely skinny. Even in the rainy night, there was no mistaking the two.

Hands were on him then, and on Mason, helping. Jefferson growled at them, but they ignored him, trying to get Mason back where he would be safe. None of them yet realized that Mason was dead.

One of the corporals, a large ugly man who had spent his time bad-mouthing their new lieutenant, now came forward. He said, quietly, almost gently, "Please, sir, let me give you a hand."

Dumbly, Jefferson let go of Mason and looked up, confused. He was crying harder now, out of frustration. Mason had managed to blow up the enemy pillbox, and then had died because he had stopped to talk to him. If anyone should be dead, Jefferson thought it should be him. Not Mason.

Someone else said, "You did it, Lieutenant. You did it!"

Jefferson didn't understand that. It would be hours before he would realize that everyone in his platoon thought that he had crawled out and blown up the pillbox. None of them knew that he had stopped far short and that Mason had actually done it. No one questioned him, and by the time he said anything about it, it was too late. The myth had been built by the video reporter. Mason had followed him, to lend support, but it was Jefferson who had crawled out there, according to the story that was circulating on the intership video.

And when he tried to set the record straight later, those who would listen thought that it was a final gesture for a friend killed in action. Jefferson was trying to reward Mason. No one would listen to him.

* * *

Three days later, the platoon, now in dress uniform, freshly shaved and showered, stood at attention while the commanding officer of the task group stood in front of them and read the citation slowly and distinctly. It seemed that Major David Steven Jefferson, newly promoted, had, through bravery above and beyond the call of duty, destroyed an enemy installation with minimum loss of life. Without regard to himself, he had crawled out in front of his platoon, exposing himself to concentrated enemy fire, and had blown up the pillbox. The only death in the action was Staff Sergeant Robert Mason who had followed the young officer out into the field in an attempt to support him. It was an amazing feat of bravery that had freed an entire battalion to attack the enemy. Jefferson's action was the key to winning the battle. It reflected great credit on himself, his unit, and the United States Army.

Next, they read the citation that outlined Mason's bravery. It was for a lesser award because his act had not been quite so great. It was posthumous.

When the official ceremony was over, the platoon whooped its approval of the awards. Several couldn't wait to tell Jefferson about their roles in securing the decoration for him. They all stood around, patting him on the back and congratulating him. Even the corporal who had hated him before the pillbox episode was there, explaining that he had initiated the citation. There was nothing too good for their lieutenant.

A final time, Jefferson tried to explain that he had been the one who had stayed back. It was Mason who had taken the chance. It was Mason who had blown up the pillbox. What Jefferson didn't know was that the Army preferred a live hero to a dead one. So, even if the platoon hadn't been sure that it was the lieutenant who had gone out first and who had blown up the pillbox, one of the brass hats would have found a way to make it so.

Just as the celebration was beginning to roll, and as Jefferson was beginning to unbend enough to admit to himself that the tall private with short brown hair was kind of attractive, the general moved to the center of the room one last time.

"I have one more announcement. I know that none of you will like it, but there is nothing that can be done. As of the 27th of the month, Major David Steven Jefferson is assigned as the battalion commander of the 767th Maneuver Battalion."

To halt the gasps and mumbling, the general held up his hands. "I would like nothing better than to leave Major Jefferson as your platoon leader, but we can't have a major commanding a platoon. Besides, he has abilities that demand we move him up. I know that you all will approve of the promotion because it is the best for the Army."

Jefferson was secretly pleased. He saw it as his way out of the hole he felt himself in. To the others, he expressed his disappointment, but said, "You know the Army. No good deed goes unpunished."

An hour later, with the party in full swing and everyone totally drunk, Jefferson, escorting the tall private with the short brown hair, slipped away. Neither was missed until the next morning.

1

ON BOARD THE FLEET STARSHIP

MAJOR DAVID STEVEN Jefferson sat in the miniature office that was his battalion headquarters while they were on the ship. It was barely big enough for him: a small table that served as a desk that held a built-in keyboard, a small screen for information retrieval, a printer, and a narrow chair for a visitor, in case one showed up. Everything was molded plastic, including the bulkheads, floor, and ceiling. The ceiling was translucent, letting light through. Above the hatch that served as a door was a digital clock snapping off the minutes.

Sitting there, alone, Jefferson wasn't sure what he was supposed to be doing. Actually, he was trying to review the personnel records of his top staff people, but he felt like a thief. It was an irrational feeling because he was authorized to review the records; it was just that having been commissioned only three months before, and then suddenly promoted to major and given a battalion to command, he didn't have a solid background. He was not used to seeing the records of other officers because only COs and personnel officers normally saw the files of others.

The light knock at his door got his attention.

"Yeah?"

A voice from outside said, "Captain Torrence to see you, sir."

"Send . . ." Jefferson hesitated, not knowing if Torrence was male or female. Quickly he typed Torrence's name into his computer, saw that Torrence was a woman and said, "Send her in, please."

He turned from the computer screen and watched her enter. From the file, he knew that she was five seven, and now he could see she had long brown hair, and was wearing a full uniform of dark brown that had been carefully tailored to her. This struck him as odd because very few of the people in his battalion wore full uniforms. They opted for comfort when possible.

"Captain Victoria Torrence reporting," she said.

Jefferson returned her salute, unsure of what to do. He glanced at the screen, scanned the information displayed there and then waved a hand at her. "Ah, please. Have a seat, Victoria. Or do they call you Vicky?"

Torrence sat down stiffly, folded her hands in her lap and stared at him. "Vicky. Or Victoria. Either is fine, sir."

"You're the executive officer."

"Yes, sir."

Jefferson touched a button and scrolled on down. All he saw were facts and figures. Dates for the completion of various military schools, awards, including one for bravery on Cetus Tau Six, dates of assignments, and qualifications. An impressive record that told him nothing of the person. "Well," he said finally, "I guess the one thing for us to do is to get to know one another."

"Yes, sir," agreed Torrence. She crossed her legs and leaned back slowly, relaxing slightly. Idly, she plucked at the crease in her trousers.

"Maybe you'd like to tell me something about yourself."

"Not a whole lot to tell."

"Must be something," said Jefferson, pressing. He suddenly felt like a high school student, trying to impress the head cheerleader. To cover his embarrassment, he continued. "After all, you've been made the executive officer of a battalion. That suggests that you have something on the ball."

"Well, sir, I'm from a little town in Missouri. Grew up there, went to college in Kansas and took ROTC. Joined the Army to see the world and have seen too many of them now.

Didn't realize that Ryerson was going to ruin my life. Then I . . ."

"You're pretty flip about it," said Jefferson interrupting.

"Maybe," she said, "but I'm very good at my job and Major Chamberlin had no complaints."

"I wasn't implying any complaint. I was commenting on an attitude."

"Yes, sir." She shifted around, glanced at the deck and then back up toward Jefferson. "My major in college was astronomy, so it is somewhat coincidental that I ended up flying among the stars. I had hoped that astronomy would get me into astronaut training." She smiled briefly. "Funny how some things work out."

"Yes," agreed Jefferson. He kept his eyes on the computer screen. He then glanced at Torrence. "Why is it that no one in this battalion wears a uniform?"

Torrence laughed out loud. "I guess that is an outgrowth of our last assignment on Cetus Tau Six. Damned planet had a average temperature of about a hundred and ten degrees. When we weren't on duty it seemed easier, cooler to wear T-shirts and shorts, if that much. That's why we had the arm bands with rank insignia on them made up. Now it's sort of a tradition that we brought with us."

"Tradition."

"You're not planning to change it are you, sir?"

"Right now I don't plan to make any major changes. I want to look over the standing orders and operational procedures before I start making wholesale changes."

Torrence sat forward, uncrossing her legs and putting both feet flat on the floor. She rubbed her hands on her thighs as if the palms were wet. "Major," she said, glanced at the nameplate on his desk and then continued, "Major Jefferson, maybe I shouldn't say anything at all."

Jefferson waved a hand. "You shouldn't be afraid to say anything to me."

"Yes, sir," said Torrence, nodding. She shrugged and then plunged ahead. "I think you should know that there are some people in the battalion who aren't happy about this."

"Happy about what?"

"This assignment. Your assignment here." She stared at him and pressed on quickly. "Some of us, some of them, think that the new commander should have been promoted from within. The majority of us have been together for two or three years. We know one another and work well together."

"Uh-huh."

"There are qualified people in the battalion. At least a dozen officers who could command."

"And you're one of them."

"Yes, sir," nodded Torrence. "I think I could. But it's not that. . . ."

"Listen, Captain!" snapped Jefferson. "I'm in command here now. I don't need you blowing in here to tell me that I shouldn't be. I earned this job."

"Yes sir, I'm sure you did."

"I've been going through this same thing ever since I won that damned medal. People telling me that I'm lucky. Telling me not to screw up. Telling me that they have their eyes on me." His voice was rising, the anger becoming unmistakable.

"Sir, I didn't mean . . ."

"But this is just what I expected. I knew you people would be like this. I just knew it."

"Sir," said Torrence trying to break in. She had only wanted him to know that some of the officers were resentful so that he could prepare to deal with it. "Major, I didn't mean to suggest that I wanted the job. I thought . . ."

"You're not paid to think," shouted Jefferson. "I'm the one who is paid to think. You're paid to obey."

"Sir."

"I think this interview is *over*, Captain." He emphasized the word, making it sound like something unpleasant.

Torrence sat there for a moment and then stood up. "Yes, sir."

Jefferson ignored her salute. He stared at the screen, suddenly fascinated by what he saw there. He was vaguely aware that she was there. After a few moments, she turned and exited.

Outside the hatch, Torrence closed her eyes and took a deep breath.

"Well?" asked Captain Judy Sinclair. She was a tall, skinny woman with jet black hair. There was a long, white scar on her shoulder that was visible because Sinclair was wearing only a sleeveless T-shirt and shorts. Her captain bars were fastened to an arm band.

Torrence opened her eyes, glanced at Sinclair and then at Jason Lynn. He was a young man, not much older than the major, but with a hard look in his eyes. Like Sinclair, he was thin and like her, had black hair.

Torrence ran a hand through her hair, as if to pull it back off her face. "I think we're going to be in real trouble with this clown. I don't think he's got the faintest idea of what he's supposed to be doing."

"Come on, Vicky," said Sinclair. "He can't be that bad."

"He blew up when I suggested that there was some resentment about his promotion."

"Good God! You told him that?" Sinclair rolled her eyes. "No wonder he blew up."

"I was just trying to get him to cut us some slack."

"I'm sure he'll be happy to, now," said Lynn.

"Besides," said Sinclair, "he's going to know there will be resentment. You didn't have to tell him that. Probably made him feel real welcome."

"I was trying to get things off on the right foot," said Torrence.

"Sometimes," said Sinclair, "you do some real stupid things."

After Torrence closed the door to his office, Jefferson slammed a hand down onto the molded plastic desk. He swept everything from the top of his desk and kicked at the debris. He spun and looked up at the holographic print from an old army lithograph called the *Wagon Box Fight*.

There were so many things that he didn't understand. So many things that he hadn't been given the time to learn. It seemed that one minute he was crawling through the mud on some second-rate planet and the next he was standing on the brightly lit hangar deck, a band to the right and the general staff in front of him. Martial music, flags waving, and the general handing him, pinning the medal, to his chest. None of it made sense.

He wished, for the thousandth time, that Mason hadn't been killed. The big staff sergeant would have sat across from him and made a series of sarcastic remarks, but, at the very least, he would have known what to do. Jefferson felt lost, mixed in with people he didn't know and who didn't like him.

The one thing that he had learned from Mason was that you couldn't show weakness. Image was all important. If the image slipped, the troops would be on you like buzzards on a rotting carcass.

For a moment he sat there, his head in his hands, wishing that he had been killed along with Mason. That would have made everything so simple. But then, slowly he began to get angry. Who in the hell were these people to question him? Who were they to say they resented his being given command? He didn't have to prove a thing to them. *They* had to prove it to *him*.

He stood up, jerked at the hem of his tunic, and started toward the hatch. Then, remembering who he was, he dropped back into his molded plastic chair. "Sergeant," he bellowed, "get your butt in here."

A second later the hatch flew open and the sergeant stood there, at rigid attention. "Yes, sir."

"I want a staff meeting, senior officers and company commanders, in ten minutes."

"Yes, sir. In the staff conference lounge?"

Jefferson hesitated for an instant and then nodded. "Of course." He didn't have the faintest idea of where that might be, but he wasn't about to admit that to the NCO. He just hoped he could find it easily.

Twelve minutes later he found the conference lounge and opened the hatch. Inside, in the muted glow of recessed lights, seated around a long, highly polished tabled, were the staff officers. All were dressed in dark brown uniforms, black shoes, and wearing all their awards and decorations. Someone had jumped through hoops to get them all assembled, in dress uniforms, in under fifteen minutes.

As Jefferson opened the hatch, one of the officers said, "Ladies and gentlemen, the commander."

They all got to their feet and Jefferson moved across the soft carpeting of the lounge to sit in the chair reserved for the CO. Before saying anything to the others, he looked across the table at what happened to be a huge window that showed deep space. Distant stars and a couple of planets, one of them with rings like Saturn's. Off to one side was the remainder of the fleet, visible as glowing specks.

Finally, almost as if it were an afterthought, he said, "Please. Be seated."

Carefully he looked from one face to the next, trying to read something about each of the officers. He should have taken the time to read the files on each of them before calling the meeting, but he hadn't thought of that. Their faces revealed nothing about them.

"Captain Torrence," he said quietly, "would you be kind enough to introduce the others?"

Torrence nodded and gestured across the table. "These are your company commanders: Captain Sinclair, Captain Mitchell, Lieutenant Lynn, and Lieutenant Rider." She turned and pointed at the others at the far end of the table. "This is Lieutenant Winston, your S-1. Next is Lieutenant Carter, the S-2, Captain Peyton, the S-3 and finally Lieutenant Norris, the S-4."

Jefferson nodded at each of them in turn, but refused to smile at them. His eyes lingered on Norris because she looked to be younger than he was, and she had pretty eyes. Deep blue eyes.

When the introductions were finished, Jefferson said, "I don't know what you people have been told about me, but it doesn't matter now. We find ourselves stuck with one another, so we're going to have to get along. I will tell you that I do know something about small-unit tactics and I know something about combat operations and that's probably why I was given this assignment."

He stopped talking, waited, and then hoped that one of them would have something to say, but the silence stretched until it hung in the air like yesterday's laundry. When he'd entered, he had been angry, but the anger had evaporated, leaving him with nothing to say.

Finally, to break the silence, he said, "I think that we can work together." He held up his hands, as if in surrender. "I know that everyone here was fond of Major Chamberlin, and everyone was shocked when he was killed. But that accident should have nothing to do with our relationship. There is no reason for us to blame one another for that. All we can do is make the best of a bad situation." As he said that, he wished he could bite his tongue. It wasn't a bad situation. It was just the way things were. To try to distract them he said, quickly, "Until I have a chance to review the policies and procedures, all standing orders will remain in effect."

Again there was a long silence. Jefferson looked around the table and then stared at Norris. "You're supply?"

"Yes, sir."

"You got everything you're supposed to have?"

"Last survey was run right after we redeployed to the ship. All battalion equipment that was lost on Cetus Tau Six has been replaced. Some of the older stuff needs to be repaired, but we have everything we need."

"I'd like to have it all up to speed in the next week."

Norris shrugged, not understanding why it had to be done quickly. "Yes, sir."

Turning to Winston, he asked, "We up to the TO and E?"

"Full strength now that you've joined us, Major. Oh, we're missing a couple of people here and there but nothing that would affect our combat efficiency."

Jefferson went around the table like that, asking each of the officers a question or two about his or her job or company. He tried to fix names with the faces, but seemed to forget the names as soon as the person was introduced to him.

Finished with that, he turned toward Torrence and said, "Let's see if we can get the people to dress in a more military manner—at least when the divisional commander is around."

"Yes, sir."

Jefferson nodded and then said, "Now that I've had the chance to shoot my mouth off, would any of you care to have the chance to do the same?"

The officers around the table looked at one another waiting for someone else to break the ice, but no one spoke. For an instant it looked as if Torrence was about to say something, but the moment passed before she could speak.

"All right, then," said Jefferson, standing. "I will be calling on each of you separately in the next few days." He stood, looking at them and then turned on his heel, walking out.

As soon as the hatch was closed, Carter, one of the youngest, said, "Christ. What a jerk. Sounded like he read the manual that said you have to take an interest in each of your subordinates."

"That's not going to help us," said Torrence. "He's going to be around here for a while."

"He's still a jerk," said Carter.

"If you don't have something constructive to say, keep your mouth shut," warned Torrence. "Now, if there is any problem between us and him, I'll absorb it. That's my job. The rest of you have to do your best to make him feel welcome."

"That's not going to be easy," said Rider. He was junior among the company commanders. "He's not . . ."

The interruption this time came from the public address system. The metallic voice of a divisional clerk said, "Attention please. All officers and senior enlisted personnel from the Seven Sixty-seventh Maneuver Battalion are asked to report to the main briefing room. Formal briefing to begin in thirty minutes."

Torrence looked at the rest of the staff and said, "You heard that. Let's roll out."

"What about the major?" asked Peyton.

"The major will find his way there, I'm sure," said Torrence, ignoring the real question.

The briefing room, which held about a hundred officers and NCOs was crowded when Jefferson arrived. It was set up like a movie theater back on Earth with high-backed chairs facing a raised platform and holotank in the front. Jefferson walked down a narrow, carpeted aisle, past the NCOs, to the front where the officers waited. To one side of them was a single, empty seat, which Jefferson figured was his. He moved to it and sat down.

The chairs were narrow, soft, with high backs that partially wrapped around the head and shoulders. There was a thick lap strap, rather like a seat belt, made of molded plastic and containing a variety of controls.

As soon as Jefferson sat down and had pulled his lap strap into position, the lights dimmed. An officer, dressed in a dark brown uniform walked to the center of the raised platform. As he reached his position, the holotank flashed once as a mist appeared, swirled, and then began to solidify into an image of the fleet's crest.

"Good afternoon," said the officer at the front. "I'm Lieutenant Colonel Karl Streeter, the Division Intel officer.

This briefing, in accordance with various military regulations is classified as secret. It will not be discussed with those not cleared to hear it."

He stopped long enough for the holotank to shift again, this time displaying a star system. Using a light wand he had carried with him, he pointed at the star system.

"Recent mapping surveys revealed a series of inhabitable planets circling the Class M star here. Exploration resulted in contact with the intelligent lifeforms and diplomatic contact resulted in a request for military and economic assistances."

Before anyone could ask a question about the request for military and economic assistance, Streeter rushed on. The image next to him vanished and the clouds of the glowing gas swirled and then coalesced into the form of a humanoid.

"The inhabitants of the planet, as you can see, are very tall, measuring between seven and eight feet. They have light blue skin with a yellowish fuzz that covers the whole body, growing longest on the head, the chin, and from the shoulders to the wrists." He used the light wand again. "The hands have three digits and an opposed thumb. They all, male and female, wear a poncho-like garment and pants underneath. The very young wear just the poncho."

Again, the holograph shimmered, dissolved, and solidified. This time it showed a planet spinning on its axis.

"The planet has three major factions fighting one another for supremacy. One group on each of the three major continents. These continents are connected by isthmuses. The planet is a third again the size of the Earth, so gravity is higher than Earth normal. There is also a higher oxygen content.

"The environment is hot and humid, running about a hundred, a hundred five degrees Farenheit with a correspondingly high humidity. This is a hot, wet world and because of that there are vast areas of rain forest and swamp, and very little dry land."

Again the picture dissolved and then solidified, becoming a map of one of the continents.

"There are few large cities. These are situated mainly along the coasts. The agricultural areas generally lie from the coastal plains toward the hills. These are surrounded by the swamps. There is some farming in the hills, but the locals seem to prefer to stay close to the coasts. Complete details will be provided before planetfall. Our current information is sketchy, but we have a couple of drones traveling toward the planet for a remote fly-by."

The holograph image faded and vanished. Streeter moved away from the tank as the lights came up. Looking at the audience, he said, "This mission is the normal support package for locals who request aid and who advocate a democratic policy.

"This package will contain arms, training, and support personnel. Our role is advisory. The locals will be in control of their own military forces and will operate on their own terms."

Streeter nodded and the holotank flashed, showing the chain of command throughout the entire battalion. "You can see that the battalion will be broken down to its major elements for this mission. Battalion headquarters and the headquarters company will establish a main base. Once that is accomplished, each of the line companies will be detached to establish more bases along the main lines of communication. Training of aliens will begin just as soon as possible."

With that, Streetcar paused and Carter interjected, "What about the alien's language?"

"During the upcoming two-week training phase, you will all be rotated into the hypo tanks for a crash language course. You won't be fluent, but you will be able to communicate. The S-2, and several of the NCOs will be given more extensive training."

Streeter looked down at Jefferson. "Major, what's the level of training in your battalion?"

Before Jefferson could speak, Torrence spoke up. She glanced at Jefferson but didn't give him a chance to say a word. "We've undergone a series of stiff exercises during the last seven weeks. Prior to that we were stationed on Cetus Tau Six. That was a normal support mission, although we didn't have to build from the ground up. It was a divisional-level mission. We've had very few replacements or transfers in the last two years so the whole unit is experienced."

Streeter listened to the report, nodding periodically. He looked at Jefferson once, but said nothing to him. When Torrence finished, he said, "Thank you, Captain. That tells me that I don't have to lay everything out in minute detail."

"Yes, sir," agreed Torrence. She hadn't noticed that Jefferson was burning. She said to Streeter, "What about maps, the terrain, the major cities?"

"As I said, we have the recon probes out now. We'll know more about the planet once we receive that information. The landing zones, as soon as they are determined, will be announced."

From the rear, someone shouted, "What about disease?"

"Again, we'll know more once the recon is finished. But, remember, there has been some contact between us and the aliens and no new diseases have been detected." Streeter didn't bother to mention that the latest scientific thought was that humans would not be able to catch alien diseases because the biological systems were too diverse. He let them think that the probes were checking on it.

"What weapons will we be using?" shouted someone else.

"Probably use the standard assault rifle and projectile-type bullets. Contact has been kept to a minimum, so we don't want to introduce anything that is too far advanced. The level of introduction should be circa mid-twentieth century, or a little earlier. We're going to stay away from the laser weapons, cluster bombs, sonic disruptors, and the like. We may use some aircraft in a recon role as opposed to close air support or strategic bombing."

Finally Jefferson had a question. "How many other units will be involved?"

"Right now, we don't plan to use anyone else. We don't anticipate any problems that would require anyone other than your battalion to handle them."

Another voice began a question. "What about . . ."

"Please," yelled Streeter. "I think that everything will be covered in the pre-planetfall briefing. There are two weeks before we land. Division is planning a series of exercises that will incorporate the local environmental features. Anything that we learn during the next two weeks will be included."

Streeter continued in that vein for another fifteen or twenty minutes. Jefferson thought of dozens of questions as Streeter talked, but didn't interrupt to ask them. He figured that as more information became available, it would be given to him. As the reports from the probes came in, Division would let him know. In fact, he could tell Carter to check with Division so that they wouldn't miss anything. They had two weeks to prepare, and there was no way to learn everything they had to know in the next hour.

At last Streeter began to wind down, but he had talked for so long that when he asked if there were any more questions, no one said anything. He thanked them for their time and obvious interest and told them that he would see to it they got any new information that would be of interest. He then cautioned them again that the briefing was classified, and escaped to the right.

Jefferson stood then and watched the men and women of his battalion exit. Most of them he had never seen before, and was suddenly frightened to realize that the majority of the battalion hadn't even been in the briefing. There were hundreds of men and women in the battalion and he didn't know one percent of them. Soon he would be making decisions that could kill them.

As Torrence stood to leave, Jefferson said, "Captain, I would like to speak to you for a moment."

They stood quietly for a couple of minutes, watching the rest leave. Torrence wasn't sure what to make of it. She could tell that Jefferson was annoyed about something, and she tried to think of what she might have done. They had already had words about her attitude but she didn't think that Jefferson would want to bring that up again.

When they were alone, Jefferson turned to her, his face bright red. "Who in the hell do you think you are? Just who in the hell?"

"I'm sorry," sputtered Torrence. "I don't know what you're talking about."

"You don't know," shouted Jefferson. "The Division intelligence officer comes down here and asks about the level of training, and you stand up to sharpshoot."

"I didn't mean to sharpshoot. I just thought that since you were new, you might not be completely familiar with the training of the battalion. I was only trying to help. Coordination of the training effort is one of the primary responsibilities of the executive officer."

"Come on, Torrence. I wasn't born yesterday. I know what you're thinking. You're thinking that there is still time for Division to repair the damage it did by putting me in here, and give the job to someone who deserves it. Well, it's not going to be that easy. I'm going to have my eye on you and if I find the slightest reason, I'm bouncing your ass out of here. You got that?"

"I'm sorry. I didn't think. I was . . ."

"That's right. You didn't think. And let's have a *sir* at the end of those sentences. You got that?"

"Yes, sir."

After Jefferson left, Torrence stood there, nearly shaking, unable to speak. She was dizzy, and sick to her stomach. She wished there was something she could do to change the way the relationship with Jefferson had started, but now everything she did seemed to be wrong.

2

IN SPACE WITH THE MAIN FLEET

THE SIMULATOR SHIP could be attached and detached, moving through the fleet to link with vessels where there were training requirements. Originally it had been a colony ship, hauling thousands of Earth men, women, and children among the planets of the solar system. First they had gone to Mars, later to Venus, and then spread out among asteroids before moving to the moons of Jupiter and Saturn. When the interstellar distances were eliminated by the invention of the Ryerson Drive, the ships were converted to it, and the coming of the wars had demanded a second conversion. Now some of them housed the men and women of the army and navy, and others were used for training or carrying material, while surrounded by warships designed for interstellar travel and protection of the unarmed transports.

Orders from Division had moved Jefferson's battalion from its semi-comfortable quarters on the battalion ship, and into the training vessel. They had been issued obsolete shelter halves, ponchos, field gear, and training rifles that could have been used in the Second World War. They found the ship had been converted to a tropical environment by using heat lamps and water jets that added mist to the already wet air. And, to make it more uncomfortable, a spin had been added to simulate the gravity to be found on Procyon Two.

Jefferson was introduced to the control room late on the first day. With the official scorers from Division, he would watch the progress of his battalion as they played the games designed to prepare them for the landing. Unlike them, he would not play the games, live in the ship, or eat the food. He had moved from being just another of the soldiers to being one of the leaders, and many of them felt that the leaders could do the job best from glass-enclosed booths that held a dozen TV and holograph monitors that let them see "the big picture." Besides, these were training missions and the battalion commander should already be trained. The junior officers should run the show.

On the first morning, after the first night, Jefferson met with his officers in a small clearing near the main hatch and the monitoring booth. He was supposed to give them their assignments. It wasn't anything shattering. Division had prepared the orders of the day and all Jefferson had to do was fill in the names of the people. Torrence would be given command for the first day. The aggressor role would be assigned to A Company, and the others would be responsible for establishing bases. Three other companies meant three such sites. Members of the Headquarters Company would be assigned to one of the maneuver companies.

Jefferson, holding a sheet of computer print-out paper, read the contents to the officers. "Enemy forces in the area are estimated to be small and ineffective. They have no armor or heavy weapons, and are thought to be guerrillas with little or no military training."

He folded the paper and stuffed it into one of the pockets of his starched and camouflaged battle fatigues. "I guess you know that anything can happen during the exercise. You all have your maps and selected locations for your bases. Remember that the aggressors will be assisted by a platoon from Division that does nothing other than train everyone else."

Each of the officers nodded his or her understanding. Torrence asked, "Where will you be, sir?"

"I'll be in the scorer's booth watching. Orders. I'd rather be with you. Exercise will begin as soon as the simulated landing is made. Any questions?"

When no one spoke, Jefferson turned and walked down the jungle path toward the booth. He triggered one of the booby traps, a simulated cross bow that fired a dulled bolt that struck him on the chest raising a welt that would later turn black and blue. Since he was part of the umpiring team, it didn't count against the battalion.

Jefferson entered the scorer's booth and sat in one of the plastic chairs that faced the monitors. He let his eyes roam from one to another as each of his companies moved through the simulated jungle, toward the jump-off points that would signal the beginning of the exercise.

One of the umpires, a short, pudgy lieutenant who claimed her name was Janice Ramon Dupress, pointed to the company being lead by Torrence. "She's going to make the first mistake."

"How do you know?"

"Because, like all the others, she's going to anchor one side of her perimeter against that rocky bluff that leads to the river, assuming that the enemy won't be able to cross there. When we ask, she's going to tell us that she was thinking that she could basically ignore that side and stack her defense on the side that faced the jungle."

"Makes sense to me," responded Jefferson.

"Of course. It's good tactics," said Dupress, "except that it ignores the fact that the enemy might be able to cross the river and climb the rocks. While it would be difficult for humans, there are many alien species that can easily swim the river and climb the bluffs. We purposely said nothing about the enemy's physical capabilities in that realm. Just wait. You'll see."

They had been in the simulator ship for over an hour, beginning with the briefings, and then moving toward the jump off points. The first few minutes hadn't been bad. The gravity made each of them sluggish, but the heat and humidity wasn't a bother. Within minutes after they began walking toward the jump-off point, however, they found their uniforms soaked with sweat, their mouths filled with cotton and their muscles beginning to revolt under the higher simulated gravity.

At the jump-off point, an umpire with them warned them that the exercise would begin in thirty seconds. The simulated landing had put them down unopposed. Now they had to form the units and move them to the areas where the bases would be built. Anything could happen.

Torrence checked her maps and compass. She found that the compass was spinning wildly. There were no magnetic lines of force around the ship and no magnetic north. There were, however, metal sides to the ship, electronic fields, and electrical currents, and those made the compass worthless.

Torrence got down on one knee and spread the map out on the ground in front of her. She discovered that one tree looked basically like another, and there were no real landmarks visible anywhere around. That meant that she would have to send out scouts to learn the lay of the land and give her some idea of which way they had to move. There were pathfinders assigned to the headquarters for just that purpose, but none handy.

Before Torrence could say anything, there was a burst of firing from the right side of the line. First firing from a single machine gun and then the rattling of small arms, punctuated by several explosions. Torrence, with two of the commanders, rushed forward to see half a dozen troopers sitting on the ground with their electronics flashing, "Killed." Then from the jungle came a rattling of machine-gun fire and a final explosion.

The umpire informed Torrence, "Ten or twelve of your people gave chase and were ambushed. These six were killed here. You have lost points for not having sentries out and for allowing a pursuit before the size and distribution of enemy forces had been determined." He stared at her grimly.

"But we haven't started," protested Torrence.

"In an actual combat environment, the enemy will hit you at any time and in any place, even when you don't think he should."

Torrence wanted to tell the idiot that she was aware of all that. She had been in combat before, as had nearly everyone in the battalion, but didn't. Instead she spun on Sinclair and snapped, "Get some security out. Right now!"

Two hours later, just as Dupress predicted, Torrence anchored her perimeter against the edge of the bluff, figuring that no one would attack from that direction. She overloaded the side of the perimeter nearest the jungle. There was a small, rocky ridge that ran through the selected area that made it a little difficult to get from one side to the other, but that would also provide a secondary line of defense.

This time she wasn't going to be fooled by the enemy sneaking up on her. She set out sentries and even put out a couple of listening posts. From there, she determined that there would be half alert until midnight and then a three quarters alert until four. She felt that she had it wired. There had been no sign of enemy activity since the brief attack right after their simulated landing.

The perimeter itself was a half moon, butted against the bluff. The shelter halves had been put together to form two-man tents protected by a strand of concertina wire thrown around the area. A line of foxholes had been created as the outside defense. It was close to simulated dark when they finished the work.

About midnight, Torrence called the officers together. There was a makeshift bunker constructed of impervium slabs erected near the ridge. Using a shelter half to block the light from the Z-like entrance, they were able to use their battery-powered lanterns.

"I think," said Torrence, kneeling on the packed dirt floor and looking up at her officers like a quarterback in a huddle, "that we'll be left alone tonight. I really don't think they'll have anything to throw at us. After all, they'll need some time to teach the aggressors how to operate. Keeping that in mind, I want you to turn everything for the rest of tonight over to the junior officers and senior NCO's. That way you'll be fresh during the next few days when I think they'll hit us with the majority of the stuff."

"I don't know about that," said Sinclair. "They hit us once all ready."

"Sure they did. But that was just to keep us on our toes. It was to show us that they could hit us at any time and in any place. Okay. We believe that. Now, I think they'll back off and we'll have tonight to get ourselves better organized. Besides, if they do hit us, we'll be right here. Shouldn't be a problem."

"Sounds like wishful thinking," said Carter.

"More like realistic," countered Torrence. "The aggressors have to get their training too."

"And tomorrow?" asked Sinclair.

"We scatter a couple of twelve- or fifteen-trooper patrols around the perimeter. We cut down some of the jungle and consolidate our location. And we make contact with the other two companies and establish our lines of communication so that we have the whole area under our control." Torrence grinned at the simplicity of her plans. "Questions or comments?"

"I would like to check the perimeter before I turn in," said Sinclair.

"That's fine. Anything else? No? Then I'll see you all in the morning."

In the scorer's booth, Dupress was sipping a cup of coffee with her feet propped on one of the banks of monitors. She nodded toward the one that showed Torrence and her command. Dupress said, "If they follow the pattern, they'll figure we won't do anything tonight. I don't know what it is, but they always assume that. No matter how many of these exercises they participate in they always assume that we'll give them the first night free. Of course, two of the companies are right this time."

"What's the plan?" asked Jefferson.

"Our people are going to cross the river and hit them about two-thirty, or a quarter to three. Most everything is at its lowest ebb then. For psychological and physiological reasons, people just aren't very alert at that time, no matter where they are or what they're doing."

The attack came quietly at 2:45. The aggressor platoon slipped into the tepid water and swam the river, ignoring the weak current. The lead unit of twenty reached the shore below the perimeter. Slowly, the cadre from Division leading the way, the aggressors started to climb the bluff. It wasn't very steep and they made it easily.

Once they were near the top, a second group of twenty more began to cross the river, and once they had reached the shore, a third party of twenty followed.

The first of the aggressors reached the top of the bluff and rolled out onto the flat grass. Carefully, staying low, they crawled among the low bushes and short trees, heading toward the perimeter. The cadre was silent, moving with the silence of a mist slipping through the jungle. Those selected from

Jefferson's battalion made some noise, rattling leaves and snapping twigs, but no one inside the perimeter heard them.

The first of the cadre reached Torrence's lines. They slipped behind the men and women dozing on guard and used their laser knives to simulate slitting the throats. The combat badges quickly changed to "Killed."

Once a path into the center of the perimeter had been cleared, meaning that the guards were dead, they slipped to the left and created a second path for exfiltration. When they had completed the tasks, quietly eliminating the opposition, they returned to the center of the perimeter and waited. The second group joined them there. To that point, none of the defenders had any idea the perimeter had been penetrated. As far as they knew, the night was quiet, the enemy had yet to attack, and probably wouldn't until the following day.

The beginning of the assault was signalled by the explosion of an artillery simulator, taking out the command bunker. That told the men and women at the edge of the bluff that they could start firing at targets inside the perimeter, as the defenders, now confused, tried to figure out what was happening to them.

The explosion nearly shook Torrence out of her sleeping bag. She leaped up, crouched, and then dropped to her stomach, crawling toward the command bunker. She found Sinclair near it, her weapon out as if searching for the enemy. "What's happening?" she asked Sinclair. "What's happening?"

"I would think," Sinclair said sarcastically, "that your assessment of the situation was wrong." She kept her head down, out of the line of fire. Weapons were rattling all around the perimeter and firing was coming from the bluff.

"Where's the attack coming from?" asked Torrence.

"Hell, Vicky, I know as much about it as you do."

"Get out there and check the north and east side. I'll check the south and west. I'll meet you at the command post."

"You mean the remains of the command post."

"Whatever. Just get at it." As she started to crawl off, she could see the flashing of the laser rifles. There were more explosions among the positions all along the perimeter. She got to her feet, bent forward like an old woman facing a stiff wind, and ran toward the perimeter. She then fell flat, crawling among the stimulated dead. Bright red and green laser beams crisscrossed over her head.

On the south side of the perimeter, she found nothing. The men and women there were lying flat, wide awake, but not shooting. They were staring into the night, searching for an enemy that refused to show himself. Random shots came from the jungle.

"Keep alert," she told them. "but don't forget to watch your backs."

"What's happening, Captain?"

"Probe of the perimeter. Nothing major. Stay alert." She hoped she sounded more confident than she felt and then didn't wait for any one to ask anything else. She crawled to the left, staying close to the perimeter, ordered the troops to stay alert, and moved on.

Before she could get to the west side of the perimeter, she ran into one of the enemy. A man standing, his back against the trunk of a tree, lobbing simulated grenades into groups of defenders, causing confusion. Torrence stood up behind him, grabbed him under the chin, and used her laser knife. He shook himself, cursed, and then sat down as his badge switched to "Killed."

A shape came at her, from the direction of the command post and she assumed that it was one of her own soldiers. But when the person got close, Torrence saw that it was a member of the aggressor company. She didn't react fast enough, and the aggressor hit her in the stomach before running off.

On the other side of the perimeter, Sinclair had been doing the same thing, but then discovered a gap in the lines. She found seven troopers sitting there as if they didn't have a care in the world, chatting quietly.

"What in the hell is this?" she demanded.

"Can't talk to you. We're dead," said the senior NCO present.

"Oh, shit," said Sinclair.

"How do you think we feel?" said the sergeant. "Being dead and all."

"Keep talking," said the umpire appearing from nowhere, "and I'll mark down that you cheat."

Sinclair shrugged, realized what the gap meant and headed

back toward the command post. She ran right into a group of aggressors who were there to create confusion, and in the confusion, they cut her down. Her badge began to flash "Killed."

An umpire glanced at her. "Have a seat until the battle is over."

Torrence worked her way back to the command post, dodging the incoming fire and artillery simulators. Explosions were flashing around her, making it look as if a thunderstorm had settled to the ground in the center of the perimeter. She couldn't enter the "destroyed" command post: That meant that the radios and communications with the fleet were gone too.

Then, from the center of the perimeter came a single, shrill whistle. The laser firing, the hammering of the machine guns, and the crash of the artillery simulators stopped abruptly. The enemy soldiers turned, running from the center of the camp, sprinting for the gap in the wire.

As soon as they had cleared out, the troopers left on the bluff tossed grenades to cover the exfiltration, and retreated the way they had come. Those who stayed near the shore covered them, and then, as they all crossed the river, the last of the aggressors, who had remained on the distant shore, covered them all, preventing any kind of counter-attack.

In the scorer's booth, Dupress was doubled over, laughing. "God, they're making all the mistakes. Every one of them. It's like we planned their side of the scenario. Now you know why we take the CO out of the exercises. Give someone else a chance to make the mistakes."

Jefferson nodded. He was certainly learning a lot. He had been watching Torrence carefully throughout the attack and he couldn't see one thing that he would have done differently. She seemed to be responding to the attack quickly, though there hadn't been any coordinated effort to stop the enemy. The aggressors had slipped in and then out without any organized resistance.

From the results, it was obvious she was making all the wrong moves, but the point was, he would be making them too. He didn't know how she could have prevented the destruction of her force. While he would never say it to

Torrence, or anyone else on the staff, he was glad that he was out of the loop.

Sergeant Mason would have known what to do. Mason would have told him how to handle the attack. But Mason was dead. Jefferson had to forget about Mason and concentrate on learning everything he could before someone else died because he was afraid or just plain stupid.

It all struck Jefferson as a little strange. Here was an experienced battalion. They had been on Cetus Tau Six. They had been in combat before. Yet there they all were, making dumb mistakes that were getting people killed.

Almost as if she was reading his thoughts, Dupress said, "The problem here is that you're now dealing with a guerrilla war. They don't operate the same as conventional troops. You're all used to fire-and-maneuver, artillery support and close air, but in the guerrilla war those things often aren't available. The enemy may attack, but as you see, the enemy wasn't there to capture the camp, just harass it. Made a path in and a different path out and then killed some people, stole some equipment and destroyed some. Different kind of war."

Dupress turned from the screens and holograph tanks and smiled, "But I guess I don't really have to tell you that, Major. You already know it."

"Feel free to make any comments you want," said Jefferson magnanimously. "It doesn't hurt to review the lessons."

As soon as the aggressors had withdrawn from the battlefield, the overhead lights came on, giving the scene a strange, yellow-orange cast. The umpires signalled the end of the exercise and called a time out.

"You can count your dead and wounded, if you like," the senior umpire told Torrence. "A chance to see how you've done."

Torrence stood up, brushed ineffectually at her mud-stained uniform and then slowly walked out toward the perimeter. She discovered that there were twenty-six dead, eighteen wounded, and a lot of equipment that had been destroyed. They lost a large number of weapons including a heavy machine gun, apparently carried off by the attackers. Torrence, after learning that, walked slowly back to where the command post had been and sat down on a rock near it. She stared at the ground and felt like crying. She couldn't believe that she had failed so badly. She couldn't believe that only a few days earlier she had been telling Jefferson that there were a number of officers in the battalion who could have assumed command. She had just learned that she was not among them. In her very first attempt at command, she had nearly fifty dead and wounded, and from the looks of the field, had killed only three of the aggressors.

Jefferson, Dupress, and the chief umpire, left the scorer's booth to grade the battalion on the exercise. The chief umpire, a lieutenant colonel named Freeman, said, "Well, they certainly blew that. You going to relieve the CO?"

"I don't think so," said Jefferson. He was still thinking that he had learned a great deal without the embarrassment that Torrence had undergone. "I think we'll just pretend that this didn't happen and start fresh."

"That's your choice, of course, Major, but I remind you that she has done nothing to warn the other three companies that she has been attacked. If it was a coordinated effort, her warning might keep the same thing from happening to them."

"But it won't," said Jefferson. "And, when I talk to her, I'll let her know that. I want her to get the experience in the field and if I pull her out now, she won't get it."

Freeman shrugged and walked to the ridge at the center of the perimeter so that he could address the whole group. When they were gathered, including those with their badges blinking, he said, "On the whole, a pretty lousy showing. I think that most of you know what you did wrong, but it was such a marvelous screw-up, I think I'll belabor the obvious.

"First, this is a guerrilla war, and that's something that you should keep in mind. You're not interested in taking and holding territory and neither are they. Your job is to inflict casualties. That is exactly what they did to you.

"You have to turn your thinking. Get the large-unit tactics out of mind. Think small. Think of inflicting casualties and think of destroying equipment. Don't think of pushing the enemy off land and occupying it. It's not that kind of war.

"There will be, of course, a complete analysis of the night's activities available later. I would suggest that all the officers and senior NCO's read it very carefully. It wouldn't hurt if all of you took a look at it."

Freeman paused, looked at Jefferson and said, "Anything you would like to add, Major?"

Jefferson stepped up, onto the ridge next to Freeman and looked down at his troops. He could see the disappointment in their faces. They had failed in their first test and they weren't happy about it. In a sudden insight, he understood that anything he said would only worsen the impact of the night's activities. He shook his head, then changed his mind. "Just want to let them know that there will be no more action until after 0800 tomorrow so that everyone can grab a little sleep. And to say that I would like to see Captain Torrence as soon as we're done here."

"Okay," said Freeman, "it's your battalion." To everyone, he said, "Tomorrow, all the badges will be cleared. The dead are alive, the wounded are healthy, and the equipment will be returned. We'll start operations again." He stepped down, and without another word started back to the scorer's booth.

Dupress leaned close to Jefferson and said, "I'm going back with the colonel. You better take care of the problems and get on out of here."

Jefferson nodded and then turned. "Captain Torrence," he said formally, "please come with me. Captain Sinclair, take over for the time being, get everything cleaned up and then have everyone get some shut-eye."

"Can't do it, Major," she said. "I'm dead."

Jefferson shot her an angry look. "As of right now, you are alive again. Now, do as you were ordered. And tomorrow I'll want you to select three people to go into the hypno tanks to learn the native language." He directed his attention to Torrence. "I'll want the same from each of the companies, and probably three additional from the headquarters. Intelligence sections get priority."

"Yes, sir," said Sinclair. Her voice was hard, as if irritated about something else.

Jefferson stared at her for a moment, but nothing more was said. He motioned at Torrence and then walked toward the perimeter.

As they moved out of hearing range of the others, Torrence said, evenly, "Are you relieving me?"

"No. No I'm not."

"Why?"

Jefferson stopped walking and leaned against one of the plastic rain forest trees. "Because, watching you work, I realized that you weren't doing anything wrong. As Freeman said, your orientation was off, but your tactics were faultless."

He quit talking, scratched his head, and said, "Well, I guess they weren't faultless. You let them roll up your flank because you assumed a conventional force couldn't attack across the river without making noise."

She started to protest, and Jefferson waved a hand to stop her. "Listen, Vicky, I'm not saying this right. Freeman suggested that I give someone else a chance to run the show, but I said no. I want you to get a chance to do it right."

"Thanks," she said sarcastically.

"Shit. Cut me some slack, will you? What I'm trying to say is that I understand your mistakes. I think that you're a fine officer, and I want you to get your chance to lead the battalion. Later, I might put someone else in, but that is just for the experience he or she can get, not because I've lost confidence in you."

Torrence looked at Jefferson as if seeing him for the first time. She couldn't understand exactly what he was trying to say, but she appreciated his attitude. She'd thought he was an asshole. Now she wasn't sure about that.

"Thank you, Major," she said. "I really mean that."

For just an instant, Jefferson was going to confide in her. Tell her that he would have done the same thing and made all the same mistakes, but then the moment passed, and he kept his mouth shut. Instead, he said, "After a couple of days, I might pull you into the scorer's booth to let you watch from there. Pick up some more pointers that way."

Feeling better than she had since the enemy had fallen on her and basically destroyed her command, she said, "Thank you, Major."

And do better she did. The first thing she did was to countermand the orders that put them into the indefensible clearing. It was something she should have done when she saw the lay of the land, but the orders had been to set up there and she had been reluctant to change them without consulting with her headquarters.

Rather than blunder through the jungle searching for a new location, she sent out the pathfinders. Their new position should have some high ground, a source of water, and good killing fields. She knew that the size of the ship limited her possibilities, especially with two other companies operating, but she would do the best she could. From there, she would establish her base and begin operations.

The only thing wrong was the constant heat. There was never a cool breeze to dry the sweat. Her socks and boots were soaked and rotting. Her clothes were frayed, muddy, and smelly.

Of course, all the others were in the same boat. She had to find time to let everyone sit down on the rocks, take off their boots and socks and dry their feet in the simulated sunlight. Some of them stripped to their underwear in an attempt to get thoroughly dry for the first time in days. Although she didn't like that, she felt she had to let them try. She wouldn't do it because of her position of command, but secretly envied them the opportunity.

And there was the mud. It seemed to never dry out, or just as it was about to, it would rain again. A steamy rain that came down in sheets for ten, fifteen minutes, obscuring everything around them, and then quickly let up. Everyone wanted to get inside, out of the rain, but they couldn't do that. It was the perfect opportunity for the enemy to attack. Sneak up under the cover of the rain, the jungle sounding like amplified frying bacon, and kill them.

At first Torrence had believed that the rain would wash her as thoroughly as a shower, but it didn't work that way. She had mud caked to her boots, clothes, and in her hair. She tried to wash it off and out, but could never get completely clean, even with the daily rains.

All of that was complicated because they had to worry about the enemy. The attacks came at the worst possible moments and Torrence suspected that they were planned in the scorer's booth where all was known. She suspected that they programmed the rain to cover the approach of the aggressors. She wasn't far off the mark.

There was also a lot of grumbling about the major. He wasn't around, living in the mud, the heat and the combat conditions, eating the freeze-dried rations that had the appeal of soggy cardboard. He was in the scorer's booth, wearing a fresh uniform every day, and living where there was air conditioning, hot and cold drinks, and no rain. They all thought it was only fair that the major participate too. More than one of them said that the old battalion commander, Major Chamberlin, would have been out there with them, no matter what the conditions were.

After seven days, Torrence was leading a platoon-sized patrol through the jungle. They were avoiding the path, a game trail really, because they had already had seventeen killed and forty-nine wounded by booby traps as they moved along the trails. Freeman had berated them about it, saying, "A wounded person takes two others out of the fight because they have to carry the injured to medical aid. This is a war of attrition. Always remember that."

She had a point out, three flankers on each side, and a rear guard. They were moving slowly among the trees. Around them came the sounds of animals but they were from hidden speakers and not real beasts. It added a note of realism that was lost in the knowledge that the animals were on tape.

Torrence was feeling pretty good. The guerrillas hadn't had a lot of success against them in the stand-up fights. It was only the damned booby traps that were making them look bad. But even with that, Torrence had been doing an effective job running the battalion. And even with the heat and mud and humidity, she was feeling good.

Suddenly there was an explosion at the head of the column. Looking forward, Torrence saw three or four go down. The others dropped as if they had been shot.

Around them the jungle erupted into laser fire that raked them. The umpires swarmed around the area, noting the numbers of the dead and wounded. The numbers increased rapidly.

From behind a tree, Torrence could see the ambush. She wondered how they had known the direction being taken, and then realized that it wasn't important. She had to do something before the whole platoon was wiped out. Lying on the trail wasn't going to get them out of it.

She pulled a grenade simulator and tossed it among the trees where she thought the ambushers were hidden. As it detonated, she leaped to her feet, and yelled, "Come on. Let's go! Let's go! Let's go!"

For a moment, there was hesitation. But then the rest of the platoon scrambled up and forward, firing their weapons as they charged into the trees.

Torrence led them, using her laser rifle. She saw some of the enemy forces there, and fired at them from the hip. She saw that she was scoring hits. One man came at her, but she was faster and gunned him down.

In seconds it was over. The ambushers who survived fled the scene. Some of her patrol started after them, wanting to finish the job, but Torrence remembered the first day and the second ambush that had killed those who followed.

"Fall back," she ordered. "Everyone fall back." Once she saw that she had them stopped, she said, "Security out. Check the dead and wounded and police up the goddamned weapons."

"That's it," yelled an umpire. "Everyone back to the briefing area for the out-processing. The exercise is hereby terminated."

One of the corporals came over to Torrence. "Excuse me, Captain. Can he do that?"

Torrence smiled. She knew exactly what the corporal was thinking. There had been so many tricks thrown at them in the last few days, that no one was willing to believe that it was over just because the umpire said that it was.

"This isn't part of the exercise, is it?" she asked.

"No, Ma'am, it isn't. The operations have been concluded."

Torrence turned to the corporal and nearly laughing, said, "I guess he can."

There was a single whoop from the corporal and then an explosion of cheers as everyone realized that they would soon be out of the simulator.

3

THE SIMULATOR SHIP WITH
THE MAIN FLEET

THE LOWER-RANKING ENLISTED men and women were allowed to leave the simulator almost as soon as the exercise was declared over, the corporals in charge of them. Debriefings for those people would be held the next day. The officers and senior NCO's were required to meet immediately with the Division scorers and Major Jefferson. A group of bleachers, looking as if they had been modeled after those of World War II, had been set up close to the scorer's booth, and the officers and NCOs were led to them.

Jefferson stood to one side, his starched fatigues beginning to wilt in the heat of the simulated tropical afternoon. He watched his officers and NCOs arrive and climb, slowly and sluggishly, into the bleachers. They all looked tired. Torrence had bags under her eyes and lines on her face. Her uniform, like those of the others, was filthy. Mud was caked to her boots and her pants below her knees, and there was a rip that showed a scrape on her thigh as she walked. There were mud splatters over the rest of her and her hair was matted. She didn't look particularly happy.

"Buck up," Jefferson said quietly as she approached him. "This shouldn't last more than an hour."

"An hour isn't long," she agreed, but didn't say anything

40

else. She just sat down and stared, tiredly, at the ground between her feet.

When everyone was settled, Freeman came from the scorer's booth and stepped to the center where the makeshift stage and lectern had been erected. He lifted a thick book to it and let it drop with a thud, getting everyone's attention quickly.

"Don't worry," he laughed. "This is just a copy of the fleet standard-operating procedure. I bring it in and let you all see it so that when I pull out the real report, you're all relieved that it's so short."

There was almost no response from the audience. They were all too tired and dirty to care for jokes. They stared at him with blank faces and exhausted eyes.

"First, I would like to say, that although your performance during the beginning of the exercise was less than spectacular, your recovery was good. We went over the problems of the first day at that time. The written report on it has been completed, and is available on the mainframe for access at your convenience, so I won't go into that now.

"The lessons you learned in the last few days will be valuable in dealing with your next assignment. Since we covered most them as they happened, I won't go over that again, either. The completed report will be available on the mainframe tomorrow morning."

Torrence glanced over at Jefferson by turning her head. Her elbows still rested on her knees as she sat hunched over. Jefferson noticed the glance and shrugged, telling her that he didn't understand it either.

"The reason," Freeman continued, "that we cut the exercise short is that we're nearly there. We had thought we were going to have to divert for supplies, but the supply vessel was dispatched from port to meet us near the target, allowing us to proceed at full speed."

Freeman consulted his notes. "I understand that you've already received your initial briefing. Since the return of the probes, there is some updated material for you and a little more in the way of background."

He glanced at the tired men and women. He studied Torrence's face for a moment and realized that they would retain almost nothing he told them. He flipped through his notes and decided to hit the high points for them.

"There are three major land masses, all of them connected with thin strips of swampy land and there are three local governments. Each has been at war with the other two, on and off, for centuries. The allegiances change as the reasons for conflict change. Not unlike our own history in that respect.

"Government standards change but currently there is one democratic government, one dictatorship with an emperor appointed for life, and one theocracy.

"Your battalion has been selected to support the democratically elected government which has come under pressure in the last few years. According to the reports, although the planet was only recently discovered, the democracy was asking for aid almost as soon as contact was established."

Freeman hesitated and then added, "The level of technology on the planet is late nineteenth, early twentieth century. We'll be using the assault rifles with full automatic capability, some lasers, but those are aiming devices only, and hand-held anti-tank missiles. Some body armor will be issued, and the radio equipment will be light with full secure and long-range capabilities. A complete equipment list will be provided, but that gives you the idea."

Freeman consulted his notes for a moment and then said, "Now for the real change. We are going to attach a captain to your intell section. He will not be an intelligence officer, but is a cultural anthropologist. His job will be to study the aliens and their society much in the same way an anthropologist on Earth would study a group of human subjects. You might say that he's gong to be an exo-anthropologist."

He pointed to the side where a captain dressed in fresh khakis stood. He was six feet tall, had brown hair and looked more like a soldier than a scientist.

"That is Captain Joseph Tyson. His orders are already cut. Now, are there any questions? No?" Freeman turned to Jefferson. "Do you have something you want to say, Major?"

Jefferson stood and moved to the front but didn't bother stepping up onto the stage. Facing the group, he said, "I know that the last thing any of you want to do is listen to me, so I'll keep it short. First, the good news. Tonight, we'll be celebrating our escape from the simulator ship and the exercise."

"Escape from what?" someone mumbled. "You weren't there."

Jefferson ignored the remark, though he felt his face grow hot with embarrassment. "We're going to have a party in the main rec center beginning at 1900 hours. Gives you all a chance to clean up and relax before the party. Tomorrow we're going to rest. The day after, we'll make sure that our gear is ready to go and begin assigning the marshalling numbers. We'll also begin the main hypno briefings."

He stopped dramatically, searching the dirty faces in front of him. Only a few looked up at him. Torrence had kept her eyes focused on the ground between her mud-caked boots. Finally he said, "Planetfall is in three days."

For nearly an hour, Jefferson sat in his office, staring at the computer screen as the reports dealing with the upcoming operation scrolled by. He saw little of it, other than the parading green words and numbers. The screen blurred as his mind wandered. He needed to talk to someone, anyone. A friendly face in the sea of hostility that threatened to wash over him.

In the good old days of a month ago, he would have sneaked down to the NCO quarters and found Mason. They would have slipped away, found a beer, or some other alcoholic beverage, brewed on the sly, and shot the shit. But now there was no one for him to talk to. Just an unfriendly battalion, filled with officers and NCOs who didn't like him. Who believed he had cheated them out of promotions and that he had achieved his rank through some shortcut.

He snorted once, realizing that they were right. He had cheated. Mason had done the work, had died, and now he was left reaping the awards and benefits of Mason's bravery. He wasn't qualified for the job and he shouldn't be sitting in the CO's chair.

He realized that he was accomplishing nothing by staring at the screen but not reading it. He called a halt to the parade, closed the file, and shut down the computer. Standing up, his fists pressed into the small of his back, he thought about going to the party, but the whispered comment about him missing the dirty duty still rang in his ears. He could still hear the resentment in the quiet voice.

There were a couple of questions he wanted to ask Torrence. Simple things that could easily wait until the next ship day, but he still had the desire to see a human and to speak with her. If she hadn't left for the party, he could get the details out of the way. It was a good excuse, anyway.

He slipped out of his office and walked the dimly lit corridors. Red lights glowed in them all the time, as if the ship's captain believed attack was imminent and that night vision of all crew was important. He ignored the cables that had been added to augment the power or to direct the new defense turrets added during the last refitting.

He reached the infantry quarters and found Torrence's cabin, knocked on the hatch, but heard no response. He touched the glow plate next to it and heard the bolt slide back quietly.

Once inside, he called, "Captain Torrence? Victoria? Are you in here?"

From the rear of the tiny cabin, in the shower room shared with another officer, Jefferson heard someone call, "Just a minute. I'm in the shower. Have a seat."

Jefferson dropped into the one chair. It was molded plastic and bolted to the deck. He looked around the tiny cabin slowly. It was a standard room for a low-ranking officer, providing barely enough space to live in. It was no more than six feet long, four wide and just over six high. It had a cot attached to the bulkhead, a couple of pictures on the wall, a bright overhead light, and a small reading lamp above the bed. There was a tiny night table that held a paperback novel.

Jefferson had never really thought about the incongruity of the situation before then. Books where there should have been computer terminals. Individual rooms that wasted space. Showers that recycled a few gallons of water through a filter system that poured it right back out of the showerhead so that the individual could have the impression of privacy. Jefferson thought that there should be more efficient ways of handling these problems.

He was still wondering about it when Torrence walked into the room. She was scrubbing at her hair with a small towel. Water from the shower glistened on her naked body. A thin, trim, solid-looking body.

Without looking up, she started to speak, and then saw that it was Jefferson. "Oh . . . sorry. I didn't expect you." She didn't try to cover herself.

"Listen," said Jefferson, standing suddenly, "if it's inconvenient, I can see you in the morning. Just a couple of things I thought we could clear up tonight."

Torrence sighed and sat down on the cot. "No, that's all right. I was just waiting for a couple of the others to show up and then we were all going to the celebration." She grinned weakly and rubbed the towel over her hair.

"Oh, yes. I forgot."

Torrence dropped the towel she was using on her hair to the deck. She sat there, waiting, oblivious to her own nudity.

"Is there something that you wanted, Major?" she asked.

Jefferson sat there trying not to stare at her. He kept his eyes focused on her lips, not wanting to even look into her eyes. A hundred responses ran through his mind, but he couldn't bring himself to utter any of them. Finally, to fill the silent void, he said, "The exercise seemed to go very well."

Torrence leaned to the rear, her shoulders against the smooth metal of the bulkhead. "Not in the beginning. Really stepped on it there, but once we understood the parameters of the game, we did a lot better."

"I guess the guerrilla war isn't something that you've been involved with much."

"Not in the other campaigns. Mostly you trade lives for real estate, and when you have enough of the real estate, you win because the other side has nowhere to go."

Again Jefferson fished for a comment, realizing his excuse for coming to her cabin was transparently thin. "I'll be looking forward to using some of your new-found knowledge after planetfall."

"I'm sure you will," she mumbled in response. "Is there something else?"

Jefferson stood up then, ready to leave. Deliberately, he stared at her body, examining her from the ankles upward. The scrape on her thigh was an angry red welt but didn't look serious. There was a bruise on her stomach and another on her shoulder.

Torrence sat there, letting him inspect her as if she was a side of beef. She spread her legs slightly, inviting him to look at her. When he refused the challenge, she crossed her legs and stared at him hard.

"I know that I shouldn't say anything," she said to break the silence, "but I think you've a right to know. Many of the people in the battalion, hell, the majority of them, feel you let them down."

Jefferson felt the anger bubble through him. "Let them down? How the fuck have *I* let them down?"

"By not being in the exercise. Everytime we saw you, it was just after a major conflict. We were hot, sweaty, muddy, and tired, and you come waltzing in wearing starched fatigues looking as if you just left the club. All you needed was a drink in your hand. Didn't make much of an impression."

"Now wait a damn minute here. I was ordered to sit out the exercise. They wanted you all to take over and run things your way so they could evaluate you."

"But who evaluates you?" she asked, her voice rising sharply. "None of us have seen you in action. All we know is that a new CO has been dumped on us and the only time we could have seen him, he was hiding in the scorer's booth."

Jefferson's hands were at his sides, clenching and unclenching. "I was not hiding," he hissed. "I was obeying my orders from regiment which came down from Division. Besides, it is not up to you, a junior captain, to worry about evaluating my performance. That's done on a higher level."

"The point," said Torrence evenly, "is that you took the easy way out. You could have told Division that you wanted to take a more active role in this exercise, as Major Chamberlin would have done."

"And how do you know that I didn't?"

"Did you?" When he didn't answer right away, she knew the answer, but asked again, "Did you?"

"To be honest, I never really thought of it."

"Fine. I think my point is well taken."

Jefferson felt his temper flare again. "You have no point at all, Captain. Just because I followed my orders without question doesn't mean that I'm incapable of leading the battalion."

"I didn't mean to imply that . . ."

"I'm not at all interested in what you meant to imply. I think you would do a better job if you worked to support me rather than run a popularity contest."

"That's not called for, Major."

"Whatever I say is called for," he snapped. "Now, I'll expect you in my office at zero eight, no, make it zero nine hundred tomorrow. Be prepared to discuss planetfall. Good night."

Jefferson, whirled, stepped to the hatch and then had to stand there for endless seconds while the sensor decided to open the hatch.

The party had already started when Torrence entered the rec center. Over the speakers, the latest hit music was blaring. At least it had been the latest when they left Earth. At one end of the room was a table loaded with food, and near it was a gigantic tub filled with beer. An enlisted man from another unit was tending bar, or trying to. Nearly everyone was ignoring him and grabbing anything they could get their hands on and swilling it as quickly as they could swallow it.

There were shifting patterns of lights on the floor and lights flashing on the bulkheads around them. There were a dozen couples dancing. It looked almost as confusing as hand-to-hand combat.

Torrence forced her way into the party, saw a couple of the other officers and tried to gravitate in their direction, avoiding the NCOs and enlisted soldiers. When she got close, she could hear that they had forgotten about the party and were seriously discussing Jefferson.

"I don't care what you say," Clay Mitchell nearly screamed, partly to be heard over the noise, and partly out of anger. "He should have been in there with us. He's nothing more than a rear-area progue who lucked into a command."

"He seems to know his stuff," countered Rider, quickly. Loudly.

"How in the hell could you tell? He's never done anything that would lead us to that conclusion, expect skate out of the exercise."

"I hate to interrupt," yelled Torrence, "but this is a party and we should party. Besides, it isn't bright to discuss the merits of our new commander in these surroundings. Too many ears to hear too much."

But Mitchell wouldn't let it drop. "You know him better than we do, Vicky. What do you think?"

"What I think is of no importance. Besides, I haven't seen him that much more than the rest of you. I've only had a couple of meetings with him and it's been mostly him telling me what we have to do. Very little opportunity to get to know him."

But even as she spoke, she thought about the temper tantrums she had witnessed. He seemed to get upset over the smallest things, especially when she seemed to be questioning his competence. It could be immaturity, a fear of failing in the first important post he had held, or just that he was a regulation-issue asshole. She didn't know what his problem was and had tried to explain that it was her battalion too, and if he failed then they all failed. He didn't seem to understand that. She said nothing of that to the assembled officers.

"That's just great. Going into unknown territory—shit, enemy territory, with someone we don't know and don't trust."

"He's kind of cute," said Norris.

"Oh that's beautiful, Courtney," snapped Mitchell. "What the hell kind of qualification is being cute?"

"None whatsoever," she said in a strong voice. "It was merely a comment. I was trying to divert this conversation before one of us said something incredibility stupid for the others to hear." She stared at Mitchell.

"She's right," said Torrence. "Besides, do any of you know who this Jefferson really is? He's the latest winner of the Galactic Silver Star. They don't hand those out. That's why he's here and in command."

"How did you find that out?"

"I called a friend at Division a little while ago and mentioned that we had some misgivings about our new leader. I was told to forget the misgivings because he was their fair-haired boy, complete with his shiny new metal."

Mitchell whistled so softly that no one could hear him over the music. "Jesus! He's that Jefferson? You'd never think it to look at him."

"Well," said Torrence, waving a hand to end the discussion, "let's mingle with the troopies. Eat drink and make merry for tomorrow we may die."

"Planetfall, tomorrow?" asked Rider.

"Don't be stupid. It's a figure of speech."

Courtney Norris wandered around the rec center for a while, sometimes dancing and sometimes just talking to the men and women she knew, trying to avoid the older NCOs who frightened her. She carried a glass of beer with her most of the time, and when she finished it, she found another. She wasn't really drunk, but she was feeling very good. That's what she told herself, though her face tingled and she was staggering, sometimes having to brace herself against the bulkhead to keep from falling.

After nearly an hour of surreptious searching, she decided that Jefferson wasn't going to show up. That wasn't right, she thought. He should be there for a while, and even if he didn't have to live in the field with them, he had been there in the simulator ship, working at his tasks. It wasn't right that he skip the celebration. Maybe all he wanted was a personal invitation from someone in the battalion. She figured that she would deliver it.

She left the rec center and turned toward the senior officer's quarters. She found the hatch of Jefferson's quarters and knocked quietly. When there was no immediate response, she knocked again, harder.

A second later the door flew open and Jefferson was standing there, wearing a long, blue robe. For a second he didn't recognize Norris because, unlike her counterparts, she had brought a civilian dress that molded itself to her body, and she had let her long brown hair down so that it framed her face, making her features seem sharper. It changed her appearance.

"Yes?"

"Major Jefferson. Don't you know me?" she asked as she weaved back and forth, trying to maintain her balance. Some of the beer slopped out of her glass.

"Of course," said Jefferson, recognizing her voice. "You're Norris."

"Courtney Norris, Major. Aren't you going to ask me in?"

Jefferson didn't move right away. Then he stepped back, out of the way. "Come on in."

She entered, twirled once, taking it all in. She moved to the large chair pushed into a corner and sat down. "This is a lot larger than my quarters. I have such a tiny area."

"Something I can do for you, Lieutenant?"

"Don't be stuffy," she said coyly. "I'm Courtney."

"Is there something that you wanted?" ignoring the tone of her voice and the blatant invitation of her posture.

"Well, the party is going full blast and I noticed that you weren't there."

"Most observant."

"Anyway, I thought that if I came down here and talked to you, you might put in an appearance. Thought it would be good for the morale of the troops if you did."

"I have found that the troops tend to have more fun if the CO isn't around. They don't care if the other officers are there, but something about having the CO there puts a damper on the festivities." When he had been a lowly lieutenant, he'd preferred the parties where the CO was absent and they could drink without worrying about it coming back to haunt them later.

Courtney sat back and slowly crossed her legs so that her dress rode up slightly. "I don't think we need to worry about that."

Jefferson stood up and walked over to Norris. He reached for her hand and said, "I'm about to do something that I know that I'm going to regret later."

"What's what?" She smiled, misunderstanding.

"Throw you out of here. I appreciate the gesture, but there is a lot of work to do tomorrow and I want to get some sleep. Besides, you're probably the only one to miss me tonight so don't worry about it."

She let him pull her to her feet and then stepped close pressing herself again him. "I won't tell," she said, her voice husky.

"I'm sure that you won't, but I think it's best if you leave."

She nodded once, and tilted her head to kiss him on the point of the chin. "If you really want me to go."

"I'm sure."

Norris shrugged, whirled, slopping beer from her glass, and retreated. It had not gone as she had thought it would.

When Jefferson opened his office door the next morning, he found Tyson sitting there, using his computer to scroll through a classified copy of the latest intelligence report on Procyon Two. He hadn't liked Tyson when he first saw him at the briefing the day before and liked him less now. He definitely didn't like the way Tyson assumed that he didn't have to obey the battalion's standing orders.

"Morning, Major."

"You take a lot for granted, Tyson."

"Don't go bully boy on me, Jefferson," said Tyson grinning. "I'm immune. Division controls my activities so that I don't have to take any shit off anyone."

Jefferson leaned over and hit the button to clear the screen. When he saw the report disappear, he walked around to sit behind his desk. "What can I do for you?"

"Just wanted to let you know that I've brought my gear down here, and gave it to your supply officer, what's her name, Norris. She wanted me to check with you before she manifested it."

"Tell her I said that you could do whatever you want in that respect. Tell her to obey your orders and to get you squared away. Now get out of here."

Tyson stood up and began to leave. Then he stopped and said, "Hey, did you go to school to learn to be an asshole or is it just natural talent?"

"Remember one thing, Tyson. You're only a captain. I'm a major."

"Right. And I report directly to the general and he writes my efficiency reports, so stuff it up your ass."

For the next thirty hours, they all worked getting the material ready for planetfall. They moved the equipment out of the supply bays and carried it to the shuttle area. They double-checked it, cleaned it, and repaired it. Some of it had to be replaced from the Divisional supply. Norris crosschecked her lists with the equipment being brought in. The laser weapons, sonic grenades, and electronic machine pistols were left behind. The assault rifles and hand grenades were substituted. It didn't take them long, since they had been through the drill several times before.

Eight hours before planetfall, with all the equipment stored, the lists crosschecked and all personnel given their assignments for the upcoming mission, they were told to get some sleep. The remaining hypo tank sessions were cancelled, some of the people having gotten the training and some of them not. Everything changed with the arrival of the supply ships and the change in the lead time to planetfall. It had been rush, rush, rush, and then it was get some sleep.

As the time for planetfall approached, the troops moved to the shuttle bay. The landing would be made in pods ejected out the rear. These had limited flight capabilities and needed little room to land. They had to be airlifted out and existed only because they could use a short field, or no field, and could be converted to erect a defensive wall.

Jefferson was scheduled to be in the lead ship. He hadn't been worried about the landing because he had been too busy to worry about it. As he strapped into his seat, he realized that everything was now on his shoulders. In all the other missions, there had been someone who had responsibility above him. A company commander or a battalion commander. This time, he had to run the show, make the decisions, send out the patrols, and give the orders. He was going to become the ultimate authority. Suddenly he felt that he wasn't ready. In fact, he knew it. He didn't deserve the position. He had gotten it because everyone else thought that he had been brave. That he had displayed audacity. Now hundreds of men's and women's lives depended on him, and he didn't think he could handle it.

And then, suddenly, it was too late. He was pressed back into the seat as the shuttle accelerated out of the ship, and then dropped into space. Jefferson felt pressure on his chest so that he couldn't breathe. Suddenly, a moment later, he was weightless, the pressure gone. His head spun and his stomach rotated as the shifting pressures and feelings changed rapidly. Sweat beaded on his forehead and seemed to freeze there. He thought he was going to throw up, knew he wasn't, and then they were in the planet's atmosphere.

The shuttle's lights flashed and a quiet, electronic voice said, "Thirty seconds to drop. Thirty seconds to drop. Twenty-five seconds to drop."

Jefferson knew, as the voice counted down, that he wasn't ready. He wanted to scream at them, telling them to wait. To give him a little more time. To get him the hell out of there.

He saw the lights change from red to green, heard the voice quietly announce, "Drop, drop, drop," and felt the sickening lurch that let him know they were separated from the shuttle. It was too late then. In less than a minute, they would be on the ground.

4

ABOVE PROCYON TWO

As IN ALL his other landings, both real and simulated, Jefferson felt a sharp downward pressure when the shuttle pulled out of its dive and ejected the landing pod with a shattering explosion that was felt rather then heard. Shifting feelings, first the tug of acceleration, then the weightlessness of space, and finally the pressure of gravity from the planet's surface, which changed again to weightlessness as the bottom seemed to fall out. Unconsciously, Jefferson dug his fingers into the arms of the protective chair in which he sat. He squeezed his eyes shut, blotting out the chalk-white faces of the others around him, and prayed, as he always did, that the swirling emotions and perceptions would end before he threw up.

The miniature engines of the ejection pod cut in just then, stopping the rapid fall, and the pod started on a downward spiral. Close to the ground the drag chutes popped, and then the main chutes deployed, forcing Jefferson and all the others back into their chairs.

Moments later, the pod hit, harder than it should have, the instruments having failed to record the full pull of Procyon Two's gravity. They bounced, rotated forty-five degrees, hit with a bone-jarring jolt, and rolled to a halt, leaving one half of the men and women with Jefferson hanging upside down.

The retaining straps held them tightly, preventing serious injury.

Jefferson, on his back, hit the quick release, and pushed himself up, out of the chair. Clutching the short-stocked assault rifle, he pushed his way to the bulkhead where the weapons had been secured. He flipped the mechanical lock up, jerked the restraining bar out of the way, and grabbed his rifle. Three others stood behind him and he handed them rifles.

"Get out and check the area. Set up security."

"Yes, sir."

The senior NCO spun the wheel on the hatch that was now located over their heads. The NCO pushed it up, and it fell open with a clank that reverberated through the hull. He handed his weapon to one of the others, leaped up and grabbed the edge, hauling himself up and out. He reached back for his weapon and slipped out of sight. The other two followed quickly.

As they disappeared, another trooper joined Jefferson. She had a cut on the side of her head where she had somehow jammed the edge of her helmet against the bone. Her eyes were slightly glassy and the bright blood stood out in stark contrast to her chalk-white face.

"You okay?"

She nodded dumbly and reached for her weapon with a shaky hand.

"Stay here and pass out the weapons."

Again she nodded.

Jefferson turned and headed deeper into the pod, away from the hatch. He helped one man out of his restraining harness, reaching up over his head to break the man's fall as the quick release let go. Then the two of them helped a third. They moved down the line helping while those opposite, lying on their backs, struggled to get up themselves. As they were freed, they grabbed their weapons and scrambled from the pod.

Within five minutes, everyone else was out of the pod. Jefferson lifted himself out, slid down the side and dropped into the lush, crimson vegetation. Immediately he noticed that the dark splotched camouflage battle fatigues they wore stood out, rather than concealed. The masterminds who were supposed to check such things had failed badly.

He knelt, with his back to the smooth, warm metal of the

pod, checking his surroundings. One other pod stood near the crest of a short rise a hundred yards from him. Thirty troopers from it had thrown a protective ring around it. Directly in front of him was the beginning of the rain forest. Or what he suspected was the rain forest since it resembled nothing from Earth. It wasn't just that the trees were gray and red, or that the bushes were covered with red leaves. It was something different. There were plants of bizarre shapes that didn't have leaves. A couple of them looked like parachutes propped on stiff cord. Others were a blotchy red-and-gray web that clung to anything near, obscuring the surroundings.

Underfoot was an unbroken moss of an orange so bright that it seemed to give off its own eerie light. The troopers moving around on it looked like great lumps green and brown and black.

Jefferson found an NCO, and grabbed his shoulder. "Sergeant, you have to get these people deployed. I want security established. And I mean now."

"Yes, sir. I'll give it a try."

"Do more than try. And have someone get the radio ready."

"Yes, sir." The sergeant trotted off.

Jefferson, along with an escort of three others, broke through his own perimeter and jogged up the slope to the second pod. There he found a second lieutenant who had joined the battalion just a couple of hours before planetfall. Jefferson glanced at the man's name tape and said, "Okay, Thatcher. What's going on here?"

"I have the people spread out for security. I've sent a couple of them into the ah, jungle, about a hundred yards to see if they can spot anything and to set up a listening post."

"Good. Any word on the others?"

"Well, sir, I was about to climb up on the pod and see if the additional elevation will let me see anything."

Jefferson patted the side of the pod. "Only thing wrong with these is that we see nothing coming down. However, I would assume that the rest of the battalion is that way."

"Why's that?"

"Simple. I'm the first one out. You're the second. We should be pretty much on line."

"Want me to organize a patrol?"

"Not yet. Let's get things consolidated here first. Then we

can do that. Besides, I think the others will be doing that. Trying to rally with us."

Just then, Torrence, and twelve others stumbled out of the jungle, glanced up and saw Jefferson and Thatcher. She pointed left and right, deploying the people with her before heading up the hill.

"Glad you could join us, Victoria," said Jefferson somewhat mockingly.

"The shuttle crews sure let us down on this one. We're spread all over the goddamned landscape."

"You make contact with any of the others?"

Torrence nodded. "Three other pods were in the same clearing as me. It's not that far from here."

"What's the terrain like."

"Nowhere near as good as this. No high ground at all. In fact, we're in kind of a valley. More of a depression really and the trees aren't more than fifty, sixty yards from each of the pods."

"I've got one of the NCO's setting up the radio to order everyone in here. Set up the rally beacon. Once we've got the majority of the battalion, we'll try to find our way around here."

"Where are the locals?" asked Torrence.

"Haven't seen anyone or anything. We're not in the right place, though."

"You sure?" asked Torrence.

Jefferson shot a glance at her. "If we were in the right place, the locals would be here."

"Then how do we find them?"

Jefferson was going to shrug, and then had an inspiration. "Easy. We assume that we were dropped on the proper heading. We just move in that direction. The locals will undoubtedly be able to find us, and then we'll be able to find the official battalion staging area."

As Torrence turned to head over to the NCO with the radio, one of the troops reported to Jefferson, "Sir, we have movement all over in the jungle."

"That's just our people coming in. Don't worry about it."

"Beg pardon, Major," said the soldier, "but they're making a lot of noise and I don't think our people would be making that much."

"This is an alien environment. Our experience is in normal Earthlike vegetation. I'm sure there are variations."

"Yes, sir. I still don't like it."

"You don't have to. Now get back on line. Oh, and see if you can find someone who was in the hypno tanks to learn the language. In the rush, we neglected to put anyone in the pod with me who could. We assumed that we would all come down fairly close together."

A crash of gunfire interrupted them. It wasn't the normal sharp crack of the assault rifles, but a louder, duller sound. It was followed by a dozen more shots that hit the pod near Jefferson. It was a ragged volley, not like the disciplined firing of the battalion.

The sergeant dove for cover, rolling to his right and swinging his rifle around. Jefferson stood flatfooted, staring into the jungle in front of him.

Aliens burst from the trees, holding long rifles with bayonets attached. They surged across the open ground, growls erupting from their throats. Jefferson still didn't move. But as he saw the aliens, he yelled, "Hold your fire. Hold your fire."

The aliens either didn't understand the command or didn't care about it. As soon as they had a target they shot. Half a dozen Earth men and women fell, dead or wounded. One man rolled down the hill, clutching at his belly. The aliens stabbed at him, piercing him a dozen times with their bayonets. He died screaming.

His battalion also ignored his order and opened fire. Several of the aliens were hit. They stumbled, but didn't fall. They came on, using their bayonets. One of the Earthmen leaped to his feet, fired three times at point-blank range and then stood still as the alien used his bayonet to rip him open, blood spurting onto the bright orange moss.

Another Earthman fired three more times and the alien, now dripping a yellowish fluid, toppled slowly to the ground. It tried to sit up, failed, and rolled to its side. It didn't move.

Torrence, having heard the shooting returned, rushed from the first pod, a dozen soldiers with her. She saw Jefferson standing near his pod. She saw the aliens running up the hill, a couple of them swinging huge clubs that smashed the skulls of those who got in the way. Soldiers fell, their heads crushed, their blood and brains leaking. She dropped to one knee and began pumping bullets into the nearest of the aliens. She kept firing at one until she saw it fall.

The other troops did the same. Rather than try to engage in hand-to-hand combat with the aliens, they attempted to keep their distance, using bullets. They fired and fired, the sound of the individual rifles combining until it was a single, long, loud detonation. There were screams and shouts. Everyone was running forward to form a skirmish line.

Other soldiers, from the other side of the hill, scrambled up to the top. They fanned out along the pod, aiming and then pouring rifle fire into the aliens.

More of them fell, but the survivors kept coming, running forward, toward Jefferson and Torrence, swinging their rifles like baseball bats. Torrence was firing as fast as she could pull the trigger. Once she glanced at Jefferson who stood clutching his assault rifle to his chest at port arms.

She stood up then, and stepped forward as if to put herself between the major and the enemy, her back to him. She emptied her rifle into one of the aliens, hit the release, and let the magazine drop to the ground. She jerked a fresh one from a pouch and as she slammed it home, she heard a rifle shot behind her and turned in time to see Jefferson pumping rounds into an alien to their left.

Then, as suddenly as it started, it was all over. The last of the attackers dropped under the concentrated firing of the battalion. For a couple of moments, the battalion continued to shoot, hosing down the bodies. As the firing began to taper to a sporadic rattling, Torrence stood then and began shouting. "Cease firing. Cease firing."

When it was silent, she looked at Jefferson. "Now what, Major?"

Jefferson shook himself, as if he was just returning to consciousness. "I don't understand. I thought they were supposed to be on our side."

"Snap out of it," said Torrence. She kept her voice low.

"On our side," repeated Jefferson.

Torrence saw that some of the soldiers were staring at them. She tugged at his sleeve and said, "Come on, Major, let's go discuss this. Maybe someone on the fleet will have an idea."

"That anthropologist. That Tyson. Where's he?"

"Why?"

"Because the dumb son of a bitch should know what's happening here," said Jefferson. "He should know."

"Let's get to the radio," she said. "Maybe someone will be able to tell us."

One of the NCO's appeared. "Ah, Major? What are your orders?"

Torrence studied the dazed look in Jefferson's eyes. She said, "Pull everything back to this pod. Post security and establish a solid perimeter. Get the rally beacon going and begin a muster. I can see that the medics are helping the wounded, but check to see if there is anyone who needs to be evacked right away. And check the aliens to make sure they're dead."

"How do we tell?"

Torrence glanced at Jefferson and then back at the soldier. "Get the weapons away from them and have a detail drag the bodies to the edge of the jungle. We'll burn them."

The NCO looked first at Jefferson and then at Torrence. "Yes, ma'am," he said, and ran off. Torrence realized that she had just taken command of the battalion, unofficially. She was sure that Jefferson would snap out of it, whatever it was, but they couldn't stand around waiting for him. And, she had to get him away from the others before they all saw how he had seemed to have fallen apart.

For the next hour, Torrence sat inside the pod, using the radio to coordinate the movements of the battalion while Jefferson sat on the deck and studied his boots. She discovered that almost everyone had landed safely. A couple of other small units, as they were moving to the rally point, had been attacked, but all had fought off the attackers. There had been casualties, but the losses were acceptable, given the circumstances. Torrence made arrangements with the fleet to pick up the dead and wounded.

Tyson showed up later still. He entered the pod, saw Torrence sitting by the radio with a map spread out in front of her. Jefferson sat to one side, his eyes closed and his head back, as if he was concentrating heavily on something.

"I've arrived," said Tyson to announce himself.

Jefferson opened his eyes, and shouted, "Where in the hell have you been? We need some answers."

"Got here as soon as we could. We were dropped nearly four miles away."

"Don't give me any shit. What the hell are these creatures doing? Why are they shooting at us?"

"Without a chance to talk to a couple of them, I really couldn't tell you."

"You could guess, couldn't you?" demanded Jefferson. "You can do that, can't you?"

Tyson sighed. "If I had to guess, I would say it's one of two things. Either we've been lied to, and they don't want our help, or somehow the opposition found out where we were going to land and arranged the welcome."

Before Jefferson could comment, Thatcher stuck his head in the pod. "We have another group of aliens coming in."

"Well," snapped Jefferson, "prepare to repel them."

"Wait a minute," said Torrence quickly. "How do we know that these aren't the ones who were sent to meet us?"

"Let's not take any chances."

"Good idea," said Tyson. "But we don't have to shoot at them to not take chances. If they are friendlies, we certainly don't want to open fire."

"Can you speak their language?" asked Jefferson.

"Somewhat. That was one of the things I was doing while you and your people were playing in the simulator," Tyson reminded him.

"We weren't playing," said Jefferson.

"We better get out there," said Torrence, getting to her feet.

"Yes. Let's go," ordered Jefferson, suddenly standing.

Outside, they saw a group of fifteen aliens standing among the trees. Their descriptions matched that given on the ship, right to the ponchos and pants. But then the aliens who attacked them had also fit the description. Each of these carried a rifle that was nearly six feet long, topped with a slim, pointed bayonet. They were hesitating because of the bodies lying on the slope.

Slowly, Tyson moved toward them. He held both hands in plain view, and called, in the formal mode of the alien language, "Greetings from the people of the Earth."

One of the aliens detached itself from the group and came forward. It held its weapon out, away from its body as if offering it as a gift. When it was close to Tyson, it bent from the waist as a form of greeting.

Tyson did the same, copying its movements. When they were both standing straight again, Tyson said, "I am called Tyson by my people."

"I am Zeric. We are here to assist you."

"These others," said Tyson pointing to the dead aliens, "attacked us without warning. Why?"

"They are not of my tribe. They are from far away. I think they have killed those of my tribe. Friends who are now no longer with us."

Jefferson and Torrence approached cautiously. They stopped behind Tyson, who introduced them. Torrence then handed him the map she carried and had him ask if they could locate the large, open plain shown.

Zeric took the paper and shook his head. "I do not understand."

Tyson, realizing that it would be hard to explain the concept of a map to someone who had never seen one, tried to describe the official landing zone. Zeric finally understood.

While Tyson and the aliens talked about finding the official landing zone, Torrence, under orders from Jefferson, worked to get the people and equipment organized to move. Torrence decided to leave thirty people behind. That way, as the stragglers made their way to the rally point, they would know what to do. Once the campsite was located, a group of pathfinders could be sent back to lead them all out. And, once the camp was established, they could assemble the transport and move the large pieces of equipment to the perimeter. It would all take a little time, but it was all fairly standard. The only problem was running into more unfriendlies. The intelligence reports had suggested that they would have to operate outside their landing area to find the enemy. Apparently that wasn't true.

Nearly three hundred people had gathered at the rally point when Jefferson decided it was time to move out. He had reclaimed command of the battalion by the simple expedient of issuing the orders. Torrence stepped out of the spotlight when that happened, grateful that Jefferson had seemed to have come to his senses. She was worried about what might happen later, under the pressure of combat situations, but decided to concentrate on the problems at hand and worry about the future when it happened.

With Tyson, Zeric, several of his aliens, and a dozen pathfinders in the lead, the battalion began to slip into the jungle. The rest of the battalion, divided into companies, then platoons, and finally squads, followed. They used a fairly wide path, a hard-surfaced trail that ran into the jungle, covered with a light coating of the orange moss.

It was almost dusk when the perimeter was finally set. The men and women had been required to dig foxholes for the first night. Near the center, they had erected a pre-fab structure that was a cross between the foxhole and a bunker. It had enough room for seven or eight people, firing ports, a few weapons, and the main radio equipment.

Inside it, Jefferson sat studying his map, which was little more than an aerial photograph printed out by a computer. Torrence stood looking out one of the firing ports. When she saw that no one was close, and that the bunker was deserted, she turned and said, "What happened to you today?"

"What do you mean, what happened?" he asked, looking up at her.

"I mean, you froze when the aliens hit the landing site. I mean that you stood there and didn't issue a single order."

"There was nothing that I had to do," alibied Jefferson. "The troops were handling the situation. They opened fire as soon as the hostile nature of the aliens was determined and my running around screaming orders wasn't going to make the situation any better."

Torrence turned from the firing port and moved in to where she could study Jefferson. "I'm not buying that, Major. I want to know what to expect from you."

For several seconds he didn't speak. Finally he asked, "Are you suggesting that I'm a coward?" He was almost sneering at her.

"Nothing of the kind." She groped for words. The whole episode had been preying on her since it happened. She had been so busy at the time that she wasn't sure of her impressions. It had seemed that Jefferson was incapable of thought, that he had been incapable of making a decision. But he had drawn his weapon and he had fired. But then she had to nearly lead him away from the site, into the pod. She needed some answers.

"I know that today wasn't the first combat you've seen, but you didn't do much to help us."

"Captain Torrence, I'm getting a little tired of having to explain my actions to you. Or to the other officers. All you have to do is worry about yourself and let me handle myself and the battalion. Now, do you have any questions about tonight?" He stared at her, trying to establish his dominance.

Nervous, because she didn't know what to expect, she moved deeper into the bunker. She touched the radios, and then stepped closer to Jefferson. She ignored his question and asked quietly, "Is there something I can do to help?"

Jefferson glanced at the papers that littered the field desk set up in one corner. Computer terminals and floppy discs had been left behind and records transferred to paper. He wanted to grab them, throw them at her. He reined in his emotions, and said, "Just what are you implying, Captain?"

"Not a thing, sir. It's just that you don't seem to realize that my job, as exec, is to lend support to you in whatever capacity that you require. I'm on the chopping block too."

He was about to snap at her again, and then realized that what she said was true. If he made the big mistake and lost the battalion, she would die with them. But there was really nothing he could say to her without losing his ability to command. Once he became friendly with anyone, no matter the circumstances, he believed that his effectiveness as the commander would be undermined.

For a moment, he looked at her carefully. Not as a subordinate officer, but as another human being. The heat and humidity had soaked her uniform, and her hair, piled on her head, most of it hidden by her helmet, was damp. He wished, for just a moment, that he could forget about the battalion and command and talk to her. But he knew it just couldn't be done.

Finally, he turned and moved back to the field desk. He picked up a couple of papers and studied them. "I have the duty rosters for tonight ready. Do you have any questions?"

"No, sir." She wanted to say more, but decided that it wasn't the best idea. They had already had a number of confrontations and certainly she didn't need another the first night on a new planet, surrounded by hostile aliens. She would quietly alert some of the more trusted officers and senior NCOs. She would tell them to keep their eyes and ears open and not to be afraid to act at their own discretion. She wouldn't tell them that she was afraid that the new commander wouldn't be able to handle the problems. She would tell them that the situation was fluid and they had to stay alert.

She watched the major work for a couple of minutes and felt sorry for him. It had to be difficult to be thrown into a new battalion where no one knew who you were or what you had done. And where you knew no one. Maybe that was why he seemed a little erratic. She would just have to do her job better. She would try to take some of the pressure off him and see if that helped.

Without another word to him, she left the bunker, found the radio operator and told her to get back on radio watch. They wanted to make sure that they were in touch with the fleet at all times, just in case the enemy decided that tonight would be a good night to wipe them out.

5

THE DEMOCRATIC REGION
OF PROCYON TWO

IT WASN'T UNTIL noon on the next day that they found the area that Division had designated for their main base. It was a gigantic open field that rested on top of a gentle slope. Down the back side was a wide, meandering river that held crystal-clear water. They could see the bottom easily and the fish swimming in it. The jungle ended on the far bank of the river, giving them an open area that was more than three klicks in diameter.

Jefferson checked his map, another of the aerial photos, saw that the landmarks fit, and then showed it to Carter, the intelligence officer, who agreed with him. Jefferson then folded the photograph and stuffed it into one of his pockets.

He spotted his executive officer. "Looks like we're here. Captain Torrence, I want you to call the fleet and have them drop the rest of our equipment, and make some arrangements to pick up the empty pods."

"Yes, sir."

The supply officer—looking hot, sweaty, and unhappy—approached. As she did, Jefferson said, "Norris, you better begin checking the equipment. See how we stand. What we've lost. That sort of thing."

Without waiting for her reply, Jefferson continued, pointing at the other officers clustered around him. "Winston, you better get a muster together. See how many are still missing. And Carter, you find Tyson and the two of you had better start arranging things with our allies. We've got a lot of work to do before it gets dark."

When they had run off to complete the tasks given them, Jefferson asked Peyton, the operations officer, "What are your plans?"

"Right now, most of the equipment we need is scattered all over the countryside. I don't know what we have and what we've lost. I'll get together with Norris and find that out. I'd like to get a strand or two of concertina out as a barrier, although, looking at the aliens, I don't think it will make much difference to them."

"We've got to get some kind of perimeter established before nightfall," said Jefferson.

Peyton rubbed his chin, feeling the stubble there. "We'll have something, although I don't know if it will be effective. I wish Tyson were here. He could answer a couple of questions."

"Such as?"

"For one thing, he could tell us why the first group of aliens attacked us."

"These are things that we can worry about when we have the base established. Right now, all we can do is work to get the thing built as quickly as possible."

Torrence returned. "Fleet's going to drop us a couple of construction robots. One to lay the wire and another to dig foxholes. They said they would try to locate anything we lost and bring it to us."

"They say why we were off the mark?" asked Jefferson.

"Didn't think to ask and they didn't offer any explanations. I figured they would let us know."

Jefferson smiled. "I doubt that they'll volunteer any information. Okay, as soon as the robots are down, have Peyton tell you where he wants the wire and then get busy with the outer defenses. Once that is done, we can begin throwing up the pre-fabs."

"We going to work out a training schedule?" asked Peyton.

"For whom?" asked Jefferson, somewhat annoyed.

"The aliens."

"Right now we have more important things to worry about.

Besides, there are only twelve or fifteen of them. Say, what do they call themselves? We can't go on referring to them as the aliens."

"I'll ask Tyson," Torrence chimed in.

"Anyway," continued Jefferson, "there aren't enough of them to worry about training right now. Once more of them arrive we can begin setting up the training platoons." He looked at Torrence. "You get the list of names of the people who can speak the language."

"Yes, sir. There's not very many of them. And one of those was killed yesterday."

"What do you mean there aren't many of them?"

"As I understand," she said, "there is something about the language that makes it impossible for most people to speak it. They can understand it, but they can't speak it. So, of the twenty or thirty people who were sent into the hypo tanks, only about half of them came out with the ability to speak. And one of those is dead."

"Well, that certainly is good news," said Jefferson. "How come no one bothered to tell me?"

Torrence shrugged and wiped the sweat from her face. "Administrative detail that didn't require anything from you."

"Any other surprises that I should know about?"

"No, sir," said Torrence.

"What about patrols?" asked Peyton.

"We'll start that tomorrow. I doubt that we have to worry about anything tonight."

"Major," said Torrence. "That was the mistake I made on my first night in the simulator. And we've already been hit once."

"The difference is," Jefferson reminded her, "we are not in enemy territory. We are surrounded by friendlies. And I didn't say that we wouldn't have out pickets and a couple of LP's. I just said that we would keep everyone else at home."

Jefferson turned slowly, looking at the activity all around him. Nearly the whole battalion was there. Some of them were assembling the tent city, some of them unpacking equipment and setting it up. Others were out, cutting down the large bushes that grew between the battalion area and the trees of the jungle. They were filling in depressions that would give the aliens places to hide, and creating a killing zone four to five hundred yards wide around the whole camp. No one would be sneaking up on them.

"Okay, Captain Peyton, you have your orders. Hop to it," said Jefferson. "Captain Torrence, I would like to talk to you for a minute."

As Peyton walked away, Torrence said, "You're not worried about the aliens?"

"Not right now. Fleet and Intell have assured me that the enemy hasn't really penetrated this deeply into the friendly territory. Oh, we can expect some activity, mainly harassment, but nothing of a major nature."

"That's what they told me on the first night of the exercise."

"Your problem, Vicky, is that you confuse an exercise with the real thing. This is not an exercise and there isn't anyone around to mislead us. Fleet is running surveillance of the whole area for us and will pick up any large concentrations of aliens moving toward us. However, if it will make you feel better, put out a couple of small patrols, circle the camp at no more than a klick and stay in radio contact."

"I'll see to it, Major."

"Fine." Jefferson turned his back and watched as the men and women of his battalion struggled to get the camp ready for night.

Tyson and Carter, having located Zeric, were now following him and three of his friends from the camp toward their village. They weaved through the jungle, cutting back and forth across their own trail in an obvious attempt to keep the Earthmen from learning the path to the village. The attempt was in vain, however, since Carter kept track of the direct route by eliminating the loops. Zeric didn't ask what the map that he used was, and Carter didn't volunteer the information. It took them over four hours to reach the enclave.

As they left the jungle, they found themselves on a bluff overlooking the village, which was laid out in a series of concentric circles with a large, circular building in the center. The pathways to the building were a maze of twists and turns, lined with long, thin buildings. Standing on the bluff, an officer designing an assault could map out the shortest routes to the center of the city. It would give an attacker a tactical advantage, but Zeric didn't seem to be aware of it and there was no evidence that anyone had ever erected any type of guard post on the bluff.

When they started down the bluff, Carter said quietly, in English, "This isn't such a good idea. We're out here by ourselves and no one knows where we are."

"Don't worry about it. If we get killed, Jefferson will be happy to have lost me. Figure it's one fewer problem to deal with, and it will tell him that the aliens are unfriendly."

"Except they're supposed to be our allies."

"Except for that," agreed Tyson.

"You see anything strange about the village?" asked Carter.

"Nothing spectacular. The layout is strange, but seems to be functional as well. The streets and pathways would make it difficult for an invading army. That's why many of the streets in European and Asian cities were so narrow and winding. You have something else in mind?"

"Just wondering," said Carter.

They entered the village. Tyson could see it wasn't a series of primitive structures, but was made of steel and concrete, with glass windows. If it wasn't for the fact that all the buildings, except for the central fortress, were only one story high, it would look like a city of Earth, built at the end of the nineteenth century.

The only thing missing was the inhabitants. No one seemed to live there. Tyson wanted to walk slowly, so that he could study it. He noticed that there were no electric lights. He noticed that the streets were paved and clean. And, as they penetrated deeper, he saw that there were shops. Or, at least, there were buildings that had large windows that showed all kinds of different things. Clothes in one. The ponchos and pants were universal, but the colors and patterns changed. Another held something that looked remarkably like a television.

Carter leaned close to Tyson and whispered, "This is not what I expected. I thought we would run into something primitive. Maybe thatched roofs, mud huts. Nothing like this."

"Never go into something with preconceived notions, if you're operating blind," said Tyson.

As they approached the center, they began to see signs of destruction. First it was evidence of a fire. Then a building that looked as if it had exploded, and as they turned another corner, there was rubble lying in the street. A couple of craters were near an intersection.

Carter said, "They've been bombed."

"Or rocketed," countered Tyson. "Don't assume anything until we know for sure. It does look like enemy action, though."

"Looks like it's recent, too."

"Yeah. It sure does."

With twenty fully equipped troopers, Torrence began her sweep through the jungle. The strange orange moss extended into the jungle, making it look like a carefully manicured lawn. They made easy progress, even though they stayed away from the trails. There was no thick undergrowth to fight, no steep hills to climb or wide streams to cross. It was more like a walk in the park than a patrol on a foreign planet with hostile aliens.

The patrol uncovered nothing. There was no evidence that any large group had moved through the area recently. In fact, there was no evidence that anyone had moved through the jungle, though Torrence wasn't sure they could recognize the sign if they saw it. Even their back trail looked clean and almost undisturbed. Just a slight scuffing of the moss that seemed to be shifting around as if to repair itself and conceal the path. After three hours, she returned to the camp, satisfied that there were no enemies around them. Or at least that there was no large concentration of them preparing for an attack.

Torrence reported to Jefferson about an hour before sunset. She stood, facing the sun and Jefferson, squinting despite a boiling, yellowish cloud cover. It hadn't rained since they landed, but it looked like it would at any moment. Humidity was running high, making them sweat more.

"Didn't find a thing," she told him. "There were no obvious signs that anyone had traveled through the jungle near us and no sign of troop concentrations."

"Then you're satisfied with the safety precautions?"

"Yes, sir. No problem."

Just as she finished speaking, there was a loud crump and a geyser of dark dirt and day-glo moss leaped into the air. Three troopers fell, one screaming and holding his knee.

Torrence dropped immediately, yelling "Incoming!"

Jefferson stood, turning slowly, looking for the flash of the enemy weapons, but saw nothing. He lifted a hand to his eyes to shade them. There wasn't another explosion. As the dust settled, the troops began to scatter, heading toward their battle stations on the perimeter.

"Guess I was wrong," said Torrence sheepishly, brushing at the front of her dirty, sweatsoaked fatigues.

An NCO ran up, saluted quickly and said, "We got three hurt, Major. Don't think it's serious. I think the battalion surgeon can take care of it unless you want to evac them to the fleet."

Jefferson shook his head. "If the Doc thinks they'll be all right, we'll just keep them here. If this was a couple of weeks from now, I'd let them go up for a rest."

"Yes, sir."

Jefferson turned his attention to Torrence. "First, I don't want any more saluting in the field. Tells the enemy who the officers are."

"I don't think we have to worry about that."

"Don't argue, just issue the order. Now, you were saying that you found no evidence of the enemy in the area?"

"That's what I was saying," she sighed. She took a deep breath. "Guess they're around here somewhere."

"I'm not sure that I agree. Could have been a mine. Could have been a lot of things. It doesn't mean that there are any aliens around or that there are many of them. Just the same, we'll go to half alert after midnight. Tomorrow, as I say, we'll begin patrolling for real."

The closer they got to the center of the circle, the more damage they saw. Tyson thought that it looked like a target. A few rounds outside the rings, some scattered inside them, and a lot concentrated in the black. The pockmarks on the streets were becoming more frequent and the damage to the buildings was heavier. Some of the buildings were nothing more than bombed-out shells. There was no glass in any of the windows and the stone and concrete used for construction was blackened, as if by fire. There was a stench coming from the buildings. An undercurrent of odor that suggested death by violence.

As they reached the outer wall of the central building, there were battle scars all over. Pockmarks from rifle bullets and damage done by explosions. The once handsome structure was shrapnel-scarred. The facade was damaged, making it look old and used up.

In part of the city (Tyson could no longer think of it as a village), in the fringes as they had entered, there had been shade plants, the large, red sticks covered with the parachute-like leaves. Around the central structure there were the remains of the plants. Shrapnel or concussion had stripped the leaves from them.

The buildings there had no glass in them. But, unlike Earth where the windows would have been boarded over to protect them from looters, the broken glass had been replaced with clear plastic to protect the interior from the elements. Some of the plastic now hung in strips.

The central building, made of polished stone and shining chrome, was surrounded by a wide moat. The surface of the water seemed to be covered with plants that looked like water lilies, except they were huge and red. A bridge of steel plate stretched from the bottom of the gate until it reached the bank of the moat close to where they stood.

Zeric pointed and said, "We go in here. See some of the others."

"What has happened here?" asked Carter.

"The enemy has been bombing us. They are trying to force us out of here. To make us move deeper into our country."

"And the people?" prompted Tyson.

"People?"

Tyson smiled at his own anthropomorphism. "Sorry. The inhabitants. The . . . ah . . . ?"

"Adnoly. We are called adnoly."

"All right. Where have all the adnoly gone."

"Many go to find relatives. Many are killed. Some come here for protection."

Carter whispered to Tyson, "You know, we could move the battalion in here. It would be more comfortable and be easy to defend since the defenses have already been erected."

"Unless the adnoly don't want us in here."

With the bridge in place, they crossed into the central building that Tyson now considered a castle. They moved through the entrance portal, saw evidence of thick gates that could slide into place, trapping invaders between both huge doors, and then entered a plaza. The surrounding walls had only a couple of thick doors. An upper level was ringed with windows, or firing ports, so that invaders, having penetrated that far, would have to fight their way out, using only a couple of small doors while the defenders fired down on them. It was a classic defense design.

They walked across the plaza, went through one of the doors and entered another courtyard. This one opened into a hundred rooms, some with glass fronts. There was a large pool surrounded by a hundred chairs. Male and female adnoly sat around in abbrieviated costumes. Others were in the pool, splashing around, although none of them were swimming. There was no evidence of youngsters.

To the right was a long table heaped with colorful food. Much of it looked like fruit, although none of it looked like anything that Tyson had ever seen on Earth.

Zeric gestured at the table. "You may eat."

"Ah . . ." hesitated Carter.

Tyson elbowed him in the ribs to shut him up. "We may have a problem with that, Zeric."

"Why?"

"We have never eaten any of your food and we don't know what we can eat without getting sick."

"But this is food. Everybody eats it and nobody gets sick."

"Yes. But adnoly have always eaten it. We have never tried it. Surely there are plants that the animals can eat that the adnoly can't. Until we have a chance to test the food, we'll have to pass."

"You'll not eat with the adnoly?"

Tyson studied the face of Zeric. He knew nothing about the expressions or the body language of the adnoly. And he didn't know the customs. On Earth, refusal to join certain hosts in a meal was the same as declaring war. People had died in similar situations and the insult had festered for centuries, creating gulfs between the two sides. If the meal was that important, Tyson couldn't refuse it, no matter what the consequences to him personally might be.

He grinned and nodded, "Of course I'll eat with you."

"Are you out of your mind?" exclaimed Carter, in English.

"Probably. But we have to do something. If I don't make it, tell Jefferson I died for the good of the battalion." Tyson smiled. "Actually, it's probably not that great a risk. I doubt seriously that anything they eat will be poisonous to us. I won't eat much and hope for the best. If I get sick, get me to the fleet fast."

"Good luck," said Carter.

After the sun had set, Torrence and the personnel officer, Winston, found Jefferson sitting in the pre-fab command post. It was a bunker with a heavy machine gun, the radio rack, and Jefferson's field desk.

"Can't find either Lieutenant Carter or that new man, that anthropologist."

"Tyson?"

"Yeah. Tyson. Can't find either one and no one has seen them for several of hours. And Zeric is gone with most of his aliens. Only two or three are around here."

"Now how in the hell did that happen?" snapped Jefferson.

"No one was watching that closely, sir," said Torrence. "Everyone was trying to get their jobs done before dark. I guess they just walked off into the jungle."

"Well, shit," said Jefferson. "Okay, I want a twenty-trooper patrol ready to move out in fifteen minutes. I want everyone to advance into the jungle right now and see if anyone can find a sign of which way they went. When their trail is located, the patrol will follow it and try to drag them back."

"Excuse me, Major," responded Torrence, "But the moss isn't good at retaining footprints. Unless they knocked down some trees on their way out, I don't think any signs are going to be found. That was the problem we had earlier."

"All right, keep the aliens in the center of the perimeter and break out the tracking glasses. Give the patrol leader and two senior NCO's a set and tell them not to let the goddamned locals see them. Tell them to take off as soon as they're outfitted, but to be back by midnight."

"Anyone in particular you want to send?"

"No. Don't let a company commander go. Put a platoon leader in charge of it. And once they have Tyson and Carter back here, I want to see them."

* * *

Second Lieutenant Thomas Newton and Sergeant Randi Kingsley inched their way around the perimeter until they found what they thought was the trail of Tyson and Carter and the aliens. Kingsley let her glasses fall away from her eyes and squinted into the distance. The fading light made it hard to see, but she thought that she could detect the path through the jungle.

Newton followed her pointed finger and saw the trail vividly. "Okay, Sergeant. Get the rest of the people and let's move out."

Another NCO, Tech Sergeant Dennis Garth, took the point. He would hold the glasses to his eyes, spot the trail and then move forward until he needed another look. He had two people with him who were supposed to provide protection.

Newton and Kingsley followed, near the middle of the column. Kingsley had her pair of glasses, but they had given the other set to a corporal who was in the rear guard. Newton had a starlight-type scope with him. It turned the surrounding jungle into daylight although the colors through the scope were muddied, changing to browns and tans.

For an hour they wandered along the trail. It wasn't difficult given the equipment they had. They were alert for ambush, slightly worried because they were in an alien environment, but Newton wasn't overly concerned because he didn't think that the enemy would be able to find them that quickly or that easily now that the sun was gone. He had gotten the impression from the fleet briefings that the aliens were only a little farther advanced than the Indians in the American West when the white man began the big push to California and Colorado. Streeter, and all the others, had let the impression grow uncorrected because Division felt that the men and women of the 767th needed to feel superior to the aliens.

So, when there was an explosion at the front of the column, Newton didn't react quickly. He stood in the center, trying to find out what was happening. The rattling of rifle fire, directed at them, didn't impress him. He stood searching with his starlight scope, trying to figure it out.

Kingsley dove to the ground at the first sound. She rolled to her right and kicked Newton's feet out from under him. He fell to his side, his rifle under his arm and his body hitting on top of it. Even with all the sound, the shooting and explosions around him, he heard the snap of the bones.

For the moment, there was no pain. He rolled to his stomach, got to his knees and lifted the scope to his eyes. Through it he could see the enemy positions. It was a classic L-shaped ambush, except that the ambushers hadn't found good cover.

Shakily, he got to his feet. He tossed the scope aside and grabbed his rifle. Flipping the selector to full auto, he shouted, "Let's go! Let's go!"

He ran forward, toward the enemy, firing from the hip. Single shots. Others did the same. They leaped up, fired and ran forward, screaming. Kingsley followed, bent and grabbed the belt of a man, trying to jerk him to his feet. She then propelled him at the ambushers.

When his rifle was empty, Newton tossed it aside and pulled his pistol. He fired at the enemy. He hit one of them square in the head, saw a third eye appear above its other two and saw the creature grin at him as if it wasn't hurt. It stood up, a bayoneted rifle in front of it and ran at Newton.

The startled lieutenant slipped to a halt and raised his pistol again, firing six times. He could see the bullets striking the chest of the alien. He could see the dust fly from the dirty poncho and could even see the bullet holes appear in the stiff material. But the creature came right at him, intent on sticking the bayonet through him. The bullets didn't seem to affect it.

From the right came the chattering of an assault rifle on full auto. The bullets smashed the creature's legs and knees. It stumbled, righted itself and then went down, rolling. It tried to sit up, but the hammering of the rifle didn't stop. The rounds slammed into its chest and head. With a roar like an attacking lion, the alien slipped down and didn't move.

Around him, his patrol charged into the ambushers just as the infantry manual said they should. But it didn't disturb the aliens. It didn't frighten them. They just stood to meet the threat, firing their clumsy rifles and pistols. The muzzle flashes were gigantic, orange-yellow bursts that lit the whole scene. Human and alien both, standing, firing. Human weapons now hammering away, strobing like the flash of cameras. The battle took on the jerky surrealism of an old, silent movie as the two sides came together. The noise of the battle grew until it was a din that wiped out all other sound. Weapons firing, men and women screaming, and the enemy shrieking.

When the aliens ran out of bullets, they moved in to use the long, spiked bayonets that they were all equipped with. They swung their rifles, using their superior physical strength to smash the humans.

Newton saw Garth empty his weapon into one of them. He then watched Garth throw the useless rifle away and leap at the alien feet first. The weight of the collision knocked the enemy to its back, but it rolled over and got up. When Garth got close to it, its arm flashed and it grabbed Garth around the throat with its long fingers. It lifted him clear off the ground, shook him as a dog shakes a rabbit, and then threw him into one of the large parachute bushes. Garth crashed through it to the ground and didn't move.

A burst of rifle fire exploded the enemy's head and it collapsed, its feet drumming the soft, moss-covered ground.

Kingsley ran forward and tried to pull Newton back to safety. "You okay?" she shouted. "You okay?"

Before he could answer, an alien jumped on her, knocking her to the ground. Newton kicked, connecting with what should have been the alien's ribs, but it apparently felt nothing. It was trying to pick up its rifle so that it could kill Kingsley with the bayonet.

With his good hand, Newton felt the ground around him and found a rifle. As he rolled to his back, bracing the butt of the rifle against the ground, he flipped the selector to full auto, emptying the magazine into the creature. Even after taking the full twenty rounds in the back, the alien stumbled forward a couple of steps before falling.

Now Newton tried to drag Kingsley from the field. With his good hand, he snagged the collar of her uniform. He managed to get her behind one of the parachute bushes and left her, moaning quietly. He stepped around it, crouched and studied the field. Nearby were two of the creatures, and he thought that he could see a human with them. And standing behind them was another human, all of them looking like the Indian chiefs watching the battle below them. Newton didn't recognize them or their uniforms.

He had tossed away his starlight scope so that he lost the detail in the dark, but with the scattered moonlight, he could see enough. He knew that they weren't members of his patrol and didn't think they belonged to the battalion.

He dropped to one knee and fumbled with the magazine of Kingsley's rifle. He loaded it and then tried to line up the sights as he had been taught in night-firing. He didn't use the rear peep sight, but tried to put the V of the front one on the chest of one of the humans. He pulled the trigger and felt the weapon recoil, but he couldn't tell where his shots were going because he had no tracers.

As the bullets snapped by them, one of the humans reached out and grabbed the shoulder of the other, dragging him backwards, deeper into the jungle growth. Newton lost sight of them as they fled into the dark.

To one side, he saw two of his people running toward the enemy and the humans with them. Both were firing from the hip. One of them had tracers in the assault rifle, and Newton saw the bullets wipe through the jungle undergrowth and the bushes. Several rounds seemed to pass close to the aliens and the fleeing humans.

Suddenly they stopped running and whirled. Both dropped, and then opened fire. Not with the clumsy weapons of the aliens, but assault rifles. The muzzle flashes strobed. Both of Newton's people were hit and both fell, one tossing his weapon into the air as he dropped.

The firing began to taper off into random shots. Newton tried to reload the rifle again, but sudden pain flared, and his broken arm wouldn't cooperate. Cold sweat blossomed on his forehead and he felt sick to his stomach. The pain threatened to pull a curtain of black over him.

As the aliens withdrew, disappearing into the jungle, Newton's surviving soldiers began to move. One stood and fired a parting burst and then dropped to the ground. Another shouted something unintelligible. An NCO was up, yelling. "I want a skirmish line now. To the right. Move it."

Newton staggered back to where he'd left Kingsley. He dropped to his knees near her, his head down.

"You okay?" she asked.

Newton let the rifle slip from his fingers and nodded. "Fine. You?"

"Okay. We go on?" asked Kingsley.

Newton ignored the question and asked, "How are you? You hurt badly?"

"Nah," she said shaking her head. "Just had the breath knocked out of me. Are we going on?" she repeated.

"No," said Newton, trying to keep his world from fading away. "We turn back."

"That many people hurt?"

"I don't know about casualties yet," Newton said. "I saw some humans with the aliens. They weren't our people. I think it's more important to report that than to continue to look for Tyson and Carter. They'll just have to take care of themselves."

6

INSIDE THE ADNOLY CASTLE

AFTER THE SUN had set and it was completely dark, a bank of lights on the top of the building came on, illuminating the inner courtyard. The heat and humidity of the day didn't break with the setting of the sun. But Tyson learned, as he sampled the adnoly food, that there was something in the food that made the temperature easier to take. It was as refreshing as diving in a pool of cold, clear water. For the first time since they landed, he didn't notice how hot it was.

The food itself didn't taste all that different from Earth fruits. There was one with a texture like an apple and the taste of a banana. There were several juicy fruits that ranged from the very sweet to the very sour. And there were vegetables too. Tyson, after a cautious beginning, decided that he wasn't going to get sick and started sampling everything.

The adnoly seemed to disappear with the sun. There had been dozens of adults around until it was dark. Then there were only the few that had been escorts for Tyson and Carter.

"We don't care for the night," Zeric explained. "It is not that we fear the dark, it is that we don't see well in it, and until the invention of the incandescent light, we rose with the sun and slept with sundown. Old habits are hard to break."

Both Tyson and Carter were sitting in the chairs that surrounded the pool. Zeric and his males were with them.

Carter, searching for military information, asked, "How did this conflict start?"

Zeric shrugged in a very human manner. "Who is to say? Those of the Rexoc Empire desired to have the minerals buried under our soil. They didn't want to pay for it, and attacked us. We fought back, but they have sowed the seeds of discontent among the adnoly."

"Then your own kind, the ah, adnoly, of your realm are fighting one another?"

"Not really. There are some who believe that life under the Rexoc would be better. But they are a small minority."

"Uh-huh," mumbled Carter.

Zeric didn't understand the comment and continued. "Most of our adnoly alert us when the Rexoc are near, but some help them. They have more and better weapons."

Tyson felt that Carter was pumping Zeric for too much information too fast, so he tried to change the subject. "From what you said, I take it that we won't be going back to the camp tonight."

"No," said Zeric. "It would be too hard to find it at night. And there are enemies who creep through the jungle in the night. Better to wait until morning."

Tyson sat back so that he could stare into the night sky. The cloud cover that had obscured it for most of the day seemed to have thinned so that some stars showed through. Even with that, Tyson couldn't see much. Only a couple of the brightest of the stars, and he hadn't taken enough astronomy to know which ones they were. If the night had been clear, he might have been able to identify a couple of constellations. Then he realized that he didn't know if they were in a part of the galaxy where familiar constellations would be visible. The perspective might be enough to throw everything off.

Deciding that he didn't care about that at the moment, he said, "Since we aren't going back tonight, where are we going to sleep?"

"Arrangements are being made. I hope that you will find them comfortable."

"And tomorrow we return to the camp," asked Carter, somewhat alarmed.

"Of course."

* * *

Sitting on the soft moss-covered ground, his soldiers working around him, Newton was fairly comfortable. His arm ached, but the pain that had threatened to knock him out was gone. The curtain of black had risen and he was watching his troops clean the battlefield, treat the wounded, and cover the dead.

But then he tried to stand. Pain flared brightly, a white-hot jolt that brought tears to his eyes and turned his stomach inside out. Without knowing it, he began to weave like a drunken sailor, unable to make sense of his surroundings.

Kingsley saw the young lieutenant sway and leaped up to catch him. She reached out, saw the strange angle of his arm and the blood on the sleeve of his fatigue jacket. She grabbed his shoulders and steadied him. Without a word, she pushed him gently to the rear so that he would sit down.

Newton sat down, wishing there was a real tree nearby that he could lean against. To Kingsley, he said, "Get a count. See how many we lost."

"No problem. You going to be all right?"

"I'll be fine," said Newton, gritting his teeth. "See if the medic has anything to take the edge off the pain."

Kingsley got to her feet and began checking out the patrol. She caught the sleeve of an NCO as he rushed by her. She spun him and asked, "How'd we do?"

"Seven dead and three wounded, if you count the lieutenant."

Kingsley nodded. "You can count the lieutenant. Got hurt saving my butt."

"Looked more like you got hurt saving his," said the sergeant, staring at her intensely.

She shook her head. "Doesn't matter. He saved me and I saved him and we've got seven dead."

"Including Garth," said the sergeant.

"What about the aliens?"

"We've got six bodies, but no equipment." He studied her for a moment. "Looks like they've picked up some of our equipment. Couple of assault rifles are missing." He hesitated. "And unless you or the lieutenant have an extra pair of night glasses, we're missing them too."

"Damn. Okay, thanks." She turned then, walking back to where Newton waited. She crouched near him and said,

"We're going to have to leave the dead. We've got too many dead and wounded to carry everyone out."

"How many killed?"

"Seven."

"Ah, shit! Seven! Really? Seven?"

"Yes sir," she said quietly. She could hear the pain in his voice, hear that he cared about those who had died. "I'm sorry about that. You did well, though. You broke up the ambush. Most of us survived."

"But seven," sighed Newton. "Ah, Jesus. Seven."

Kingsley wanted to say more, but didn't know what it could be. She could suggest that it wasn't important, that the majority had survived. It hadn't been anything he had done and it wasn't his fault. In fact, his performance had been good. But it would only be so many words and that wouldn't help. She decided to try to divert his thoughts.

"How is your arm?"

"It's killing me. Did you find the medic?"

"Nope. I'll see if I can find her in a second. Then we'll be heading back to the camp, right?"

"As fast as we can. Do you think that you can take over for me now? I feel sick to my stomach and I can't concentrate. I know you're not supposed to assume command, but I really think it would be best."

"Don't worry about it. It's only a short trip back to the camp, and you'll be right here if anything happens. I'll get everything organized."

"Just as soon as the medic looks at me, let's get out of here."

Inside the adnoly castle there didn't seem to be one straight line. The walls were curved, the ceiling concave and the floor dipped into a shallow depression. Tyson felt momentarily dizzy as he stepped in and was assaulted by the riot of color splashed on the walls. There were bright oranges and reds that blended into yellows on the ceiling and floor.

"Well," said Carter, "it's different."

"Different wasn't exactly the word that I had in mind," responded Tyson. "Bizarre, maybe. Strange. But certainly it is different."

"I didn't think that you were supposed to comment on other lifestyles."

"I think that I'm supposed to remain objective while observing," said Tyson. "I am allowed to have opinions, and in my opinion, this is certainly, ah, stimulating."

Carter took a step backwards, as if suddenly frightened. "Now how did you mean stimulating?"

"Oh, knock it off," snapped Tyson.

Carter shrugged and walked through the room, to the door. "I think I've found the bedroom."

"I hope the colors aren't quite so bright."

Tyson moved over so that he could look in. The beds, or cots, were attached to the walls. The colors around them were muted, compared to those on the other walls. He walked in and sat down. There was an immediate sensation of heat.

"Say," said Tyson, "have you noticed anything about this place?"

"You mean these rooms, or the city, or the planet?"

"For an intelligence officer, you're sometimes dumb. I mean this whole environment."

Carter lowered his voice. "I wish you wouldn't throw that term around. The fewer people who know I'm the intell officer the better."

Tyson was going to protest and then thought better of it. Instead, he said, "What I mean is that this is supposed to be a primitive society. On the level of the mid-nineteenth century. But they certainly seemed to have advanced farther than that. This bed," Tyson patted the plastic covered cot, "is self-warming.

"And look at this building. The engineering in it is only just short of spectacular. This is not the mid-nineteenth century."

"I wouldn't worry about it," said Carter. "After all, they only had a few weeks here before we landed. Survey team just missed a couple of clues."

"Maybe," agreed Tyson. "Maybe. But there are still a lot of questions to be answered."

"Such as?"

"How did the survey team get enough of the language learned so that we could be taught how to communicate?"

"Computers. We have shiploads of computers that could put all that together."

"But in two weeks?"

"Probably in two hours, if they wanted," said Carter.

"A language is a very complex thing. To unravel it in only two weeks and prepare a program to teach it is a miracle."

"Forget it, Joe. It's not that important. You want something to worry about, I'll give you something. When we roll in tomorrow, Jefferson is going to hit the roof."

Tyson leaned back, against a wall that was slightly soft and yielding, and said, "Yeah. He's going to be pissed." Tyson was smiling.

It didn't take Kingsley long to organize the survivors of the patrol. In only a couple of minutes, they had fashioned stretchers out of the parachute plants and the stiff cords that supported them. The cords were as strong as saplings and the plants had a canvas-like texture. They also used some of the leaves to wrap the bodies of the dead, hoping that it would protect them from predators. They had seen virtually no animal life but that didn't mean the ambush site wouldn't be teeming with it seconds after they left.

They slowly worked their way back to the camp, avoiding the path they had followed from it, stopping every ten or twenty minutes to listen for the sound of pursuit and to switch the litter bearers.

Finally, two hours later, they approached the perimeter without being challenged, walked through it and right up to the command post. Newton directed the wounded to be taken to the battalion surgeon for treatment, but refused to go himself until he had talked with the commander.

Jefferson was sitting in a web chair, his feet propped up on an ammo crate. When he saw Newton and Kingsley, he sat up and said, "Did you find them?"

"No, sir. We were ambushed."

"Oh, shit. Did you . . ." Jefferson stopped talking, took a deep breath and said, "Tell me exactly what happened. From the beginning."

"Well, sir," said Newton, "we left here at . . ."

Jefferson noticed that the sleeve of Newton's uniform was torn and covered with blood. He saw a bandage hidden in the material of the uniform. "You okay?"

"Yes, sir."

Jefferson waved at one of the corporals who was standing nearby. "Get the Doc over here. Bring a couple of beers and see if you can round up some hot food. That okay with you two?"

Both Newton and Kingsley nodded approval.

"Sorry to interrupt. Go ahead."

Again Newton launched into his story of the patrol and the ambush, including how the starlight scope had helped spot the enemy positions. He underscored the difficulty in killing the aliens with the small caliber weapons they carried. He also detailed the aliens withdrawal procedure.

He finished the debriefing with, "I saw two people with them."

Jefferson didn't understand the significance of the comment. He blinked, as if a bright light had been flashed in his eyes and then asked, "You saw people? You mean human people? Our people?"

"No, sir," said Newton. "I mean that I didn't recognise them and they weren't wearing our uniform. I don't know who they are but I do know they were human."

For a moment Jefferson sat quietly, his mind racing. He knew that the people with the aliens couldn't possibly be anyone from his battalion. Everyone was now accounted for, except for Tyson and Carter. Nearly fifty of them were back with the fleet waiting to be redeployed, but everyone else had straggled into the base camp.

And, according to everything he knew, there were no other humans on the planet, except for some political types who were in the capital. They wouldn't be outside that city. It meant that there were some humans operating on the planet that no one knew a thing about.

Jefferson got up, walked around his chair twice, sat down and rubbed his face. "You say that you didn't recognize them. Any possibility that they were either Tyson or Carter?"

Newton glanced at Kingsley as if she might have the answer. He shook his head and said, "They were working with the enemy. Is there any reason that Tyson or Carter would be working with the enemy?"

"None that I can think of," said Jefferson. "They were working with the aliens?"

"Hell, sir, they shot at us."

"Okay," he said, "okay. I guess we need to give this to the

fleet. Ah, Newton, I guess we'll send you up for treatment for your arm. That way you can fill in Division Intell."

"Yes, sir."

"Sergeant," called Jefferson, turning and trying to get the attention of the radio operator. "I'll need to send a scrambled message to the fleet."

"I'll get the equipment fired up, sir."

Jefferson turned his attention back to Newton. "Anything else you can tell me about those people? Anything you noticed about them?"

"Just that they stayed in the background. If it hadn't been for the starlight, I would never have seen them."

"Damn!" said Jefferson. "There's something here. Something wrong, but I just don't know what it is."

"There's a couple of people working with the enemy, that's all," said Kingsley.

"No," said Jefferson, slowly. "It's something more than that."

"Sir," said the radio operator. "I have contact established and the signal is secured."

"Thank you." To Newton he said, "Anything else?"

"No, sir."

Jefferson moved to the radio, took the mike and told the fleet intell officer what he had learned. Then he asked, "Who are they? What status do they hold?"

"Wait one," came the response.

While they waited, Torrence entered the command post. She glanced at Newton and Kingsley. She locked eyes with Newton and quietly asked how he was. He held up a hand to indicate that he was feeling all right.

She turned to Jefferson. "What's going on?"

"Tell you in a minute."

The radio crackled to life. "Headhunter Six, be advised that the humans are renegades from Earth. If encountered again, you are advised to withdraw. They are not to be engaged in combat. Do you copy?"

Jefferson sat silently for a moment staring at the radio as if it had turned into something ugly that smelled like an open sewer.

"Do you copy?"

"Roger. Understand," he said, even though he didn't understand. The instructions were odd.

"Also, we would like the patrol leader and the NCOIC to report to fleet as soon as possible. Transport will be arranged for first light."

"Roger."

"You will be advised if additional information becomes available. Out."

As soon as he had signed off, Jefferson said, "You two are dismissed. Catch some sleep. Be ready to leave tomorrow morning and don't discuss this with anyone else."

When they were gone, Torrence said, "What's going on?"

Jefferson explained the situation as he understood it. Then he said, "What I don't understand is how those renegades got here. I mean, according to the information, we haven't known about this place all that long. How could those people get here so fast without us knowing about it?"

"Not to mention," said Torrence, "the fact that nobody has their own interstellar ship."

"You know," Jefferson mused, "there are a lot of things that seem fishy about this whole deal. There's something bothering me about it, but I just can't put my finger on it. I mean other than the fact that those people are out there."

Torrence moved to a table set up in the corner of the command post where there was hot coffee. She poured a cup and then leaned back so that the table was supporting her hips. "You want something else to worry about?" She sipped the coffee waiting.

"Why not? I don't have enough yet."

"The patrol walked in here without being challenged."

"They what?"

"Walked right out of the jungle, through the perimeter and into the command post without once having to tell anyone who they were. I asked some of the troops why they didn't challenge them and they said because they could see that it wasn't the aliens. Figured it had to be our people."

"Great. Just fucking great."

"And that doesn't explain where Captain Tyson and Lieutenant Carter got to," said Torrence.

"Yeah," said Jefferson. "I'm looking forward to seeing them again. I really am."

* * *

The morning dawned bright. For the first time since they had landed on the planet, they could see the sky, and even though it was green, it was pleasant to see it. Tyson, dressed only in boxer shorts, stood on the balcony of the room that he and Carter had shared. Three stories below him, he could see some of the adnoly. Again, it was just males and females and no children. They were circulating among the tables and chairs, in some kind of strange ritual.

Tyson leaned against the rail, arms folded across his chest. He kept his eyes locked on the scene spread out below him.

The adnoly all finally went to the pool. They knelt in front of it, but rather than washing, as Tyson thought they might, they began to drink. First one half of them, and then the other. He could see no reason for it. The first group was made up of both males and females, so it wasn't broken down by sex. There may have been some hierarchical reason for it, but Tyson couldn't be sure.

When the drinking was done, they did wash, and as a group, stood up. They moved to the tables where the food had been the night before. Tyson couldn't tell whether there were new piles of it or not because everything looked the same.

The adnoly had now broken up into smaller groups, some containing only two individuals. As each group reached the table, one of them took a large amount of food, while the others took a very little. Those with a little food moved to a pit near the end of the table and tossed the food in. Once everyone was served, the pit was set on fire.

It looked like some kind of sacrificial ritual, or a thanking of the gods for a bountiful harvest. Or maybe it was an offering to ancestors. There were a hundred things that it could have been. Tyson wished that he had a video so that he could record the event. Then he wished that he would be around the next morning to see if they went through it again.

Once all the adnoly had food, those with a large amount now shared it with the others in the group. They sat down and began to eat. From that point it looked like any community type breakfast that Tyson could have seen on Earth.

Carter joined Tyson then. "Say, Joe. The sun."

Tyson looked at the sky. "Yeah. Not very bright, though."

"What's happening down there?"

Tyson laughed. "Damned if I know. They're eating breakfast now. That's about all I can tell you."

"I suppose that we should think about getting back."

"Jefferson is probably flipping out right now."

"I guess," said Carter, "that we better find Zeric and see if we can get back to the camp."

7

THE 767TH'S BASE CAMP, PROCYON TWO

At dawn, Jefferson was asleep in the command post, having decided to wait there, rather than try to get a tent set up. Besides, it was a little drier and cooler inside. He woke with a start, sat up, and rubbed his face. He looked over at the two NCO's on radio watch, but didn't speak to them. Instead he stood up, walked stiffly to the hatch, and exited.

Outside he stretched and quickly surveyed the area. There were people moving around the perimeter, getting ready for the day. Then, off to the right, he saw Torrence and wondered if she ever slept. He walked over to her and asked, "Tyson and Carter reappear anytime during the night?"

"No one approached after the patrol came back. I think they're probably off with Zeric and the other aliens."

"Okay, I'll want to see Sinclair or Rider. Have them get a patrol ready to go out again. Let them get some breakfast first, but I'm afraid that it will have to be cold, and then send them out."

"Why cold? We have the self-heating rations."

"I meant that I didn't want them to take time to go through the battalion mess facility."

"Yes, sir. Would you like to go?"

Jefferson shot a glance at her, wondering if she was being

sarcastic. There was nothing in the tone of her voice, or in her face to suggest that she was baiting him.

"No. I'll want to stay here in case Tyson and Carter return. Once you get that taken care of, come over to the command post and we'll work out a schedule for patrolling. I may go out this afternoon."

"Yes, sir. Oh, Newton and Kingsley are ready to blast off. Shuttle is supposed to land about ten to take them out."

Jefferson sighed and scratched his face. "You know, Vicky, that is really strange. Don't let the aliens know how far advanced we are, but land a shuttle in here. Not to mention the fact that we're here, physically. I mean, that implies some kind of space travel."

"Ours is not to reason why?" She said it like it was a question.

"Exactly. Let me know when the patrol is ready to leave."

Zeric showed up while Tyson and Carter were still standing on the balcony discussing Jefferson and the state he was probably in.

"We go eat and then go back to your camp," said Zeric.

"That's fine," said Tyson. "What's happening this morning?"

"Nothing."

"Nothing," repeated Tyson. "You mean that activity is normal?"

Zeric looked completely puzzled, Tyson thought, and ignored the question.

"We must hurry."

"Why must we hurry?" asked Carter.

Zeric shrugged as he had seen the humans do a dozen times and said, "To get back to the camp."

"Well, there is that," agreed Tyson.

Long before Tyson and Carter were back at camp, Jefferson knew that they were on the way. One of the listening posts that he had put out during the night told him that they had seen Tyson and Carter and a group of aliens moving through the jungle. When they finally left the jungle, Jefferson was there, waiting for them.

Tyson and Carter saw him at the same time. Carter leaned

close to Tyson and said, "He doesn't seem to be too happy, does he?"

"I haven't hung around your major long enough to tell, but no, I don't think he's too happy."

Carter wiped a sweaty hand on the front of his fatigues. "Yeah."

As soon as they were in yelling distance, Jefferson shouted, "Where in the hell have you people been?"

Carter started to answer but Tyson put a restraining hand on his arm and said quietly, "Officers don't go shouting all over the command."

When they were at the wire that had been erected by the robot the day before, Jefferson hissed at them. "I want both of you in the command post in two minutes." He turned and stormed away.

In the command post, Jefferson had taken up residence behind a field desk and was suddenly engrossed in a paper that was sitting there. He wouldn't look up as the two officers entered. It was an old and worthless trick.

Rather than play that game, Tyson said, "We're here. If you have no questions, I'll go prepare my report for the general."

Jefferson looked up startled, as if he had just heard a dog bark. "What'd you say?"

"I was saying," said Tyson, conversationally, "that I'll go prepare my report for the general if you have no questions or objections."

Jefferson felt his hands begin to tremble and heard the paper he was holding rattle. Slowly, he set it on the desk and turned his whole attention on Tyson, ignoring Carter.

"I don't know where you think you get off, Tyson, but I've had about all I'm going to take from you."

Tyson leaned forward, one hand on the desk, his face only inches from Jefferson. He said quietly, "And I told you that I don't bully. I operate for the general. Not for you. If you have a problem, let's talk about it, but don't sit there and think that you're going to dictate to me. You don't frighten me with your juvenile games."

For a moment they stayed like that, noses inches apart and eyes locked. Finally Jefferson rocked back in his chair. "While you're on this planet and assigned to this battalion, you'll answer to me. You will not go wandering off without informing me of your intentions. You will not take anyone from this battalion with you without permission. Is that clear?"

Slowly Tyson grinned and then nodded. "Okay. I'll apologize for leaving yesterday without telling anyone, but I had an opportunity to study the adnoly and if I hesitated, I might lose it."

"The what? Study the what?"

"Adnoly. It's what the aliens call themselves. Zeric wanted to show us his village, it's a city really, and if we didn't go, we might not get another opportunity."

"You saw where they live?" asked Jefferson forgetting that he was supposed to be angry.

With that, Tyson launched into a detailed description of all that he and Carter had seen the day before. He described the damage that looked as if it had come from either bombing or long range artillery fire. How the outer section of the city was abandoned, but how the inner ring and central building were inhabited.

He finished saying, "You know, that outer ring is large enough to house the battalion. It would seem to me that it would be easier to defend and it would provide the troops with some protection from the elements."

"I can't go moving the battalion all over the countryside at a whim."

"Why not?" asked Tyson. "You are the commander. Besides, if I read the signs right, we'd be that much closer to the main access to this continent. We could effectively seal it from overland threat."

"Now you're an expert in tactics?" asked Jefferson.

"Not an expert, but I've been in the army long enough to understand that you don't march your troops through a valley, but you do guard the access to the valley. A few well-placed people can hold off divisions."

"But this field," alibied Jefferson, "has a long, flat surface to receive shuttle flights."

"And so does that city. Your battalion, stationed there, would be in the perfect place to inhibit enemy flow onto this continent. Tactically and strategically, it's the perfect place for you."

Jefferson was about to tell Tyson to mind his own business when he heard the quiet voice of the late Sergeant Mason telling him that subordinates sometimes had good ideas. Never reject anything out of hand because it would come back to haunt you.

He got up and moved to one of the aerial photographs taped to the wall. It had been taken from deep space and showed the land masses of the hemisphere. Large detail like lakes and mountain ranges were resolved, but the cities and villages were lost in the blurs of the environment. Jefferson reached out and touched the map and mumbled to himself, "I don't understand."

Tyson overheard the remark and asked, "What don't you understand?"

"There seem to be so many things that don't add up. What we were told on the ship doesn't exactly jibe with what we've learned here."

"Are you going to move us out?"

"I don't know. Division selected this place based on their photo and aerial recon."

"Before they had people on the surface who had new intelligence."

Jefferson looked at Carter and asked, "Why is the intelligence we've gotten so far off the mark?"

Carter shrugged. "I've given you the best that I have, that Division has. Gathering methods have left something to be desired."

Jefferson turned his attention back to Tyson. The anger that he had felt at the two officers was gone. Now he had a problem. Division had let him down.

"The only intelligent thing to do is shift the battalion to the city," said Tyson.

"Captain Tyson, I wish you would remember your position here. In fact, I wish you'd tell me exactly what your position is because I don't understand that either."

Carter finally broke in. "Sir, I think that I should make my report to Division. They'll want to know what I observed during the last few hours. Some of it could be important."

It was at that moment that Lieutenant Rider entered. He stood in the background until Jefferson waved him forward.

"Company's ready to go."

"All right, Alex. I've changed my mind since Captain Tyson and Lieutenant Carter decided that they would rejoin us." He led the young officer over to the aerial photograph. "Now I want you to explore this area. We have some information that it is being used as a line of communication between the enemy capital and the troops fielded here."

"Where did this information come from?" asked Tyson.

Jefferson turned so that he could see the captain. "It makes sense since this is the only way they could get from their continent to this one, as you've pointed out yourself not five minutes ago. Now, let me brief Rider."

"Yes, sir."

"From the map, it doesn't look like it is more than thirty or forty miles wide, and those mountains running down the center like a spine should effectively limit the enemy activities. You stay on this side. Don't cross."

"Yes, sir."

"You move out in fifteen minutes. I'll be going with you."

"Ah, Major," Tyson interrupted again. "What about the upcoming move?"

"First," said Jefferson, "there may not be an upcoming move. Second, I want to check with Division before I go relocating the base camp. There might be a sound reason to put it here. Someone may actually have studied the problem. Third, you and Carter will have to make your reports to Division. And fourth, we do have a job to do here, even if you don't go along with it."

Tyson looked to his left and saw a chair. He collapsed into it and then said, "Fine."

"And fifth," said Jefferson, the anger flaring again, "I'm not going to explain all my decisions to you. Now get out of here."

The patrol, a company-sized sweep commanded by Jefferson, left about mid-morning, after the shuttle had roared out of the sky, touched down long enough for Newton, Kingsley and Carter to get on. Tyson had opted to stay on the planet and radio his report in coded transmission to the fleet when he had it ready.

Jefferson had told one of the platoon leaders and a senior NCO to take the point. There were protests, but Jefferson said the more experienced the people, the more likely it was they would survive. So, before the company had cleared the perimeter and entered the jungle, there was already dissension in the ranks. Jefferson chose to ignore it since he was the battalion CO.

As they moved away from the battalion area, the shape of the jungle began to change. First, there had been hundreds of the parachute plants. Then they came to places where there were large columns that looked more like marble than anything living. There were no leaves at all on them, just limbs that branched until they ended in bright yellow buds. If nothing else, the surface of the planet was colorful.

The jungle floor was covered with the same day-glo orange moss that seemed to carpet everything. There was very little in the way of bushes, probably because the little light that did filter down through the parachute plants and the marble trees was already weak. What there was had sharp spines, broad leaves to catch the spotty sun, and thick, tough stems that resisted cutting or bending.

The sun had finally reached high into the sky and the heat that it brought did not help the attitudes of the people on patrol. The humidity was close to one hundred percent, and they were all covered with sweat. The heat and humidity was draining the energy of the patrol. They all began muttering until Jefferson told Rider to enforce noise discipline or he would.

As they moved deeper, the company spread out. Each person could see the one in front, but couldn't see many more than that. The thinness of the undergrowth made it possible to keep everyone widely separated, so that an ambush would have to be nearly a mile long to take them all at once, yet they were all close enough to support one another in case of an ambush.

The piercing scream rang through the jungle about an hour after they had started. Everyone dove for cover and waited to find out what would happen next. There was a burst of firing and then several single, spaced shots. Jefferson leaped to his feet, dodged to one of the marble trees, peeked around it, but could see nothing ahead. He began working his way forward, bent low and dodging from tree to tree toward the front of the column.

Ahead of him, there were angry voices, one outshouting the others. Jefferson sprinted forward, past the prone forms of many of the troopers, telling them in turn, "Stay here. Keep your eyes open, but don't move until you have orders."

As he ran forward, he kicked something and looked down in

time to see a human skull roll away with an irregular bounce. He stood and stared at it for quite a while, and then the voices he had heard shouting at one another broke through into his consciousness.

In front of him, he saw a misty substance that looked like a red and grey web. It clung to the parachute plants and the marble trees, reaching upward about forty or fifty feet into the air. It laced outward, covering everything until it was lost in foliage and distance.

As Jefferson hurried forward, Rider said, "Don't touch the web, Major."

One of the others said, "We can't get Joubert out of there."

"What happened here?" asked Jefferson, forgetting for a moment that they were on patrol and he was letting a group of them bunch up.

The NCO who had been on point, Forbes stepped forward. "Joubert was trying to avoid that web when there was a sudden scream off to the right. I turned in time to see that thing," he pointed to a thin, fur-covered humanoid creature almost obscured by the web, lying on the ground near Joubert, "leap out of the tree, there, and land on his back. The impact knocked Joubert back, into the web and onto a sharpened stake. That thing clung to his shoulder and was biting at his neck and throat."

Jefferson moved to the web and reached out to push some of it aside so that he could see Joubert and the creature better. A hand shot out and stopped him.

"Please, Major, don't touch the web."

Forbes continued glancing at Rider and then at Jefferson. "The thing finally got a hold of the jugular or something because there was a splash of red down Joubert's side. Joubert grabbed it then and tossed it to one side. I put a burst into it and so did a couple of the others," Forbes gestured at some of them. "We killed it before it could escape."

Jefferson studied the web and then Joubert's body, which seemed to be impaled on a thin wooden stake. His helmet was crooked, the strap twisted under his chin as if the creature had tried to rip it off. Blood had spattered over the ground around him, stained the front of his uniform and the side of his fatigues, and had pooled near his hand. The corrosive web had eaten away parts of his uniform, and his coffee-colored skin, some of it puffed and scarred where the acid had touched it, showed through.

Now Forbes tried to point. "See where his uniform is burned. I think the web did that. It's like acid."

"Lieutenant Rider," said Jefferson, "I would suggest that you get your people deployed for security."

"Yes, sir."

"We'll take a ten-minute break here before we move out."

"What about Joubert?"

"We'll send someone from the battalion out after we get back. Someone who is prepared to deal with an acid web and the other problems here. Right now we have other things to do."

"Yes, sir."

Jefferson didn't notice the resentment on the faces of the men and women who stood around him, listening to his orders.

After they had eaten lunch, two platoons guarding while two ate, they began moving through the jungle again. They kept the pace slow and steady but even so, the heat of the afternoon began to drain them. All around, Jefferson could hear the men and women grumbling about the heat and the length of the march, the quick cold meal, and his lack of emotion at the death of Joubert. Finally, knowing that there were still several hours of daylight left, Jefferson told Rider to call a halt.

Although he stopped earlier than he thought necessary, he still planned to keep it a military mission. He told them to dig in, and even when they complained about that, he wouldn't back off. He remembered reading that the Marines in Korea in mid-twentieth century had survived an onslaught by the Chinese because they had taken the simple precaution of digging in. Besides, with no aliens around, they could use automatic foxhole diggers.

The old U.S. Army had had such a device. It was a tripod with an explosive charge that blew a crater into the ground. The one that Jefferson's people had was much more sophisticated. It used an intense laser to burn a hole into the ground melting the silicates in the dirt to form a smooth surface. With careful use, it could make a very elaborate, cylindrical hole with glass-like sides.

In the center of the perimeter, Jefferson created his command post. This was another hole in the ground. It was just a little bit bigger, a little deeper, and dominated the whole area. Near him were the company radios and two NCO's.

As night fell, Jefferson told Rider that he wanted only a quarter alert, that is, one person in four had to be awake. He thought about increasing it after midnight, and decided against it. With one person in four awake, he didn't see how anyone could sneak up on them, and he knew that the people needed to get some rest. It had been a rough day.

The enemy stumbled onto them sometime after midnight. It wasn't a surprise for the patrol because they heard the aliens coming, and Jefferson had inadvertantly put his night laager down on the center of the line of communication.

Without waiting, the men and women on the perimeter opened fire as soon as they had a target. The clouds that obscured the sky most of the time had begun to return so the moonlight wasn't very bright, but the dark shapes of the aliens, moving against the brightly colored backgrounds of the jungle, made the targets easy to spot.

The first two aliens fell in a hail of bullets. The others, hidden by the night and jungle dropped back for a few moments to regroup.

Jefferson was awakened by the firing. He jerked awake, his heart hammering and his hands shaking, and peeked over the top of his foxhole. He saw the flashes of the weapons. He ducked back, pulled his pistol and cocked it and then didn't move.

Rider, also awakened by the shooting, crawled from his position to Jefferson. He looked down, into Jefferson's hole and saw the major crouched there, his weapon out, but his eyes tightly closed.

"We have enemy action," said Rider, not because he had to tell Jefferson that, but to announce that he was near.

Jefferson seemed not to hear and didn't respond. Rider spoke louder and still got no response. With that, he left, crawling toward the perimeter where the shooting had been.

When he got there, one of the women told him, "We saw some movement, sir. It's stopped now."

"You sure you saw something?"

The woman pointed outward. "If you look closely, you can see one of them lying out there."

At that moment there was a crump from deep in the jungle. A second later there was a whistling overhead and an explosion far to the right.

"Mortars?" someone whispered.

Rider hugged the ground. "Not accurately aimed."

There was a series of pops then and the explosions walked their way to the perimeter, but they stepped over the foxholes and began to detonate harmlessly on the interior of the camp.

As that happened, fifteen or twenty of the aliens ran from the cover of the jungle, across the open ground. The men and women began to fire, flipping to full auto. The enemy, even those taking hits, continued to rush forward. A couple stumbled and one fell. Firing from the perimeter increased. The muzzles strobed, looking like heat lightning. The detonations of the weapons combined into a single explosion.

And still the enemy came. Running across the open ground, screaming. They fired their weapons, worked the bolts and fired again, never stopping their attack.

Two more fell, rolling over and over and then were still. More and more of them died as the humans poured out a steady stream of hot lead until there were only a few of the enemy left for the assault. And then the attack broke, the enemy whirling and fleeing for the safety of the jungle.

The mortars stopped falling as the last of the enemy disappeared, and the firing from the perimeter tapered but didn't stop. Rider leaped to his feet and ran along the edge of the perimeter, checking his people.

Some of the troops kept firing, even after the enemy had disappeared, putting rounds into the jungle where they had last seen them. Single shots and short bursts. Glowing red tracers flashing into the vegetation and then tumbling high, into the night sky.

Jefferson appeared out of the dark and commanded, "Cease firing. You're only giving away your positions."

"They already know where we are," responded a male voice sarcastically.

"But they don't have the exact location of each foxhole, and won't have it if you don't tell them. Cease firing immediately."

"There!" shouted someone. "There they are!"

At the edge of the jungle a dozen of the enemy appeared. They crouched in the vegetation, as if waiting for reinforcements.

"Fire!" shouted Jefferson. "You have targets!"

The aliens surged forward then, as if responding to Jefferson's shouted command. More than a dozen of them, two, three times that many, running in a strange, long-legged lope that ate up the ground. A dozen of them fell to the intense fire from the Earth weapons, but there were too many of them this time.

One of the attackers leaped over the foxholes and was standing behind the first line of defense. Jefferson saw the creature standing there, seven feet tall, its weapon held high over its head as if it wanted to smash someone's skull. Jefferson jumped toward it and shoved his pistol into its stomach, pulling the trigger. He felt the recoil and heard the shot, but the enemy didn't flinch. Again he fired, and then again and again. He felt the hot blood of the creature wash over him as it spurted, and smelled the odor of melting rubber, but the creature didn't seem to be hurt.

As it tried to wrap him up, he ducked under its arms. Again he fired, aiming for the head. The round hit the enemy in the mouth, snapping the head back and the shock of that toppled it. As it fell, it dropped its rifle.

One of the women was plucked from her foxhole by an enemy reaching down and grabbing her head. It hauled her out, held her at arm's length and shook her, breaking her neck. When she went limp, the creature threw her to the side so it could grab another.

Jefferson hit the creature in the back with two rounds from his pistol. He dropped the magazine, shoved another one home, and fired three bullets into the creature's chest when it whirled to face him. It stood there staring at the holes leaking its blood and then fell forward.

Two of the men tackled one of the aliens that had entered the perimeter. All three fell into a heap, but the creature held the men down as it clambered back to its knees. It knelt there and slammed its huge fist into the chest of one man and then the other, crushing their ribs, killing them.

Another man rushed over and hit the alien in the side of the head with his rifle butt. He succeeded only in shattering his weapon, but as the creature turned on him, a woman opened fire, putting all twenty rounds from her magazine into the enemy's body in a single, long burst.

"Capture one," shouted Jefferson. "Take one of them alive."

With that four men and two women jumped from their foxholes and tried to tackle an alien. For a moment, they held it down, but none of them had a clue as to what to do next. The creature held on its back, kicked its legs, shaking them free. With a piston-like motion, it struck out, hitting one of the women in the stomach. She flew nearly thirty feet in the air before hitting the ground, the inside of her abdomen a series of smashed organs and internal hemorrhaging. It took her three minutes to die from the massive blow.

The others jumped clear almost as if someone had shouted an order. They surrounded the creature, but none of them knew what to do. The other woman jerked her pistol free of its holster and fired two rounds into the knees of each leg.

Using its arms, the enemy rolled to its stomach. The woman put a bullet into each of its elbows and it fell forward on its face. It made some feeble attempts to get to its feet but it's legs and arms wouldn't cooperate. The joints were all smashed.

Seeing the alien was helpless, they turned their attention back to the battle raging around them. They saw a couple of creatures standing behind the line of foxholes and all of them opened fire, cutting down the enemy.

Jefferson had finally abandoned his pistol and found a rifle dropped by one of the dead troopers. He moved to his right and saw one of the enemy leap to the edge of a foxhole as an Earthman fired at it wildly. Apparently he didn't hit anything vital because the creature didn't even stagger. It used its bayoneted rifle to pin the man to the side of his hole like an insect on a board.

Jefferson dropped to one knee and fired single shots until the attacker collapsed. Then, deliberately, he aimed at the creature's head, putting bullets into it until the skull seemed to sag.

Two of the enemy leaped the foxhole line to try to help their wounded fellow. With one swipe of a huge hand, one of them sent one of the women troopers sprawling. She rolled twice and didn't move. The other grabbed one of the men, lifted him high, and tossed him backwards, toward the jungle.

Jefferson spun toward that fight. As the creature let go of the man, he poured the rest of his magazine into it. It took two steps toward him and died, falling slowly, like a giant tree.

The other being turned and tried to grab two of the men, but missed. Both of them opened fire with their weapons and kept shooting until the enemy was down.

Jefferson turned to run back toward the radio. He wanted to make contact with the fleet, to prepare them in case he needed reinforcements quickly. He saw another group of aliens among the trees. He slid to a halt, and ordered, "Kill them. Open fire!"

All at once, it seemed that the enemy was trying to retreat. One of them reached into a foxhole and grabbed a woman, but rather than kill her, it stripped her weapon from her and hit her once in the side of the head as if it wanted to knock her out. It then threw her over its shoulder and ran for the protection of the jungle.

Another alien grabbed a man and did the same thing, but as it ran for the safety of the parachute plants and marble trees, a dozen weapons opened fire, stopping it far short of its destination. It fell and the unconscious man rolled free.

Two or three of the Earth people leaped from their fox holes. One shouted, "After them!"

"Hold it!" yelled Jefferson. "Everyone hold his position. No one move."

There were still some shooting but that soon tapered off and died as the last of the targets disappeared. Jefferson ranged over the perimeter, checking on the conditions of the people and making sure that there were no gaps in it. He directed the injured to the center of the perimeter where one of the battalion's surgeons was supervising the medics as they treated the wounded. Those who couldn't move themselves were assisted.

As the wounded were being cared for, Jefferson made sure that the rest of the company was on alert. They watched the jungle, but saw no sign the enemy was still out there. He pointed to a couple of men and said, "Let's go recover that wounded man."

All together they jumped to the front of the perimeter and hurried forward. Jefferson crouched by the body and felt the throat. When he found a pulse, he said, "Let's get him back inside the camp."

Once there, Jefferson let the men take the wounded man to the medics. Then, finding Rider, he said, "Let's stay on full alert the rest of the night. Check everyone. Make sure that we haven't overlooked any wounded." He couldn't bring himself to say that they should check the dead to make sure they were dead. "Are there any wounded aliens out there?" he asked.

Rider, who had seen the men and women try to capture one, said, "I think so."

"Have one of the medics look at it and see if there is anything he can do for it. We'll take it back to camp tomorrow."

"We go in tomorrow? Before the patrol is over?"

"Lieutenant Rider, we have wounded. We have learned that the enemy is moving supplies over the isthmus. We have a prisoner who is wounded and will probably need more treatment than we can give it. We have to go back."

"What about the woman who was captured?"

"I will take a platoon and go after her at first light. The majority of the company must return to the main base."

Rider stepped back, surprised. "You're going to take out the platoon?"

"Unless you have an objection to that, Lieutenant."

"No, sir." Rider was quiet for a moment and then said, "Will a platoon be enough?"

"I doubt that it will be, but I don't think it matters. I don't think we'll find her alive, but I can't take the chance."

"What does that mean?"

Jefferson looked around. Everyone else was busy with the wounded and dead, or watching for the enemy. Quietly, he said, "It means if word gets out that we lost people and don't try to get them back, we're going to lose the support of the troops. Even if the effort is futile, and everyone knows it is futile, we still have to do it. If we knew she was dead, we wouldn't waste the time, but we know nothing of the kind."

He glanced at his watch and realized that he had no idea what time the sun would come up. He was still on Earth time and according to his watch, the sun would have been up two hours earlier. To Rider he said, "We all move at first light."

8

AT THE AMBUSH SITE

SUNRISE SAW THE whole camp ready to move. Using the parachute plants, they had made stretchers for the wounded. The dead were buried where they fell with a tiny marker left for the graves registration people. Later a small monument with a nuclear powered beacon would be left at the site, making it into an informal but permanent cemetery.

Jefferson sat at the edge of his foxhole, his feet dangling down. He was eating a combat meal. Unlike those given to armies in the past, these were not packaged in cans but in plastic pouches and freeze-dried. By adding water and a single tablet that reacted with the water to produce heat, a hot meal could be prepared in seconds without fire.

Jefferson held the package up, watched it bubble as it cooked, and realized that it was another evidence of the great technology that supported them. Here was something that should have been left behind, but which had been on the list of legitimate supplies for Procyon Two. If the aliens saw it, they were going to wonder about it and want it, if they understood it.

"We're going to move out now," Rider announced. "We're going to head directly to the camp. Some of the wounded are in pretty poor shape."

Jefferson dropped his plastic fork back into his pouch. "You realize that in a couple of days we'll have transport down here so that you wouldn't have to carry them out."

"Yeah, I know. Too bad that the fleet didn't think of wounded before they dropped us in here. Makes no sense not to provide for rapid transport."

Jefferson looked at the remains of his meal and decided that he wasn't hungry anymore. He dropped the whole thing into the bottom of his foxhole.

"Well, I think we ran into trouble a little faster than they thought we would. If we had anyone who was in immediate danger of dying, we would have arranged something."

"So we let them suffer."

Jefferson shrugged. What could he say to that? "They'll be fine once you reach battalion."

Rider nodded. "Right. Well, then, we're off."

"See you at camp, later."

Ten minutes after the majority of the company left, Jefferson and the remaining platoon moved into the jungle, trying to follow the path taken by the enemy the night before. Finding where they had camped wasn't hard. The bodes of the dead aliens pointed the way. Jefferson was interested to see what happened to the dead aliens, to see if there were scavengers to take care of the problem. So far, they had seen very few animals.

Then he wondered if Rider would pass the area of the web and try to recover Joubert's body. He hoped that he wouldn't. It was something that they didn't need to worry about.

As they entered the trees, they found little evidence of the enemy. The resilient ground and the tough orange moss hid the signs left by passing aliens.

They did find three more enemy bodies. It appeared that the creatures had been wounded in the fighting and had managed to drag themselves to the jungle where they died. Apparently the aliens didn't care about their wounded anymore than they cared about their dead.

Jefferson had his people check the bodies for anything that might be useful. They could find no pockets in the clothing and there was no jewelry. It was as if they had no concept of personal property. Or it could be that they left their valuables home when they went to war. Or that their friends robbed them once they were dead. Whatever the reason, the new bodies produced no more of intelligence value than all those that had been left on the field.

They spread out from there, moving slowly through the jungle, looking for signs that the creatures were near, or had been close. They found nothing. Even the marble trees had no scrapes on them.

After an hour, Jefferson called a halt. He put out security and then sat down to rest. Although the search had begun fairly early, his uniform was already soaked from perspiration. He took off his helmet and ran a hand through his damp hair. He then looked at the men and women with him and saw that they too were hot and sweaty. It seemed they didn't want to continue searching for the missing woman. Jefferson was tempted to call a halt and head back, but then remembered what had happened to Custer. During one of his attacks on an Indian village, twenty or so soldiers had gotten separated from the main force. Custer refused to go after them and a couple of days later the bodies were found. Many members of the Seventh Cavalry hated Custer after that.

He took a deep drink from his canteen and then told everyone that it was time to move out. As long as they had a clue as to direction, he would pursue the enemy. Once the signs disappeared, which would probably be shortly, he would turn back. At that point they would have no choice.

Rider and his people entered the main camp about noon. Torrence, who had been left behind to take command, was there to meet them. She saw the reduced size of the unit, the stretchers, and the badly wounded alien and demanded, "What happened?"

"You want a report out here?" asked Rider, glancing at the troops standing around.

"Don't get smartass," she warned him. "Briefly. What the hell happened?"

"We got hit. Late last night. They captured one of ours and there's a patrol out looking for her."

"Okay," nodded Torrence. "Get your people taken care of, and meet me in the command post in five minutes. We'll need to get something off to Division. How many did you lose?"

"Including the wounded?"

"Including the wounded."

"Thirty-seven. That's twenty-one dead, fifteen wounded, and one missing in action."

In the command post, Rider sat down opposite Torrence. He looked at the two NCOs on radio watch and said, "Do they have to stay here?"

Torrence raised an eyebrow in question.

"There's a couple of things we need to discuss and I don't think we need any extra ears."

"Okay, you two," said Torrence looking over her shoulder, "split. We'll take care of the radio."

When the NCOs were gone, Rider said, "We've got trouble with the new commander."

"I'm not sure that I want to hear this, but go ahead. Tell me about it."

"Last night, when the aliens hit us, Jefferson froze. He was in the bottom of his hole, clutching his pistol to his chest like some long-lost love. He stayed in there while the battle started and didn't provide any guidance. We could have been wiped out before he showed his face."

"But he did come out."

"Well, yes. Yes, he did."

"And directed the operation from that point?" Torrence asked, not sure of what she was doing.

"Yes."

"How did he do?"

"What do you mean?"

"I mean, was he a good leader? Did he make mistakes? Did he command with authority?"

"Well, yes. I suppose you could say that he did."

"Then what in the hell is the problem?" She thought that she knew. She had seen the same thing the first day on the planet's surface. In fact, Jefferson hadn't really come out of it during the short engagement, but then it hadn't mattered all that much. There was nothing he could have done to change the outcome.

"The problem is that he froze. He froze when the first shots were fired."

Torrence was suddenly nervous, although she didn't know why. She stood up, walked around the chair and then to the aerial photos. She realized that she did that frequently when she wanted to avoid facing a problem so she turned around and sat down.

"You say he froze but then directed the battle. Was he competent during the fight?"

"I don't know. He was shooting and giving orders. Directing the action. I was pretty busy myself. I did see him go outside the perimeter to help rescue one of ours. He did seem to be in the thick of things. If it wasn't for those first few moments . . ."

"Let me ask you one other question. Where is the major now?"

"He's out with the patrol, looking for Edison."

"Okay, Alex. Let's just do this. We haven't really seen the major in action. A couple of glimpses that have given us pause. Let's not do anything drastic. Let it ride until we have more data. It seems that he might have had a problem but I think he's worked his way out of it.

"Or, it could be that he doesn't have a problem but there was something going on that we aren't aware of. Hell, from what you said, he did a good job last night."

"But it took him a while to get started. We could have all been killed before he got started."

"The same could probably be said about half the people who were there last night. Let's just hang loose."

"And?"

"And nothing. Besides, we're not supposed to be analyzing the commander. He's supposed to be analyzing us."

"I just don't know if we can trust him."

"We can trust him," snapped Torrence. "And it would be best if you kept all this under your hat. Don't go spreading this around."

"Some of my people might have seen something."

Torrence took a deep breath. "You keep it under your hat and you squash any rumors you hear. We've enough troubles without a lot of wild rumors about the CO."

Rider nodded. "I'll do my best."

By mid-afternoon it was obvious that they weren't going to find either the enemy or the missing soldier. Jefferson kept them moving, until he heard the sound of surf in the distance. At that point he knew that they had taken a wrong turn somewhere and that the trail had fizzled out. To stay out any longer would only invite trouble.

They turned back without even seeing the ocean. With a destination in mind, especially when that destination was their home base, they moved faster but still had to camp for the night. When Jefferson ordered them to dig in, no one questioned the order. They remembered the night before and how digging in had probably saved some lives.

The next morning they were all up early, anxious to return. With only a cold breakfast eaten in ten minutes, they moved out. By noon they were back at the battalion site.

As they entered the camp, Torrence was right there to meet them. She moved to Jefferson and said, "Division wants you to report as soon as you're back."

"Let me scrape a layer of the crud off and I'll join you in the command post."

"Division said as soon as you were back. Said they would dispatch a shuttle to pick you up."

Jefferson searched her face to see if she was joking although he could think of no reason for her to kid about it. "What's the big deal?"

"They didn't confide in me," shrugged Torrence. "Just said to report in and they would dispatch a shuttle."

Jefferson grabbed one of the NCOs who had been out with him. "See that the people get their weapons cleaned, some hot food, and then some rest."

"Yes, sir."

"Now," he said, turning his attention back to Torrence, "let me get this straight. We're down here to aid these aliens, these, ah, whatever Tyson called them. We're supposed to keep the level of our technology secret but everytime we turn around, we're landing shuttles."

"I suppose so."

Jefferson shook his head, not understanding. "All right, let's go over to the command post and let Division know that I'm here. While we're waiting I can grab something to eat."

As they reached the door that opened down into the bunker, Jefferson laughed. "Hey, I get it. You like command. It's just another excuse to get me out of here so that you can stay in charge."

"Well, sir," she said, "I hadn't thought of it that way, but I guess it's not such a bad idea."

Before they stepped inside, Jefferson stopped. He looked around and saw no one near them. He said, "You know, when we're alone like this, you can call me Dave, or David."

She looked at him before speaking. It was almost as if he wanted to be friends suddenly. It didn't understand it. Especially after some of the things that had happened; she wondered if he thought he was about to be called on the carpet and would need an ally in the battalion. He was trying to prove to her now, before the shuttle-ride to Division, that he wasn't such a bad guy. If that was his motive, it was as transparent as glass. She would have to wait until she had more information.

To him she said, "Yes, sir. I understand." Then she ducked under his arm and stepped down into the command post.

In less than twenty minutes the shuttle touched down. It rolled to a halt only a few feet from where Jefferson waited outside the perimeter with a force of thirty troopers. The ramp opened and as Jefferson started toward it he yelled to Torrence, "I don't know how long this will take. Keep everyone close to camp tonight."

If she responded, he didn't hear it over the roar of the shuttle's engines. As soon as he was inside, the ramp began to close and the loadmaster nearly pushed him into a seat and then buckled the belt for him. Immediately, they began the take-off roll. The loadmaster dropped into the seat next to him as they lifted from the planet's surface and reached escape velocity.

When they docked an hour later there were people waiting. Jefferson stepped down and saw several staff officers come at him almost like the police surrounding a drug dealer. The man in the lead, a full colonel, said, "Major, we have a meeting scheduled in fifteen minutes."

"What's going on?"

"Ah, Major," said the colonel, "when was the last time you took a bath?"

Jefferson stopped moving and looked at the man. He was wearing a fresh khaki uniform. His salt-and-pepper hair and the lines on his face suggested that he was about forty. Certainly young enough to have a combat assignment or to have participated in some combat at some point.

"The last bath was sometime before planetfall. One of the last things we take with us are bathtubs. Field bathing leaves something to be desired."

"I guess it can't be helped. You could have put on a clean uniform."

"Listen, Colonel, I've just been yanked out of the field. We've barely got our base established. We don't have access to all the luxuries of the fleet. I'm sorry if I offend you, but there is nothing I can do about it." Jefferson was something less than sorry.

They moved out of the docking bay, through the corridors of the main battleship, and up to the level where the general's conference room was located. The colonel opened the door and waved Jefferson in.

The room stunned him. He had never seen it. It was dominated by a huge table of highly polished mahogany. Plush chairs surrounded it. A huge screen for two-dimensional projection stood in one corner and a holographic display tank, larger than any Jefferson had ever seen was in the other. Thick, light-blue carpet covered the deck.

But the most impressive feature had to be the window. Jefferson had seen nothing like it on any of the ships. He had seen portholes. Usually they were tiny and most of the time covered with metallic hatches. This was massive and gave an unobstructed view of deep space. They were facing away from the planet and its sun so that Jefferson could see the star fields. Galactic center was a dense mass of brightness in the distance.

"Take a seat, Major," the colonel instructed him. "I think the operations officer wants to see you first."

The lieutenant colonel disappeared without another word. Jefferson realized that he didn't know who he had been. He had never seen the man before.

Moments later the door opened and a young man entered. He said, "Colonel Prescott will be here in a moment. Is there anything that I can get you?"

Although Jefferson had been in the heat and humidity of the surface for only a couple of days, he had dreamed of an ice cold beer. In the air-conditioned comfort of the fleet, however, he found that he was slightly cold and the dream of the cold beer had faded.

To the man, he said, "No. Thank you."

He left then, but the door opened again almost immediately. A large man, with colonel's eagles gleaming on his collar and four rows of combat decorations above his breast pocket, entered. He was followed by two women and one man.

Jefferson, his military training taking over, got to his feet. "Good afternoon, Colonel."

"Sit, sit," said Prescott. He took a file folder from the aide on his right and opened it as he sat down. He handed the floppy disc from it to one of the women who plugged it into the micro computer that stood on its own tiny desk. "Now, then, Major, what in the hell is going on down there?"

"Going on?" parroted Jefferson.

"Going on. What in the hell are you doing?"

Jefferson rubbed his face with both his hands. "What I'm doing is establishing a base as I was told to."

"You were told to begin training the locals, not make war. Your job is not to fight."

"If you have the full reports there," said Jefferson pointing to the computer, "you'll see that we were attacked almost the moment we landed, and that we have been attacked by the enemy on a number of occasions."

Prescott looked up from the computer's screen. "There's your first problem. There are no enemies on the planet. There are only those we wish to aid and those we don't."

"Yes, sir," said Jefferson. He hesitated and then asked, "How am I supposed to do my job?"

"Your job is to train the aliens in the use of our weapons and to teach them basic tactics. It is not to go out and engage in firefights so that you can win another medal."

"I am not looking to win another medal."

"Let me say this," Prescott continued. "The general is not happy with the way things have been going. You have lost too many people in an operation that was only supposed to involve training and advising. You've lost too much equipment."

"All we have done is protect ourselves. I might say that the weapons we have are not adequate. They are . . ."

"Not adequate?" interrupted one of the women.

Jefferson turned to look at her. She was very young and it looked as if her second-lieutenant bars hadn't been out of the wrapping long. "They don't have the stopping power to knock down the aliens," he said. "We have to hit them five, six, ten times to stop them. We need something a little heavier. Maybe some laser weapons."

"Lasers are out," said Prescott. "And you're not supposed to be engaging in combat operations anyway."

"But they attacked us," Jefferson protested.

"Because you were operating on the isthmus. That's something else. You stay out of that region. You restrict your operations only to your base and the immediate territory."

"We were surveying the lines of communication," said Jefferson. "We've run into too many enemy, ah, aliens to believe our original estimates of their activity was right. They even attacked the bunch that was supposed to meet us."

"You let us worry about that, Major," said Prescott. "We have the big picture up here and know what's happening. Your job is to train the aliens. Now what have you done to accomplish that?"

"We've just gotten there. We have made contact with the aliens and Captain Tyson and Lieutenant Carter made a recon into their village, or city, or whatever. In fact, Tyson suggested that we move the camp into the city. He thought . . ."

"We have no problem with that. It would make your job that much easier."

Jefferson sat there, surprised. He had thought that the last thing they would want was for him to move his battalion into an alien city.

Prescott turned to the other woman. "Major Martin, you have something you want to say?"

"Yes, sir. Major Jefferson, we're going to need a complete accounting of all your equipment losses. We're going to have to have a complete record of everything you give to the aliens from rifles right down to combat meals. Everything they use is going to have to be logged and documented."

"What?" Jefferson couldn't keep the surprise out of his voice.

"I said that we're going to need a complete record of everything you give to the aliens. We have to have some way of judging the costs and charges. After all, we are not providing this aid free of charge."

"What?" Jefferson repeated. The last thing he expected was to have to explain where he was spending the money, or rather, tell them where he was losing equipment.

"It's not that unusual. Have your supply officer, Lieutenant Norris, prepare the paper work. It's not big a deal."

"You have a problem, Major?" asked Prescott.

"No, sir. It's just not quite the way we've operated in the past."

Prescott stood up for a moment. He moved around the room. "Somebody has to pay for all this. It's not free. We learned long ago that we could bankrupt ourselves if we considered ourselves the police officers of the galaxy. Someone asks for our assistance, we provide it, but we don't give it. They must pay for it."

"Pay for it how?"

"Don't be stupid. With raw materials, of course. With food supplies. With new drugs. There are hundreds of things that we need and we trade our technology for their raw materials."

"But we don't give them the best of the technology."

"That's not quite fair, Major. We don't want to escalate their internal struggles into a planet-wide conflict. We don't teach them anything that will escalate their wars. We help them to win with their own technology."

Jefferson was going to protest because he had already seen that the rule wasn't strictly enforced. The constant shuttle flights showed the aliens a higher level of technology. But then he figured there probably were things that he didn't know, so he kept his mouth shut.

Prescott sat down again. "All right. So we understand one another, I'm going to make it clear to you. You are not to engage in any combat operations. You are to train, equip, and advise the aliens so that they can fight their own battles. You can defend yourselves, but you are to initiate no actions. You will advise the aliens on how to proceed but you will not take command in the operations. Is that clear?"

"Yes, sir."

"All right, Major. I think we understand one another. Look, your second in command, this Captain Torrence, is she any good?"

"One of the best." Jefferson surprised himself there. He hadn't really thought about it. He thought about the problems he had with her on a personal level. They were mostly over trivial matters, but she had always come through for him when he needed her. There was no question that she was one of the best. He had to admit that.

"Then why don't you stay here tonight? Get cleaned up, have a shave and a bath. You can actually get a bath here and not a shower if you want, have a steak in the club and return tomorrow."

"That's it?"

"That's it."

"You mean you called me up here just to tell me these things? Hell, you could have used the radio."

"I'm not in the habit of explaining my motives to my subordinates, but I will say this. I felt, and the general agreed, that a face-to-face meeting would have more impact. Now, unless you have some questions, I have other duties to attend to. Feel free to stay the night. A shuttle flight will be arranged whenever you are ready to return."

Prescott got up to leave and turned to the male aide. "Jim, get the floppy. Laura, you want to escort the major around? He may not be familiar with this ship."

The lieutenant smiled and said, "Sure, sir. I don't mind."

As soon as Prescott and his staff had gone, Laura held out her hand and said, "I'm Laura Garner. What would you like to do first?"

Jefferson looked at her closely. He rubbed his hands on his thighs and said, "I'm intrigued by the bath, I think."

She got up and said, "Follow me. I'll take you to the senior officers club. Colonel Prescott arranged for you to use the facilities."

The club was almost as big a shock as the general's conference room. The main chamber was gigantic and filled with small dining tables covered with white-linen cloths. The walls were all panelled, except the one opposite him. It was like a picture window, a huge picture window that showed Procyon Two, its moons and its sun. Jefferson couldn't believe it, until he realized that it was a projection picture. Still, the money spent so that the colonels and generals could look at the space around them was appalling. Especially when the lower-ranking enlisted troops lived in cubicles little larger than coffins.

Garner said, "Come on, Major. I'll show you to the bathhouse."

He stopped short and said, "Hell, you can call me David."

"All right, David."

She showed him the ropes in the bathhouse, and while he was changing into a robe, she took his dirty uniform to the disposal chute. As she left, she yelled through the curtain to him, "I'll be back in about an hour with clean clothes for you."

He found a pile of light blue and green towels and grabbed a couple of them. He moved to the tub area, leaned down and turned on the water, holding his hand under the faucet. When it was hot enough, he closed the drain and stood up. As the tub filled, he dropped his towel, found a razor and soap, and then lowered himself into the water. He sat back to relax, opened his eyes once to see some of the dirt soak off him and float to the surface. He felt himself falling asleep, struggled with it briefly and then figured what the hell.

He was startled awake nearly thirty minutes later when a pair of hands began to wash his shoulders and chest. He jerked upright, splashing water around.

"Hey," said Laura, "you're getting me all wet." She was wearing a tiny pair of shorts and a skimpy halter top. Her long brown hair was drawn back in a ponytail. He noticed that she had big, brown eyes, a small nose and full lips. Until that moment he hadn't noticed how good looking she was.

And then he realized that he was sitting naked, in a tub of water where she could see his every reaction. Momentarily embarrassed, he wanted to grab a towel to hide himself, but didn't want to look ridiculous. To cover his discomfiture, he said, "You supposed to be in here?"

"I didn't think you would mind."

He was about to say that he did, but just couldn't bring himself to form the words. He wondered if it was because he was really enjoying himself, or because he didn't want to look stupid.

"Lean forward so that I can get your back," she said.

He did as told and when she had rinsed it, she asked, "Anything else I can do?"

"No. No, I can handle it. You can wait for me outside."

"You're sure?"

"Yeah, I'm sure."

When he came out, he felt a hundred times better. His hair was still damp, but he didn't care. The air conditioning of the main dining room contrasted nicely to the bathhouse. He saw Garner sitting at a table by herself. She had put on a khaki uniform that had a knee length skirt, knee socks, and a tailored shirt that had epaulets with her lieutenant bars pinned to them.

As he sat down, she said, "I took the liberty of ordering for you. I hope a steak is all right. I told them to cook it rare. That way, if you want it done some other way, you can send it back."

"You seem to have this well thought out."

She looked momentarily hurt and then said, "I was just trying to please you."

"Why is that?"

Before she could answer, a man approached them. He was not wearing a military uniform and in fact looked nothing like a soldier. His hair was long and shaggy and he had a soft look about him. Too many large meals and not enough exercise. He snagged and chair and dropped into it. "You that Major Jefferson?"

"I'm Jefferson."

"Thought so." He held a hand over the table to be shaken. "Jason Garvey. Intergalactic News."

"Reporter," said Jefferson.

"And camera man, editor, writer, and a little bit of everything else."

"There something I can do for you?" asked Jefferson.

"How about me coming down to the planet with you?"

"No," said Jefferson. "I'm not authorized to take civilians down there."

"I'll get the authorization."

Jefferson studied the man for a moment and then said, "You get the proper papers and you can do anything you want."

Garvey pushed back his chair and stood. "Knew you'd cooperate. You stick with me and I'll make you a star."

He wandered off. As he did, Jefferson turned his attention back to Garner. She sat there, quietly, waiting for him to do something. He closed his eyes for a moment, replayed the conversation before Garvey had arrived. He opened them and asked her again, "Why are you trying to please me?"

Garner studied the tablecloth in front of her. She hesitated and then said, "I'm sorry if I've done anything wrong. If you would like me to leave, just say the word." She started to rise.

"No," said Jefferson reaching out. "Please. I was just wondering why I'm being given the red-carpet treatment. Not to mention the fact that while I'm taking hot baths and eating steak, my battalion is on Procyon Two eating combat rations, living in the heat and not even getting a chance for a shower."

"I don't know," shrugged Garner. "I just know that Colonel Prescott said that you had won the Galactic Silver Star and we should take care of you. I should take care of you. You deserved it."

Jefferson shook his head but didn't speak. He thought that it went a lot deeper than that. He thought that it had to do with some of the questions that he had raised earlier and some of the things he had seen. This was a subtle bribe. They were showing him that if he watched his step, kept his nose clean and didn't ask a lot of difficult questions, then all this could be his. He would be admitted into the inner circle of great rewards and great power. If he wasn't careful, he could find himself in a dead-end job on some hellhole of a planet.

He glanced across the table at the young officer. He wasn't sure if Garner was part of the deal or not. He decided to give her the benefit of the doubt. He told himself that she was assigned as his escort, but she was putting more into it than required because she was impressed with his damned medal.

He decided that he would enjoy himself as much as he could and then he would forget all about this. He wanted to get back to his battalion and do the best job he could. He also decided that he would not allow himself to be alone with Garner because he found her very attractive but didn't want to take advantage of the situation.

9

THE BATTALION'S CAMP

IT WAS JUST after dawn when Jefferson returned to the battalion. After spending the majority of the night in the club, he knew that taking a nap would only make him feel worse. He could have stayed on the ship until he felt rested, but his battalion was on the ground and they had no comfort, just the heat and humidity of the planet's surface and the constant threat of an attack. So, he had made the arrangements for a shuttle flight, landing in the first light of the new day. Once on the ground, he could brief Torrence, order her to prepare the battalion to move, and then could catch a nap.

In the command post he found Tyson, who was sitting on the floor looking as if he was half asleep. Jefferson stood over him, his hands on his hips and announced, "We're moving to the city. How do your adnoly feel about that?"

"They'll probably be thrilled," he said, snapping awake. Awkwardly, he climbed to his feet, rubbing at his eyes. He wiped a hand over his mouth. "When do we go?"

"As soon as we can get it organized. Later today. You need to do anything to break the ice?"

"I'll get with Zeric and we'll move over there in a couple of minutes."

"You take a squad with you." Jefferson moved around a field desk and fell into a chair. He leaned his head on his hands.

"I don't want you wandering around without some kind of escort. Now you're sure that the outer ring is abandoned?"

"We saw no sign that anyone was living in there. I doubt that there will be a problem. And it might make it easier to get the adnoly to work with us."

"Okay. Get out of here. Take off as soon as you can. We'll probably be several hours behind you. Take an officer who can determine the placement of our troops for the defensive advantages."

"I am qualified to do that," said Tyson. "I am trained as an infantry officer, and I do have some experience."

"I know that, but I want you working with the adnoly. You'll be too busy to adequately check the terrain. I want someone else to do that."

"Yes sir."

He was about to order him to find Torrence and send her in, but she entered before he could do that. He said to her, "Before you sit down and get too comfortable, I should tell you that we're going to move the main base."

"Oh, goody. Just the news to make my day," she said. "Do I have time for coffee?"

"Grab a cup," said Jefferson. "Then I want you to let the company commanders know. We'll take most of the equipment but we'll leave D Company here. This will be our first satellite base."

Torrence moved to the pot, guarded by the NCOs on radio watch, and poured a cup. She gulped her coffee. "How soon do we leave?"

"Just as soon as we can get organized." He pointed to Tyson. "Tyson is going over to coordinate with the adnoly."

"I'll take an RTO," said Tyson, "and let you know if there is a problem."

"Okay." Torrence drained the coffee and put the plastic cup down, by the pot so that one of the NCOs would wash it. "I'll get on it."

When both Torrence and Tyson were gone, Jefferson put his head down on the desk and fell asleep almost immediately. He'd regretted not taking the opportunity to sleep in the air-conditioned comfort of the ship, thinking that he would have a hard time sleeping in the heat of the planet's surface. He was wrong.

Torrence woke him up about an hour later. She had chased the radio watch out of the command post. When she saw that Jefferson was awake, she asked, "Can I get you something to drink?"

"Unless you've got a cold beer stashed somewhere, I think I'll pass." He took a sip from his canteen, swished the water around in his mouth and was going to spit it out, but didn't know where. He swallowed it instead.

"Major, we have to have a serious talk."

"I don't think that this is the place or the time. We've got a lot to get done before nightfall. Not to mention having quite a distance to travel."

"I know all that, but I think this is important." Torrence moved to where she could sit down in one of the chairs. The main radio was near her right hand so that she could answer any of the calls, although they were supposedly maintaining radio silence with the fleet.

Jefferson sat up straighter. "All right then, Vicky. What's bothering you?"

"There's no easy way to get into this," she said, suddenly nervous. "I mean, it would be easier if something had just happened. We're coming into it cold."

"Well, let me see if I can make it easier for you. I've been impressed with all that you've done. I'm sorry that we got off on the wrong foot. I know that some of it was my fault, but you should know that it was because I was coming in here new. I didn't know anyone and was afraid there would be resentment. Then, when nearly the first thing out of your mouth was about the resentment, I kind of blew up."

"I guess you could say that this is an outgrowth of that," she said carefully. "Ah, Lieutenant Rider came in, what, yesterday, and said that he thought, that you, ah, you froze during the battle the other night."

Jefferson felt the muscles in his stomach knot and the anger flare. He forced it down, fighting to control himself. He stared at her, looking her straight in the eyes. Into her deep, blue eyes. He had to handle this just right, because to fail now would be to fail for the rest of his time with the battalion. He looked down, at his clenched fists and slowly uncurled his fingers.

"I did not freeze," he said. "I took a couple of minutes to

survey the situation and then ordered the troops to the proper position."

"Yes, sir. I talked to Lieutenant Rider quite a bit about this. He said that he tried to get your attention but that you seemed to be out of it. I had the same problem that first day. You remember. When the aliens hit us right after we touched down here."

Jefferson remembered it all too well. If it hadn't been for that, he probably could have bullshitted his way through this, telling Torrence that Rider had not been in full possession of the facts. But she had seen him fold. She knew. She knew that he was the coward that Mason had saved in front of the rainsoaked pillbox what seemed like years ago.

"What's the status of the battalion?"

"Sir?"

"How close are they to being ready to move out?"

"Should be an hour or two."

"Okay, Vicky, I'm going to tell you something here because I consider you to be a friend. I don't know why, but there seems to be something there. You seem to be an honorable person. I don't want what I say to leave this room."

"I understand."

"I hope you do." Jefferson stood up, sat down, and then took another drink from his canteen. As he leaned back in his chair, he said, "I never deserved that medal. The Galactic Silver Star. I told everyone at the first that I didn't deserve it, but no one would listen to me. They were too busy being impressed with what I had done, or what they thought I had done. It was really Sergeant Mason, an NCO with my platoon, who did it, but I got the credit. I told them that, too, but they thought I was being loyal to a dead friend. Now you must understand, I didn't actively seek the award and tried to tell the truth in the beginning, but no one wanted to listen."

He stopped talking and realized that he wasn't making much sense. He wanted to open his eyes and look at her, but couldn't do it. It was easier to talk to her if he didn't have to look at her.

Finally, quietly, he said, "I'll start at the beginning. Please, don't interrupt me because I'm not sure that I'll be able to do it if you interrupt me. When I'm done, maybe you can understand how hard it's been for me."

From there he told the whole story from the moment that he

took command of the platoon to the moment that Sergeant Mason had died in his arms as he begged him to hang on. He explained that he had been so scared that he couldn't move until he saw Mason crawl past him, and when the sergeant died, everyone had just assumed that it was Jefferson and not Mason who had blown up the pillbox. Everyone wanted to believe it and that made it so.

Then, when he came to the battalion, feeling that he couldn't really do the job, but having been forced into it by the commanding general who wanted a real, live hero, he was told, by his staff, that the new CO should have been promoted from inside. He had wanted to do a good job, but from the moment he arrived, it seemed that everyone was against him. He wasn't liked. It wasn't anything that he had done. No one had given him a chance. They all expected him to fail, and in fact, he suspected they wanted him to fail.

"Then, when we got here and it seemed that everything was going to be all right, I began to relax. If those sons of bitches hadn't come out of the jungle shooting when they did, I would have been fine. They caught me off guard. Completely off guard."

"Caught us all off guard," said Torrence.

"Yes, but not in the same way. As the commander, I felt responsible for the attack." He held up a hand and rocked forward, opening his eyes to look at her. "Yes, I know, it wasn't my fault, but I felt that way. Besides, you were handling the situation. Once again, I wasn't needed."

Torrence jumped into the momentary silence. Softly, she asked, "You going to keep freezing on us?"

"You know better than that. I thought I did a good job of organizing the defense for that attack."

"But you did freeze."

Jefferson sat quietly, listening to the hum of the radios and the shouts of the troops outside. He glanced at her face, into her eyes and then shook his head. "I've worked my way through that. I was finished with it when I crawled out of that foxhole. Something changed for me in there. I can't explain it, and I don't know when I realized it, but something changed. Maybe it was listening to Rider shout at me and then seeing the look on his face, as if I had just proven to him what he believed all along."

"You did freeze," she repeated.

"Yes. Yes, damn it, yes. I did," he snapped angrily. Then, almost calmly, as if to contrast his former self with his new one, said, "But I won't again. That's why I led that patrol. To prove that I wasn't a coward anymore. That I was scared, maybe, but I could function. I shouldn't have gone on the patrol, but I knew that you could handle anything that might come up and I had to prove that I was willing to do anything that I would order the others to do."

Now it was Torrence's turn to be silent. She didn't know what to say. Suddenly she respected Jefferson as she never had. Suddenly she had faith in him. She knew that he would be able to handle any situation that was thrown at him.

Finally she nodded, as if to say that it was all behind them now. "All right, Major. Now what?"

Something in the command post had changed with those words. He knew that there was nothing more that he had to say. There wouldn't be any more of the trouble that he had experienced with Torrence. He could count on her full support. To end that discussion and return them to the present, he said, "I need to see Lieutenant Norris. She's going to get some new directions."

"Such as?"

"We now have to keep close track of everything we use so that we can bill the aliens when this is over."

"You have to be kidding."

"Not at all. Word from on high."

Torrence stood up to leave. "I'll find Norris and send her over." Torrence moved to the door, stopped and looked back. "Thanks for talking to me."

"That's all right," smiled Jefferson. "Had to tell you so that you didn't have to worry about one more thing. We need to work together."

No matter how fast Jefferson tried to get ready, no matter what reports the officers had given him, it was still mid-afternoon when a group of the aliens arrived at the camp. They had been sent by Zeric to lead the Earth people to the city. One of them, claiming that his name was Etak, finally found his way to Jefferson and with a human interpreter, told him that everything was waiting for them.

Off to one side, Jefferson could see the robot that had laid the concertina wire picking it all up again. For some reason, Jefferson thought that it looked irritated, as if it was thinking, "Put the wire down. Pick the wire up." Jefferson knew that it was not true because it was only a robot.

Torrence came up and reported, "Three of the companies are ready to pull out. We've pulled the perimeter back so that D Company can handle it. I'm not sure this is such a good forward-operating base."

"No, but it will be good for training purposes once we get going. Far enough away to allow them some independent action, but close enough that we could support them if they suddenly need help."

"Then let's get out of here."

About two hours later, they stood on the bluffs that overlooked the alien city. Jefferson was surprised that something the size of the city hadn't been prominently featured on the maps drawn from the aerial photos, but decided it was just one more of the things that no one bothered to tell him. It was like not knowing that the vegetation ran to reds, yellows and oranges, or about the strange monkey-like creature that spun webs, lived in the marble trees and attacked anything that came close to it.

Jefferson decided to leave the majority of the unit on the bluff while he and an advance party went on down. They were met at the entrance to the city by Tyson and Lieutenant Newton who had returned from telling the Divisional intelligence officers about his run-in with the aliens. His broken arm was in a cast that didn't restrict his movements too much.

"We have everything staked out. We'll be spread fairly thin tonight, but we'll have the whole town covered. Tomorrow, when we have a little more time to study the situation, we can consolidate the positions."

"What kind of support did you get from the adnoly?"

"Zeric rounded up about thirty males who were interested in learning the finer points of small-unit tactics."

"Any females volunteer?" asked Torrence.

"None," said Tyson. "But you have to remember we are dealing with a society that is different from ours. Females are not involved in the combat roles, and if we start training them, we could undermine the social structure here."

Torrence glanced at the heavens as if she had just heard something incredibly stupid. Out loud she said, "Oh, come on."

Tyson said, quickly, "No, that is a concern. On Earth we destroyed—that means we anthropologists—destroyed a society because we began making subtle changes in a society's structure without understanding the ramifications of those changes."

"We don't need to discuss this out here," warned Jefferson.

"But, Major," said Torrence, "I can't let him say something like that without challenging it."

"The society on Earth," said Tyson, suddenly sounding like he was addressing a graduate seminar, "had only stone axes. All of them belonged to the males. To earn an ax, the male had to rise through the tribe's hierarchy. Then he was shown how to make the ax. The anthropologist arrived with a load of steel axes. These were far superior to the stone ones made by the males. To compound the error, the anthropologist began using the axes to encourage the tribe people to talk to him and cooperate with him. He began giving them to anyone who came by to talk."

"So what?"

"So, in the old society, when anyone needed an ax, they were forced to deal with someone who had one. It made some activities a village event. It held the village's governmental structure, a village-elder-type society, together. The steel axes undermined all that. No one was dependent on the elders any more. Some of the society's social functions collapsed."

"Maybe that was for the better."

"Maybe. Maybe not. The point is, that it is not up to the anthropologist to decide that. The same here. If the adnoly don't want the females to participate in combat, we shouldn't try to convince them otherwise."

"Not to mention," said Jefferson, "that we have other things to take care of right now. Captain Torrence, you and Captain Tyson can discuss this later. Right now, let's get the troops down here and get security established."

"Yes, sir," said Torrence. She turned on Tyson. "Don't think you've heard the last of this discussion. I'll see you later."

"Glad to accommodate you. My whole argument, however,

will be that we have no right to make changes in their society. We are just here to provide the aid they ask for."

"That is enough for now," snapped Jefferson. "We have work to do."

They moved into the city. At first, Jefferson wanted to put the people into the first ring only, but realized that he had nowhere near the number of troops he needed. He opted for the third ring with outposts scattered around the first. When that was done, the duty rosters established for the watches that night, and the supplies stored, Tyson took Jefferson and Torrence to the castle. They left Judy Sinclair in command, but took a radio so that she could contact them if anything happened.

Tyson and Zeric showed them around the castle and introduced them to more of the adnoly. They circled the pool, ate some of the food, since Tyson hadn't gotten sick from eating it during his first trip to the city, and toured the interiors. It seemed that the castle was more of a hotel than anything else. Finally they were left alone, sitting outside in an evening that had turned cool for once.

Torrence said, "I'd like to get back to what you were saying earlier."

"I wouldn't," said Jefferson, fearing the worst.

Before Tyson could say a word, the radio crackled to life. "We have movement in the streets."

Jefferson said to Tyson, "Find Zeric and tell him. Find out if there are any of his adnoly out and about. Vicky, get on the radio and find out all you can."

"They say," said Torrence, "that there seems to be a great deal of movement in the outer ring of buildings. The adnoly didn't come from in the city but from outside it. No one reported anything moving forward from here."

Tyson approached. "Zeric says that everyone is inside. No one ventures out after dark. Except for the soldiers, nearly everyone disappears with the sun. They don't see well at night."

"Okay. We'll assume that it's the bad guys. Let's get back to the battalion. Tell them to hold their fire until they absolutely have to shoot and then to pick their targets carefully. Tell them that any adnoly in the street are assumed to be the enemy but not to shoot any humans they may see."

The three of them had just crossed the bridge to leave the castle when firing broke out. It sounded distant and hollow. Jefferson realized that some of it was echoes from the buildings.

There were clouds overhead again, but some light from a moon showed through. The light color of the street and the buildings reflected it so that they could see with little effort. They stayed close to the buildings, dodging from doorway to doorway, working their way through the city. As they did, the firing intensified and was punctuated by explosions from grenades.

They were close to the battalion when they saw the first of the enemy adnoly. He was standing on the corner, looking around as if he was lost. Jefferson saw him, grabbed Torrence by the shoulder of her uniform and jerked her back, into the shadow of a doorway. Tyson was somewhere behind them, watching.

"Do we take him?" asked Torrence.

"I would think not," said Jefferson. "One of them in here, more or less won't make any difference."

Rifle fire from behind them caught the adnoly in the midsection. It wrapped its arms around itself and fell to its knees. For a moment it stayed like that and then slowly toppled forward.

"Let's move," called Jefferson. He stepped out of the shadow and the wall near his head exploded. He saw the flash from the adnoly weapon and dove back for cover.

Torrence began to peek around the corner, but Jefferson jerked her back again.

"I think there are more than one. I saw the muzzle flash from one of their rifles."

"So what do we do?"

"Simple. Move through the building and skirt the enemy. Get back to the battalion and organize a house to house defense."

Judy Sinclair had her hands full. At first, they had only seen a couple of the adnoly moving in the street in front of them. They didn't know whether they were friendly or not, but that was soon cleared up. Now she could see that it was some kind of a major assault in progress and that struck her as strange. In fact, now that she thought of it, she was aware that there were a lot of things she didn't understand. For one, how did the enemy learn so quickly where they were? Each time they established some kind of a base, the enemy attacked it.

For a moment, Sinclair stood just inside one of the buildings looking out the window. She could see the shapes of the enemy moving through the night and counted fifteen of them.

Sinclair retreated from her window to the spiral staircase she had found, and climbed to the roof. All the buildings had rooftop patios or gardens. She moved to the edge, found a couple of her people there and joined them. Together they began shooting down at the enemy moving below them, the flash suppressors on their weapons making it hard for the enemy to spot them.

Just as in all the other engagments, the adnoly were hard to kill. Sinclair noticed that shots to the chests seemed to have no effect at all. Sometimes the creature would stagger slightly, but that was more from the impact than the wounds.

"They've got body armor," Sinclair whispered. "Aim for the head or the legs."

At that moment, the night was filled with the slow chug of a heavy machine gun. Far to the right, near the entrance to the city, Sinclair saw the weapon. White and green tracers laced through the night, bouncing high as they ricocheted off the concrete and buildings. The muzzle flash lit the surrounding street and structures.

Across the street, the building began to disintegrate as the rounds from the heavy machine gun pounded it. Then, to make matters worse, grenades began to detonate around her as the enemy vanished from the street. It was as if someone had just taught them fire-and-maneuver tactics instead of frontal assault.

Sinclair said, "You people hold here for a while. I've got to get down to check things out. This is getting weird."

She whirled and, staying low, ran back to the spiral stairs. She fled down them and rushed into the front room. She collided with an adnoly there and both of them fell. Sinclair was on her feet first. She had lost her weapon in the dark but came up with a knife. She thrust out with it but cut only air. She couldn't see anything in the room with her.

She heard a scrambling and swung the knife toward the sound but missed. She kicked out and her foot connected wrong and she felt bones break. As she fell back, she rolled to the right, over the top of her rifle. She picked it up and fired on full automatic, spraying the inside of the room.

Although she couldn't see what she was doing, her luck held. The adnoly was wearing body armor, but part of the burst hit it in the throat, nearly severing its head.

Sinclair struggled to her feet, leaped over the body, landed on her broken foot and fell forward to roll under the window. At that moment there was a burst of laser fire that cut through the glass and began slicing the opposite wall.

Sinclair stayed on her back, staring at the ceiling and watching the ruby-colored beam from the laser flash overhead. When the light vanished, she got to her knees and peeked out the window. She could see the lasers combining with the tracers of six or seven heavy machine guns that lit the night in a bizarre pattern of pyrotechnics.

Under Jefferson's orders, Tyson and Torrence had entered one of the buildings and began searching the back of it for an exit into the street. Jefferson was up on the roof, trying to see what was happening, when the whole interior seemed to explode. The roof shifted and tilted and Jefferson began to slide down it.

Inside the building, both Tyson and Torrence felt the concussion of the blast but neither was in the room where it happened. Torrence, who was closest, felt as if she had been shoved from behind by a heavy, hot hand. She hit the wall in front of her with the force of a linebacker nailing the vulnerable quarterback. She fell to the floor, momentarily stunned.

The window that had been in front of Tyson was blown out. Tyson followed the glass into the street. He rolled over several times and ended up in the gutter on his side. Across from him he saw three of the enemy, but they apparently hadn't seen him. He stayed still, watching until they disappeared around a corner. When they were gone, he scrambled to his feet, felt the stiffness of a dozen bruises, and then leaped through the broken window to try to find either Torrence or Jefferson.

Jefferson scrambled his way back up the slanting roof so that he could see into the street. He saw several of the aliens running below him. Three of his people stepped into the street and opened fire with their weapons. One of the adnoly dropped to its knee and used a laser to cut them in half.

"Damn," said Jefferson. "Goddamn!"

He left the roof then, sliding down to the floor. He found Torrence and helped her to her feet.

"You okay?"

"Yeah. Fine."

"The adnoly have lasers."

"What?"

"I said that the adnoly have lasers."

"And grenades," added Torrence. "And by the sound of it, heavy machine guns."

There was another crash as the building next to them blew up. Dirt filtered down from above.

"We better get out of here."

Tyson joined them and said, "Did you know that the adnoly have lasers?"

"We've seen," responded Torrence.

Jefferson said, "Let's rejoin the battalion and see what we can do to get a defense organized."

Sinclair didn't like the machine gun that had been set up at the end of the street, which was raking the fronts of the buildings around her with a devastating fire. It was heavy enough to tear huge chunks from the walls, and more than one had collapsed under it.

The only good thing that could be said was that it kept the enemy from attacking in force. They could just hold back while the machine gunners destroyed the city.

She limped back through the building, to the other side and saw a couple of the aliens slowly moving from doorway to doorway, pausing long enough to clear the interiors. She stepped up on the spiral stairs and yelled, "Everyone get down here."

When they were assembled, she said, "I saw three of the adnoly moving down the street. I think one of them had a laser. Now if we can take them and get that weapon, we can probably silence the machine gun."

Quickly she outlined what she had in mind. Then, before the three adnoly were out of sight, the soldiers exited the building, and stayed in the shadows. Two of the people peeled off to act as a rear guard while the others pursued the creatures.

The enemy turned a corner and Sinclair ran forward,

favoring her injured foot. She saw them stop about fifteen or twenty feet from the corner. They were facing away from her.

When the others joined her she signaled them to spread out. Then, as one, they moved into the street, working their way toward the enemy. When they were all close, they opened fire and sent the adnoly reeling. They collapsed as a hail of bullets ripped into them, exploding their heads. All three dropped to the street.

Sinclair ran forward carefully and looked. "That's weird," she said. "No body armor for the back. Just some kind of protective plate for the chest and abdomen."

One of the others grabbed the laser rifle. "Let's go," he said.

"Get the rest of the weapons," ordered Sinclair.

They then ran back up the street to where the rear guard waited. Together, they inched forward until they could peer down a side street. By watching carefully, they found the location of a heavy machine gun.

Sinclair pulled her head back and leaned against the wall of a building. "The trick here," she said, "is to hit them from a couple of directions at once. That way, any of them wearing armor will be partially exposed to us."

"How do we do that?"

"First, half of you go back through the building and begin firing at that machine gun. You don't even have to aim. Just hose down the area to draw fire. The rest of us will try to take the building next to the machine gun and then clear the top. That way we can fire down on it."

Without another word three of the people turned and entered the building. A couple of minutes later, Sinclair heard their weapons open fire. That was immediately greeted by renewed shooting from the machine gun.

"That's it. Let's move."

She sprinted across the street limping badly on her injured foot, the pain flaring up her leg. She knew that when the adrenaline faded, she wouldn't be able to move. But now she could. She dove through the front window of one of the buildings. She rolled once and came up ready to fire, but the room was empty. She then moved to the doorway so that she could cover the others as they crossed the street.

One by one, they came at her without drawing any fire. They then leap-frogged forward, one covering while the others moved along the street. When they made it close to the heavy machine gun, Sinclair signalled them to enter the building, figuring they could gain the roof there. Once they moved across, they could look down on the enemy position.

"Let's coordinate this," Sinclair whispered. "Two of you move to the next door and come up on the roof in two minutes. That way, if they have anyone there, we can catch them from behind."

As the two troopers moved, Sinclair stepped on the bottom of the stair. Again the pain flared up her leg and into her belly, but she ignored it. Cautiously, she worked her way upward, until she could see out, over the roof. Incredibly it was empty. She climbed out, and as the two from the other room appeared, she crawled forward.

All three of them came together, stepping over a short wall in the center of the roof, and continuing to the edge of the building. They were directly above the heavy machine gun. They could easily see its crew and the adnoly detailed as protection for it.

Near the fifth ring of the city, Jefferson was still trying to work his way back to the battalion. He was running down the street, dodging around the decorative bushes that had grown there. He was making good time and was nearly knocked over when a man stepped into the street in front of him.

Jefferson slid to a halt and asked, "What's the status?"

There was no response. Jefferson moved closer but in the dim light, didn't recognize the man. The uniform looked strange, as did the weapon the man held. "What's your unit, soldier?"

The man grinned and tried to snap his rifle up. Jefferson leaped back and tried to swing his weapon toward the man. From behind him there was a short burst that snapped by his head. The man pitched back, into the building.

Torrence ran up. "What in the hell is going on?"

"I thought he was one of ours."

"Not armed like that, he's not."

Jefferson moved forward and grabbed the man's belt, lifting him slightly. "Help me. We've got to get him to Intell."

"Where the hell is Tyson?"

"He'll be along. Help me. And make sure you get his rifle."

* * *

Sinclair sat with her back to the wall holding the laser rifle and said, "Anyone know how to fire this thing?"

"I think I do."

She handed it to the man and said, "Okay, you got it. Now, on my command, we all fire down, into the street. Kill everything that moves. Got it?"

When there was no answer, she said, "On three. One. Two. THREE!"

As one, they all opened fire. The laser flared a dozen times, cutting swaths through the enemy position and chopping the barrel from the machine gun. Before the enemy knew what had happened, they had all been hit a dozen times from both the assault rifles and the laser. They never even returned fire.

"Cease fire!" ordered Sinclair. As the shooting ended, she realized that the whole city was now silent. She checked the streets below her and could see no movement. Over her shoulder, she said, "I think they've split."

"You mean they retreated? Like the exercises on the ship?"

"Just like on the ship," said Sinclair. "Let's secure the area and then report to battalion." Then suddenly, the pain from her foot flared into brilliance, and she slipped to the rooftop, unconscious.

10

THE BATTALION'S NEW HEADQUARTER'S
IN THE ADNOLY CITY

WHEN DAWN FINALLY came, it was obvious that the nature of
the war had changed. Jefferson stood on top of one of the
buildings and surveyed his surroundings like a king studying
his lands. There were a number of fires still burning and the
black smoke from them obscured much of the inner city.
Toward the outskirts he could see evidence of the attack. He
could even see some bodies lying in the streets, dark lumps
against the light stone and concrete of the streets. Many of
them were from his battalion.

He climbed down from the roof and found Torrence sitting
on the floor, her head between her knees.

"You all right?"

She looked up. There were dark circles under her eyes and
there was a bruise on the side of her face. Her hair was a
tangled mess.

"Yeah," she nodded. "I'm fine. Just fine."

"We have things to do. We have to get a count on the
casualties, and see what we've lost in the way of equipment.
And we've got to get that body up to Division so they can
identify it."

"If they can," she said.

"If they can."

For the next hour they talked to the various company

commanders, including Judy Sinclair who had her foot and leg in a makeshift cast until she could get up to the fleet. As Jefferson pieced it together in his discussions with his officers, the attack had been some kind of strong probe of the defenses. Although his battalion hadn't yet formed an effective ring, the enemy hadn't penetrated too deeply. It was like all the other contacts the battalion had experienced. The aliens found them, started a fight, and then withdrew after inflicting casualties. Jefferson didn't like it, but there wasn't a lot that he could do about it. It was the classic guerrilla war.

After he had talked to each of the officers, he asked for a written report. He was curious about the weapons being used. In the first encounters, the enemy had carried rifles that were single shot. They were breechloaders which meant they weren't the worst that could be had, but they were nowhere near the best. While the aliens still had a lot of those, they also had assault rifles that would fire in a fully automatic mode. During the first encounters, there were no support weapons. Now they had heavy machine guns. And more importantly, they had laser weapons. Someone, somewhere, was giving a lot of valuable military aid to the enemy and if Jefferson couldn't get similiar help, the enemy was going to be able to push him off the planet.

He found Carter who had been examining the body of the human they had shot.

"What can you tell me?"

"He's definitely human, if that's what you want to know. I would guess from eastern Europe which means practically nothing. His uniform is like nothing I have seen, although it seems to be a modification of standard Soviet design."

"Any papers or ID?"

"Absolutely nothing. Not even labels in the uniform. He's obviously operating on a covert level, and they believe in sterilizing themselves."

"How about his weapons?"

"Well, I'm not sure which one was his. There were two or three lying around there. Not that it matters. All three could have been manufactured by us, or by the other side, or any of about fifteen Third World nations.

"Then he's from Earth?"

"You expected something different? Where else would the enemy get the technology to produce the new weapons?"

Jefferson shook his head. "Shuttle should be down soon to pick up the body."

Jefferson barricaded himself in one of the rooms of an undamaged building, leaving instructions about what he wanted done. He left Torrence to carry out the details. She knew what he would want. He also told Peyton, the operations officer, that he wanted to see a training schedule for the adnoly troops. Things that had to be done even as they were recovering from the attack.

Then he retired to the room and began drawing up a plan to stop the harassment raids against him. He saw it as a way of challenging the enemy on his home territory and possibly convincing him that a continued conflict would only result in more destruction of his own territory and the death of his fellows. If it worked right, he could see a negotiated peace.

When the shuttle touched down some four hours later, Jefferson was ready to board. With him were Mike Carter and Courtney Norris. Also loaded were the bodies of the men and women killed the night before, a couple of the aliens for the biologists, and the dead human that no one recognized, for the Division intelligence officer. As in the other conflicts, the wounded who were only slightly hurt would be treated by the battalion surgeon or medics.

Norris was off to talk to the Division supply officer and Carter accompanied the body of the unidentified human to the Intell office as soon as the shuttle docked. Jefferson went toward Division headquarters so that he could request a meeting with the general. He didn't want to get sidetracked by the operations officer, or any other staff officer who might have questions.

Again he was taken to the conference room with the flat screen, the holotank, and the impressive view, and told to wait. This time, since no one expected him, the wait was long and certainly not worth it. When the door finally opened, it wasn't the general, but Colonel Prescott, this time without his staff. Prescott didn't look happy.

Jefferson ignored military protocol and didn't stand. He said, "I wanted to see the general."

"The general is busy. He asked me to see you. I can handle any problems that you have."

Jefferson decided to try a challenge right off. He said, "We are now facing an enemy who is better equipped than we are. He has heavy machine guns and lasers and even a primitive form of body armor. Our weapons are insufficient to stop them. If we're expected to win, we're going to need better equipment."

"Who told you that you were expected to win?" asked Prescott reasonably. "I see nothing in your orders that suggest you are supposed to win."

"But . . ."

"We had this discussion once before. Your job is to train the locals to fight their own war. You are not to make war for them. You are not supposed to win. You just train."

For a moment Jefferson sat there idly flipping through the papers on which he had written his plans. He studied them with a new-found enthusiasm because he didn't know what to say. What he had just been told didn't make any sense. The longer he was involved in it, the less sense it made. Why get involved in a war that you didn't intend to win? If training was the only thing he was supposed to accomplish, why not do it on the ship? Why send a battalion of combat troops to the planet's surface where they could be, would be, attacked. There was no reason for any of them to be down there.

Finally he sat back in the plush chair and dragged a finger across the highly polished table, leaving a smear. He said, "Why send combat troops to supervise training? Surely there are others who are better qualified to do that."

Slowly Prescott took out a cigar and stripped the paper from it. He lit it, puffed several times and then tossed the match on the deck. "You saying that you can't teach the aliens the use of small-unit tactics and modern weapons?"

"Nothing of the kind." Jefferson watched the smoke cloud rise toward the ceiling where hidden ventilators sucked it into the wall. He wondered why anyone would be allowed to smoke in the enclosed system of a spaceship but said nothing about it.

"You seem to have a real problem, Jefferson," said Prescott breathing out a huge cloud of smoke. He held the cigar up, at eye level, studying the glowing end of it. "Maybe you weren't the one who should have been given the assignment. Maybe it's a little too big for you."

"I can do my job," he said, "I never said I couldn't. I would just like to know where the enemy is getting all the information about our operations they seem to have. I can't send anyone on patrol without an ambush."

"I can see," countered Prescott, ignoring the main point, "where you are at a disadvantage. We'll see that you get some heavier weapons and enough lasers to equip one company. Now you can put them all in one company, or scatter them through the battalion, whatever you think best, but you'll have to account for every one. I don't want any reported lost in combat without you recovering all the parts."

Jefferson decided to ignore that. He said, "I would still like to see the general."

"Well the general doesn't want to see you." Prescott stood, indicating the meeting was over. He blew a cloud of smoke at the table and watched as it dulled the finish.

"I have a plan I think he should see."

"You have no plan, Major. You understand? No plan. You take your people and go back to the planet's surface and do your job. You train the aliens on tactics and the use of our weapons."

"All the weapons?" asked Jefferson sarcastically. He knew the answer would be no.

"All the weapons. Including the lasers. If they're going to be fighting an enemy who has lasers, our side is going to have to know how to use them."

"Just who is that enemy? And who are those humans working with them."

"You have your orders." Prescott moved to the door and then mumbled to himself. "No, Jefferson, you'll screw it up." He raised his voice. "Listen to me carefully. You run into a unit that has any humans operating with it, you withdraw from the field as quickly as possible. You understand that? You break contact and get the hell out."

"What in the hell are you talking about?"

"We don't want any more human casualties. You are not to engage any aliens who have humans with them."

Now Jefferson was thoroughly confused. He sat there staring at Prescott. He studied the uniform, his eyes jumping from the brightly colored ribbons on the chest to the silver eagles on the collar.

"Just what the hell is going on?" he asked.

Prescott released the hatch and returned to his seat. "There is nothing going on, other than what you have been told. We are assisting a democratic government that has requested our aid. Nothing more than that."

"Then who are those humans operating with the other side?"

"To the best of our knowledge, they are renegades. Mercenaries who have been hired by the other side."

"Then who in the hell cares if we kill them?"

Prescott slammed his hand to the table. "The general cares! That's all you have to know. We do not want these aliens seeing humans fighting one another. You got that? Humans do not fight one another, for any reason."

Jefferson could see that prolonging the meeting would do nothing for him except get him in deeper. He had been given his orders and he was now expected to carry them out. If he said something about his plan again, he would probably be relieved of command. Yet he didn't like what he was being told because it meant that he was stuck on the planet for an indefinite period with his hands effectively tied. Questions swirled around, but he knew that Prescott would give him no more information.

To Prescott he said, "I understand. Sorry I was so dense."

"Don't worry about it," said Prescott magnanimously. "Sometimes we don't make the instructions as plain as we could. Sometimes we make assumptions that we shouldn't make. Now, if you have nothing else, I'll return to my duties."

"No, sir. Thank you, sir."

When Prescott left, Jefferson sat in the conference room trying to understand all that was going on. It was quite obvious that there were things that he wasn't being told. There was no way for mercenaries from Earth to get to Procyon Two so fast, if the planet had only recently been discovered. If there were mercenaries, it meant that someone on his own side was lying to him although he couldn't think of one reason why.

Of course that didn't explain the weapons. Why even start out with weapons that were inferior? Why not bring in the big guns and go for the quick win? Of course, he wasn't supposed to win. But that still didn't explain why he had been equipped with inferior weapons.

And what about . . .

Jefferson nearly grabbed his head to stop it. There was so much that he didn't know and didn't understand. He would have to talk to some of the others and see what they said. Maybe they could figure out what was going on.

Prescott left the conference room and reported directly to the commanding general. He didn't have to stop in the outer office and talk to the master sergeant who sat there or announce himself to the general's aide. All he had to do was tap on the hatch and then open it. The general waved him in.

"What did you learn, Tom?"

"Well, General, this isn't going to be easy. Jefferson wants to win and doesn't understand why we seem to be trying to stop him. I think he may try to do something about it."

"Have a seat, Tom, and tell me about it."

Prescott took the leather chair that sat to the right of the general. He laced his hands behind his head and said, "Jefferson is getting suspicious. He sees the inconsistencies that we weren't careful enough to hide. He wants to know who the humans on the other side are and he's not buying that renegade-from-Earth crap we've been handing out."

"I don't suppose you've come in here without a plan to handle this."

"No, General. I think we can turn it to our advantage. We have to let him have his victory and then pull him and his battalion out of there. Replace them with the 502nd. That way no one knows that the war continues. If someone questions us, we just tell them that the hostilities being experienced are the end of the civil war. We get what we want out of it. And the aliens get what they want. Everyone is happy."

"All right, Tom. Make the arrangements. But be careful, this is too big to blow. The mineral wealth on the planet is enough to last centuries."

Prescott stood and saluted. "Yes, sir. I think we've got it wired."

Jefferson found Norris in the passageway near the shuttle bay. She was counting boxes of equipment and checking them off on a list that was displayed on a computer screen set into the bulkhead.

"How long are you going to be?" he asked.

"Another hour. Maybe two. They've given us about everything we wanted, but they say I have to sign for it all. I'm accountable for it so I'm going to be very careful with the records."

"Fine. You seen Carter?"

"He said that he was going to the club to have a beer. He was going to take as much advantage of the air conditioning and the luxury as he could."

"I'll go round him up," said Jefferson. "We'll see you back here in about an hour." He started to walk away and stopped. "Say, if you would like to join us when you're done, feel free. It's not really fair for us to drink while you work."

"Sounds good, sir. I'll see you in the club."

Carter sat at the bar in a club that looked like it could have been on any of a hundred dirtside army bases. It didn't resemble the club that Jefferson had been in a couple of days earlier. This one was designed for the junior officers who never found their way into flag territory. Jefferson crawled up on the stool next to Carter and ordered a beer. When it arrived, he glanced sideways at the intelligence officer.

"You learn anything?"

"You mean about the body we recovered?"

"Yeah. About that."

Carter sipped his beer. "Nah. They won't talk to a lowly lieutenant. I asked a couple of questions, but got mostly ignored."

"What kind of questions?"

"Well, I pointed out that the uniform was styled like those worn in the Soviet Army." Carter took a handful of beer nuts.

"And?"

"And they said that nine-tenths of the uniforms worn by armies on Earth, or by mercenaries for that matter, are styled after either the Soviets or us, and those that aren't styled by them or us are made by them or us."

"In other words, they weren't impressed with the uniforms."

"Not in the least. I also pointed out that the weapon looked like a Soviet-made carbine, but they didn't care. Then I asked about the body armor and the laser rifle. They said that the body armor was the same cheap junk being sold all over Earth. Same with the laser."

"You ask how the mercenaries or their equipment managed to get here in such a short time?"

"Of course, sir." Carter lifted his glass and drained the beer. "I was told they didn't have the faintest idea and until I came up with some more information, they wouldn't be able to make a guess. Wanted to feel that it was my fault they couldn't answer the questions."

"This is getting stranger all the time."

Carter looked at his empty glass and then slammed it down on the bar. "You get the weapons?"

"I've gotten us some heavier weapons and enough lasers for a company, if that's what you mean. And a speech about escalating the conflict to a global scale. At least I think that was the point of the lecture."

"So, now what, Major?"

"I finish my beer and we wait for Norris. She'll be up here in a few minutes. Then, I'm not sure what we're going to do."

"Well, I can't get angry about waiting for Courtney. She kind of makes it worthwhile."

"I should remind you that Lieutenant Norris is a fellow officer and should be treated that way," said Jefferson.

Carter glanced at him, not sure whether he was kidding or not.

11

IN THE ADNOLY CITY

AS SOON AS the shuttle rolled to a stop, Jefferson was out the rear hatch. He stood on the open field and looked at the buildings of the adnoly city spread out below him. He studied the single-story structures but could see none of his troops. They were hidden in the second or third ring and the sentries were all posted out of sight. He knew they were there and was glad that he couldn't see them.

With Norris and Carter, he climbed down from the bluff that overlooked the city and entered the first ring without being challenged. As he moved deeper, into the area occupied by his soldiers, he hoped the guards would be able to recognize him and not stop him with stupid challenges and advances to be recognized. At the entrance to the third ring, he found Torrence waiting for him.

"Good afternoon, Major."

"You got a command post established?"

"Follow me. We moved that heavy machine gun to the rooftop in the fifth ring. It'll guard several approaches and the main entrance to the castle. I think you'll approve."

They walked down the street, passing the caved-in fronts of the buildings and the evidences of shattered windows. There were stains in the street where his soldiers had spilled their blood, and strange green-yellow smears where the enemy had died. Torrence had already ordered all the bodies removed.

Torrence stopped in front of a building that had a huge window that faced the sun. All the glass was gone, much of it lying on the sidewalk at the base of the wall, and there were now transparent sheets of plastic taped in place. There were a few tears in the plastic.

"We found," said Torrence, pointing at the rips, "that it got too hot in there without some openings for air circulation. It's still warm but not as bad."

"Why not hook up to the electricity?"

Torrence shrugged. "No outlets. I asked Tyson and he said that the adnoly don't have electricity in the city. They have it in that central building of theirs, but none in the outlying areas."

"He say why?"

"Nope. Just mumbled something about that is the way things are and we're not going to change them."

They moved through the door, which stood wide open. Torrence explained that it was to facilitate the cooling. It seemed pointless to close it with the windows wide open.

Torrence waved a hand around like a real estate agent showing off the house. "This is one of the few buildings outside the castle that has a second floor. For some reason, the rooms up there are cooler. I put your office upstairs. It's the only room that still had a door."

"Then we'll go on up. Carter, why don't you find Tyson and bring him to us. I've got a couple of things I want to discuss and I think he should be around for it."

Within an hour, the people were gathered in Jefferson's office. Jefferson sat behind an OD green field desk that looked as if a strong breeze would knock it over. In one corner was a dark computer screen with a key board under it. The engineers had yet to get the battalion generators on line. Torrence sat in the only other chair. Tyson stood, leaning against one of the dung-colored walls, his arms folded. Carter sat on the dusty floor. There were no windows, but an open skylight let in a cooling breeze.

Jefferson waited until each of them was settled and staring at him. "I asked each of you here to talk about some of the things that are bothering me. Each of you has been involved in some of those things. That is, each of you should understand what I'm trying to say."

"Just what are you getting at, Major?" asked Torrence.

Again Jefferson looked at each of the soldiers. Young people with responsibility far beyond what they would have found in the corporate world. Not one of them was more than twenty-five. He knew Torrence was younger than that. Great responsibility that each of them took willingly.

"Things down here on this planet are not right," he informed them. "Tyson, you mentioned a couple of things. I've noticed others. Vicky, I thought you and Mike here might have something to contribute."

Torrence nodded and Carter said, "Just what do you have in mind?"

"According to the information we have, this planet was discovered to have intelligent life just a short time ago."

"Right," agreed Carter.

"Then don't you think it's a little strange that we have as much information about their language as we do but that we landed with almost no information about local vegetation or animal life? Or that the good guys are ambushed and the bad guys hit us almost as we touch down on the planet's surface?"

Torrence nodded but said nothing. Carter and Tyson remained quiet.

"The fleet," continued Jefferson, "must be running surveillance on the planet, but they have yet to warn us about the alien movements. They have to be getting something. And we've gotten no maps. The aerial photographs tell us nothing important. This city," Jefferson waved a hand, "was not on either the maps or the aerial photographs we received. There must be better information in the fleet but they're not sharing it with us.

"We've spotted humans working with the aliens a couple of times. Hell, we killed one. But according to the people upstairs, these are mercenaries. We're supposed to withdraw if we spot humans working with the adnoly. Some nonsense about not wanting them to see humans working against one another. But the real question is, how in the hell did those mercenaries get here so damned fast?" Jefferson slapped the top of his desk for emphasis, shaking it.

"There are a dozen other things. We see signs of bombing

and artillery where there is supposed to be none. We must maintain the fiction that our level of technology is on a par with theirs, even though we must have space flight to get here, not to mention the constant shuttle flights in sight of the aliens while trying to disguise the fact we're from another planet. I mean, do we really think the aliens are that stupid?

"There is an esclation of weapons. First single-shot breech-loaders and last night, they're using lasers. We . . ."

"Major," interrupted Torrence, "there a point to this?"

"A point? Well, I don't really know. I've just seen things these last few weeks that bother me greatly and I was hoping that we could figure something out. As a kid, I watched replays of the exploration of space on television and those little ships were so crammed with gear that there was barely room for the astronauts. There wasn't an inch of wasted space but ours are full of it. Hell, we have so much that Prescott can pollute the air with a cigar."

"I've noticed a couple of things," said Tyson now caught up in the discussion. "I noticed that the adnoly are more advanced, technologically, then they're supposed to be. They're at least late twentieth century, maybe later. In some ways they're more advanced than we are."

"Okay," said Torrence, nodding. "The list is long. So what?"

"Obviously," said Tyson, "we're being lied to."

"For what reason?" asked Torrence.

"That's what I don't understand," said Jefferson leaning forward. "Hell, we're all on the same side."

"Somebody," said Tyson, "behind the scenes, is manipulating all of us. It's all being stage-managed."

Jefferson turned his attention to Carter. "You're Intelligence. You should have some information."

Carter rubbed his face with his hand, deep in thought. Finally he said, "I hand out the information that I'm given by Division. I debrief our people and send reports, but I'm not on the gathering of it, really."

"But you know how to gather it, don't you?" said Torrence.

Carter looked at Jefferson. "Major?" he said pleadingly.

Jefferson wasn't going to give up that easily. "Lieutenant Carter, your job is to provide us with the intelligence we need to run our operations. We need information badly. There must be something you can do."

"But, sir, you have better contacts to answer your questions. What you want isn't going to be found here or among the junior officers. You're talking policy here, and generals make policy."

"He's right," said Torrence. "None of us have the clout we need to learn what we want to learn."

"I want to know," said Jefferson slowly, as if he was forming the thoughts as he went, "is how did we get here so fast? Why are the aliens better armed than we are? Who is escalating this thing and why? Just what in the hell are we doing here? If it's training our side, then why don't we do it on the ship? And who's training the other side?"

He stopped talking and glanced at the other officers. "Just what in the hell is going on here?"

They were all silent for a moment. And then Jefferson snapped his fingers. "Tyson! You claim to have the ear of the general. Hell, you've beat me over the head with it. Why don't you see if he'll spill something to you?"

Tyson laughed. "You really think he'll spill something that he doesn't want to spill?"

"No, I suppose not. But maybe there will be something that he'll want us to know. On the sly."

Tyson shook his head. "Can't see that happening. But I don't like what I see around us. We're making these adnoly too dependent on us. We're giving them a technology that they're not equipped to handle." He took a deep breath. "I'll ask a few questions and see what I can learn."

Jefferson was about to respond, but a knock on the door stopped him. "Come!"

The door opened and a head looked in. "Sir, we've been out of touch with Company D for twelve hours."

"What do you mean out of touch?"

"We haven't received any radio traffic from them in twelve hours and they don't answer our calls."

"Son of a bitch," Jefferson yelled. "Why hasn't anyone sent a patrol out to take a look."

"We didn't think it was important until now."

"Didn't think it was important? We've got nearly three hundred people out of contact and you don't think it was important. Do I . . . ." Jefferson had just about asked if he was supposed to think of everything. He had realized that he was.

"Captain Torrence, I want a patrol of at least two platoons, to move out immediately. I want someone to get on the radio and try to contact Mitchell or his company. I want a shuttle flight over their position and I want that five minutes ago."

He looked at sergeant who had entered the room. "You understand what I want?"

"Yes, sir. I'll get right on it."

As soon as the door closed, Jefferson said, "Vicky, I want you to go along. Mike, you and Joe get up to the fleet and start nosing around. This thing is beginning to get out of hand."

Before she left, Torrence had a number of the laser weapons issued to the people who would be on the patrol. She also made sure that each soldier had two or more hand grenades, and that some of the heavier weapons were issued. Norris didn't want to issue the equipment until she had everything organized and was sure that everything she had signed for on the ship had been delivered, but Torrence insisted.

"Write down all the serial numbers, if that makes you happy, but get the gear issued."

She missed her departure window by six and a half minutes, but she was outside of the city quickly and enroute before the shuttle made its recon pass.

Security on the patrol was sloppy. Torrence had a point out, along with flankers and a rear guard, but they were moving so fast that they kept running up on the point and leaving the rear guard far behind. There was no noise discipline. Two platoons couldn't move through a forest quietly if they were in a hurry. People made noise. They fell. Their equipment rattled. Their clothes rustled against the plants. There were coughs and sneezes, and there was some chatter.

Torrence didn't worry about it. She kept the soldiers moving, telling herself that if Company D had been attacked, they would have heard the firing. And then, with a growing sense of horror, she realized that if the company had been attacked while the enemy was probing the city, the distant firing would have been masked by that inside the city.

Then she calmed herself, reminding herself that Company D had radios and no matter how heavy the attack, either there or in the city, there would have been radio messages. None had been passed. No calls for help had been sent.

She felt the heat of the jungle wrapping her. The sweat soaked her uniform and didn't dry. It was like walking through a steambath wearing a heavy, water-soaked towel. Cotton formed in her mouth and her breathing, like the men's and women's around her, was ragged, coming in gasps as they pushed toward Company D's campsite.

As they neared their old base, the patrol halted. Security was established and one of the pointmen slipped back to her. He whispered, "I think we're less than a klick out."

Torrence crouched in the spotty shade of one of the parachute plants. She pulled an aerial photo from her pocket and studied it. "I want to swing to the right, away from the direct line of march. Come out of the forest on this slight hill. We should get a good view of the terrain from there."

"Yes, ma'am."

"And we'll close it up a little bit. We've gotten spread too thin. You slow it down now. We don't want to walk into anything."

"Yes, ma'am."

He scrambled off and a few moments later, the patrol began to move out, now with the interval between individuals shorter. They skirted the base of a gentle slope and finally, when they were opposite the camp, they began to climb. When they reached the top, and the edge of the jungle, the point halted them. Within two minutes, the NCO was back.

"What you got?" asked Torrence.

"Doesn't look good."

"What?"

The man shook his head and then wiped the sweat from his face. "We haven't really studied the situation but we can see no sign of movement down there."

Torrence felt the blood drain from her face. When it was good news, people joked about it, making it sound bad, but when it was bad, they gave the information quickly, to get it over with.

"Bodies?"

The NCO suddenly became fascinated with the ground under his feet. "Some bodies. Fifteen. Maybe twenty. Lay of the land won't let us see more."

Torrence suddenly remembered something she'd read as a kid. It had been written by an officer of the Seventh Calvalry as they had ridden to the site of the Custer massacre. Bodies lying in the morning sun, looking like white boulders strewn across the grassy slopes leading down to the Little Big Horn.

"Show me," she said, not wanting to see.

The NCO turned and took her to the edge of the jungle. She crouched there and then using the image enhancer on her helmet, she examined the field in front of her. She touched the back of her hand to her lips.

Just as the sergeant said, she could see the bodies lying on the gentle upward slope of the land. The perimeter wire had been ripped apart and the command post was nothing more than a smoking ruin.

The bodies looked so lonely. So forlorn. Lying there in the hot afternoon sun. She looked away and felt her lunch rise in the back of her throat. She clamped her teeth and swallowed, telling herself that she would not be sick. Not in front of the troops.

Tearing her eyes from the scene, she looked at the NCO. "One platoon here as a reserve. The other, on me. I'll take the point. We'll go look for survivors."

"Yes, ma'am."

She glanced at the hardened eyes of the sergeant. "Don't you feel anything?"

"Yes, ma'am. I do." He turned without another word to her.

With one platoon stationed just inside the jungle, to watch them, Torrence and the other slipped forward, on line. They worked their way down to the shallow valley and then upward, toward the devastated camp. As they moved closer, they could see more of the remains of Company D. Now they could look down, into the foxholes and see the bodies there. They were close enough that she could recognize some of the dead.

The sergeant who had been on point asked, in a hushed voice, "What happened?"

"Damned if I know."

"Where are the dead aliens. They must have killed some of the aliens."

"Get security established," snapped Torrence. "And I want a count. Maybe there are survivors somewhere."

It was getting worse. Many of the bodies had been mutilated. Hands, feet, arms, and legs had been severed. Some had been stripped, leaving the white and black bodies scattered, looking like the boulders the cavalry officer had described that horrible morning near the Little Big Horn. Now she understood, completely, what the man had felt. They looked so white. And so vulnerable, lying there.

Again the revulsion rose in her. She whirled on the closest NCO. "I want security established. NOW!"

"Where are the weapons?" he asked. "All the weapons are gone."

"Security," snapped Torrence. Then, more softly, she added, "See to it now."

Near the body of a dead soldier was a broken bayonet. There was a stain of the greenish-yellow blood there, and on the blade, were traces of alien skin and hair.

Then, with a single squad, Torrence entered the perimeter. They found the body of Clay Mitchell near the command post. He was lying on his back, a single, large-caliber bullet hole in the center of his chest. Torrence stood there, looking down at the mangled corpse and remembered the things they had shared. They had never been close, but they had been friends. She felt the loss deeply and knew that it would get worse before it would get better.

And she understood the horror that the officers and men of the Seventh had to feel as they found the remains of the five companies that had ridden to their doom with Custer. Until that moment she had never fully understood it. Now, with the bodies of two hundred fellows scattered around her, she knew exactly what they all had felt.

Before she allowed herself to get too emotional, she turned, looking away, up into the sky, and blinked rapidly. Then she turned again, staring down into the crater that had been the command post. It had taken a direct hit. One side was caved in. The radio was destroyed and the mutilated body of the operator was lying near it, her blood staining the remains of the command post.

Torrence, for something to do, climbed down and examined the expensive piece of junk. The loss of it explained why there had been no call to the fleet, but not why there had been no call to the battalion. That radio was one of six that the company had.

They swept on past the command post and to the other side of the perimeter, checking the dead. There were no wounded, although there were indications that those wounded in the battle had been killed after the fighting ended. The enemy had taken no prisoners.

"We need to get a muster. Someone might have escaped."

"If anyone escaped," said a corporal, "he or she would have tried to return to the battalion."

Torrence nodded but didn't say anything. "Just get the muster."

"Yes, ma'am."

The platoon leader, a young lieutenant, looking as if she was going to be sick, approached. "What do we do?"

Torrence wanted to scream at her, but took a deep breath instead. She turned, surveying the field and then said, "There isn't much we can do." She glanced up at the sky. "It's going to be dark soon. All we can do is return to the battalion and call graves registration. They'll have to send someone from the fleet."

"We're going to leave them like this?"

"What the hell do you expect us to do?" snapped Torrence. "We can't carry them out and we can't bury them. No time."

The lieutenant stared at the ground and didn't say a word.

They were more careful on the return trip. Noise discipline had become important and no one violated it, partially because they were too shocked to speak. Everyone had lost friends with Company D.

Jefferson was waiting to meet them as they entered the city. Radio silence had been maintained so he didn't know what had happened. He had thought Company D might return with them but it did not.

Torrence came at him and he stood waiting for her report. "They're all dead," she said in a flat voice, devoid of any emotion. "Every one of them."

"How long?"

"I don't know." She stopped moving, looked at the curb and then sat down. She hung her head, her elbows on her knees and her weapon resting against her shoulder.

Jefferson looked at the young lieutenant who stood close to them. "You take charge and make a weapons check. Hold your people away from the rest of the battalion until I have a chance to tell them what's happened."

"There'll be rumors."

"Can't stop rumors. Just do your best. I'll have the cooks bring some hot food to you."

"No one's hungry."

Jefferson shrugged and took a deep breath. "Just get these people off the streets and hold them incommunicado until I can announce the loss. Can you do that?"

"Yes, sir."

As the lieutenant moved off, dragging the two platoons with her, Jefferson looked down at Torrence. "You okay, Vicky?"

"I need a drink. I really need one."

There were dozens of questions that Jefferson wanted to ask, but he could see that Torrence was close to the edge. He grabbed her weapon and pulled her to her feet, steering her toward the command post.

As soon as they were out of sight of the rest of the battalion, safely inside the building, she collapsed against him. He guided her up the stairs and into his office, pushing her down, into the chair. He set her weapon down in the corner and knelt in front of her. "I can only get you a beer."

Torrence shook her head. She leaned back and closed her eyes. "There's not a lot that I can tell you. Their position was overrun. I think they all were killed. There's no evidence that anyone escaped or that anyone was captured. We'll need graves registration to straighten it out."

Jefferson wanted to ask questions, but didn't interrupt her. He let her talk, telling it as she remembered it.

"I think they were hit at the same time we were. Mitchell would want to make a grandstand play. Wipe out the enemy so that he could get himself the medal." She opened her eyes momentarily and looked at Jefferson. "Never told you how impressed he was to find out you had the medal. He wanted one. I figure the main radio was taken out earlier on and by the time Mitchell realized that he was outnumbered and outgunned, all the other radios were out too."

"Or jammed," thought Jefferson.

"Evidence we saw on the field suggest the enemy had the better weapons. Heavy machine guns and lasers. There were no enemy bodies but we did see more blood smears. Or rather, I think they were blood smears."

She took a deep breath and continued, describing the scene and the mutilations. "They took everything that was useful to them."

"I suppose that's to be expected," said Jefferson quietly.

"What are we going to do about this?"

"I don't know." He stood up then and moved to the field desk. He leaned on it and tried to get in touch with his emotions. Strangely, he wasn't saddened by the death of Company D. Death was to be expected in war. The mutilations didn't bother him. He would have been angered to learn that his people had been tortured, but wounds to the dead did nothing to him.

What he felt more than anything was a rage with the brass hats on the ships high overhead. They sat there and made pronouncements about the nature of war. They sat there and demanded that all the pencils be counted and if the figures didn't jive, then someone was in deep trouble. And if Company D was sacrificed, then that was the nature of war.

He wondered if his plan could have prevented the destruction of Company D. Then he realized that he wouldn't have been able to implement the plan before the attack.

They were being attacked every night. Maybe it was just a probe of the perimeter or a harassment attack, but it was a nightly affair. He was being told to train the adnoly while the enemy was infiltrating rapidly. He was not to engage in attacks or fight human mercenaries.

He shook his head as if to clear it. "I guess it's time I made a command decision. We've taken enough casualties now. More than enough. It's time to dish out some of what we've been taking."

Torrence sat up, her eyes opened. "You have something in mind?"

"You're damned right."

12

ON THE MAIN BATTLESHIP

FOR AN HOUR Tyson wandered the hallways, looking into offices and then moving on. He was trying to work his way up to the Division commander and find out something about what was happening on the planet's surface. After the talk with Jefferson, Tyson had decided that it sounded like Division was supporting both sides in the war. He didn't think it was anything quite so simple. The real answer, hidden somewhere behind the scenes, was probably a fairly complex plan.

Finally, unable to learn anything by just walking around and dropping in on people, he headed toward the Divisional Headquarters area. He figured that the first thing he should do was find someone in operations.

Colonel Prescott was busy setting up an exercise in the simulator ship. Tyson wasn't unhappy to hear that. In fact, he thought it might work to his advantage. He found the deputy operations officer, a lieutenant colonel named Alden, sitting behind a big desk that was littered with papers. To one side sat a computer with a screen that displayed flashing lights but no message.

Tyson slipped into the office unobserved, sat down and said, "What's happening, Al?"

158

Alden jumped at the sudden voice, throwing his pencil across the room. "Shit, Joe, don't go sneaking around."

"Why not? That way I might learn what's going on up here."

"There's nothing interesting going on up here." Alden reached over and turned off the computer. He didn't worry about the disc drives or the discs in them. He just shut the whole system down. Then he carefully concealed the papers that he had been working on.

"If there's nothing interesting up here," commented Tyson, "why are you so jumpy?"

"You have something on your mind? I mean, you blow in here and start talking in riddles."

Tyson leaned back and laced his fingers behind his head. "You know, Al, the soldiers today aren't stupid. They see the inconsistencies in things and they ask questions. We pride ourselves on training soldiers who have enough initiative to take any situation in stride. Blind obedience no longer exists. Our people don't want to die in a war for no reason."

"What in the hell are you talking about?"

"I think you know exactly what I'm talking about. I think that someone up here had better take a few minutes to explain why we are not supposed to engage in military operations but only train the adnoly."

"Because this is not our war. We are here to help the adnoly, as you call them. We are not here to fight their war for them."

"Then why don't we train them on the ship so that our people aren't in danger?"

Alden smiled. "Because we don't want the aliens to see the level of technology we have."

"Good God, man, that is the most ridiculous thing I have ever heard. They have to know that our technology outstrips everything they have. They have to know that we come from another star system and that we have space flight. Even if they couldn't figure it out, the shuttle flights that Division lands nearly every hour should make that clear. And now we've been giving them lasers to use for defense. Take my word. They know."

Alden stood up and moved to a coffee pot that was set on a

tiny table against the wall. He poured himself a cup, stirred in sugar and cream and asked, "You want some?"

"No. No, thank you." He watched Alden sit down again before saying, "Well?"

"Well, the simple fact is that I don't make policy any more than you do. I know that you're the fair-haired boy of the general, but that doesn't mean that I know anything or that I could tell you if I did."

"Are you suggesting that there is something more to know?"

"Now, I never said that. I merely indicated that I wouldn't tell you if I did."

"Then what is your personal opinion of the problems I've mentioned?"

"I would say that it is something that you need not worry about. I'm sure the general is fully aware of everything and he is taking every precaution to ensure that people don't die unnecessarily."

"Would you listen to yourself?" laughed Tyson. "The general is taking precautions? The general is sitting up here with no one shooting at him. We've got to live on the surface and try to explain to men and women why they have to watch friends die. Why we have to keep a careful record of our assistance to the aliens. Why we are ambushed every time we move by an enemy who supposedly isn't all that effective. Why we . . ."

"Joe, there is nothing I can tell you. All I do is carry out my orders just as you do, or Major Jefferson does."

Tyson realized that Alden was just going to hand him the same answer, again and again, in a different form. He stood abruptly. "You've been a big help. But I'm going to keep moving around and see what I can learn anyway."

"Is that a threat?"

"Of course not," said Tyson. "It's a promise. There is more going on here than meets the eye. Somebody is manipulating this for some reason and I'm going to find out what it is."

"Even if it's classified."

"Oh, don't give me that classified shit. You people wear that like a cloak. Just because it's classified doesn't mean that I shouldn't try to find it out. It probably means that I should, because for too long, people have been classifying things when they find themselves on shaky ground."

"Be careful," warned Alden. "You'll be treading on some heavy toes. I advise you to drop it before you get yourself into real trouble but I know you won't listen."

Tyson moved to the hatch. "Not when I don't have to." He left Alden sitting there for a moment. Then the man turned and switched on his computer again.

Carter had ridden up to the fleet in the same shuttle used by Tyson. When Tyson ran off to circulate, Carter went directly to the Divisional Intelligence Office. Streeter was in the back, working on a mapping project that combined the aerial photos with radar soundings and high-intensity infrared in an attempt to discover important mineral deposits. Carter tapped on the door and then opened it.

"You have classified out?"

Streeter looked up to see who it was and then said, "Doesn't matter, come on in. You've probably seen all this anyway."

Carter sat down at the table and looked at the map. It was upside down, but he could recognize some of the landmarks. He located the city where the battalion was now camped. In red, he could see a number of enemy units. He almost said that he had seen nothing like it and then remembered that one of the best ways to learn things was to pretend that you already knew them.

He pointed at one corner of the map and said, "I don't think you've got that plotted quite right."

Streeter looked up and said, "They've moved?"

"I believe they have," he said, making it all up as he went along.

"Do you know where?"

"Pulled back, toward their base." Carter got up and came around so that he could see the map better. He saw a major base of the enemy adnoly marked. He noticed a couple of routes of travel that crossed the isthmus into friendly territory. He saw that a landing field had been drawn in near the enemy strong point.

"This is getting more complicated," said Streeter. "We keep

identifying more actual units. They seem to be moving toward our base."

"Uh-huh," grunted Carter. He had seen a manifest sticking out from under the corner of the map. It seemed to be a schedule of shuttle flights to the surface for the last several days. He noticed that it didn't agree with what he knew to be the schedule to his battalion. Several of the flights were during the night hours and there had been no shuttle landings at night, with one exception.

"We got another battalion down?" asked Carter casually.

Streeter shot him a confused look but said, "No. You're it. No plans for sending any one else down there unless you people really blow it."

On the ground, Jefferson was inside the castle in the center of the adnoly city. Zeric and a number of the older males were there, listening patiently while Jefferson explained exactly what he had in mind. He told them that it was time that they stopped taking all the punishment and it was now time that they began to dish some of it out.

The meeting had been difficult to get organized. Jefferson had trouble finding anyone who could speak the language. With both Carter and Tyson aboard the fleet, and with a number of the people who had been trained in it dead, it had seemed that they would never get started. Torrence then found an old NCO in Company A who could speak it. Her presence was requested.

When everyone was present, including Torrence and the adnoly, Jefferson tacked an aerial photograph to the wall and then turned to faced the assembled group. "I know that some of you don't understand how the symbols on this paper relate to things in the real world, but I'll try to make it clear. This," he pointed to a mark near the center of the photo, "is where we are now."

He waited for the translation. Zeric nodded as he had seen the humans do and then said, in barely understandable English, "I understand."

"Fine," he said. "Now, over here," he pointed to another section of the map, "is the camp used by your enemies." He faced the west corner of the room and pointed at the wall.

"This map shows that their city is in that direction, but a long way off."

While that translation was being made, Jefferson studied the adnoly in the room with him. He saw something flash behind Zeric's eyes and wondered if suddenly, the big adnoly didn't understand aerial photos and maps.

When the translation was completed, Jefferson continued the briefing, talking about how they would move overland, to the enemy city, wait outside it until it was completely dark, and then attack, burning and stealing as much of the enemy equipment as they could.

Finished, he went over it again, slowly, but didn't give out many details. He explained it as a training session to teach the adnoly how easy it is to move through the jungle without leaving sign, the importance of noise discipline, and the importance of responding to orders quickly. He told them that others would be relying on them and if they failed to carry out their assignments, others might die.

Zeric and his fellows nodded throughout the translations of Jefferson's briefing. And when that ended, they indicated their fascination with the fancy weapons that Jefferson and his staff carried.

As he was wrapping up the session, Jefferson felt that there must be something else to say, but knew that he couldn't cram everything into one short meeting. He asked for questions, but there were none from the adnoly. They were more interested in getting out of the hot room and beginning their personal preparations for the upcoming battle.

When all the adnoly were gone, Torrence took a deep breath, crossed her legs and leaned back. "You really think this is going to fly? The general is going to leap all over you if you try something like this."

"Let's go to my office and talk about it in private," said Jefferson. Together they left the castle and walked across the drawbridge. They entered the town proper, passed some of their guards and sentries and then entered the headquarters building. Once upstairs and inside his office, Jefferson closed the door.

He turned and looked at his exec. "I thought we understood one another now, Vicky."

"We do." She moved to the chair and sat down. "I was merely saying that the general isn't going to like this."

"Between you and me, we've got to do something to slow down the advance of the enemy. They're running all over us. Besides," he said, grinning broadly, "this is just a training mission. The adnoly are running it and we can't be held accountable if they bump into a major enemy base."

Torrence wiped a hand across her wet forehead and then rubbed it on her thigh, leaving a ragged stain. "You sure this isn't just an attempt to win another medal?"

"You can ask that after seeing the remains of Company D scattered all over that hillside? Sure, we can sit here while the enemy chips away at us, or we can do something about it."

"The best defense is a good offense."

"My point exactly."

Tyson found Carter in the club, sitting at a small plastic table bolted to the deck and talking to a redhead who was sipping beer from a long-stemmed glass. Tyson walked up, smiled, and said, "Excuse me, but I need to speak to the lieutenant for a moment."

The redhead returned the grin and said, "Please."

Carter stood and they moved away, toward the bulkhead where a holographic picture of the fleet was hanging. Tyson leaned close and said, "I don't know what in the hell is going on, but I know something is. None of the people I talked to denied it, but they wouldn't answer questions."

"I found that Intell knows a lot more about the enemy than they're telling us. They've got maps with enemy strongholds and supply depots pinpointed."

"I'm afraid that doesn't help us much," whispered Tyson. "They'll just say that they would supply the information if we needed it, but we're supposed to be training the adnoly and not fighting their war."

"The best part," said Carter, "is that I saw a shuttle schedule and it has nothing to do with us. There aren't supposed to be any other units on the planet's surface."

For a moment, Tyson didn't say anything. He held one

finger up as if he was signalling for attention and then said, "Okay. Okay. That's a beginning."

"The map I saw had a landing field marked." Carter stopped talking, savoring the moment. "And it wasn't one of ours. It also showed the infiltration routes, the main enemy bases, and a couple of their cities."

Tyson reached over and tried to pull a chair away from the table there. It was bolted to the deck. He gave up and turned back toward Carter. "I guess what we need to do is go back up to Division and see if there is anything else lying around. I'm not sure what all this means, but I think it stinks."

"There is one other thing," said Carter. "I don't know whose shuttle schedule I saw, but it is possible that there is a Soviet Bloc fleet here helping the enemy."

Tyson blinked rapidly and then said, "Hadn't thought of that. I guess all I have to do is ask the operations officer where the other fleet is. If there is one."

"Got to be," said Carter. "Remember those mercenaries we've seen."

"What the hell are you suggesting?"

"I don't know what I'm saying. Maybe that there is no way for the mercenaries to get here and therefore anything we're being told about them is not true. We ignore the fact they are supposedly mercenaries from Earth. The question becomes, again, who is running those shuttle flights and is there an enemy fleet around here?"

"So that makes the list of flights important."

"No, I don't think it's important that we have the list. You say you saw enough of it to be sure that it wasn't a schedule of flights to us. Okay, they have to be going somewhere, and we have very little information about where they're going. We can check that from two locations. Here, we find out if there is another fleet, and down below, we have the major hit the enemy base closest to the shuttle landing area to see if we can learn anything more about it."

"When do we start?"

"How are things going with your redheaded friend?"

Carter laughed. "I'm not sure how to answer that. We were just having a drink while I waited for you. I would like to finish that before I go back into the spy business."

"By all means finish your drink, but remember we've got a

flight down in a couple of hours and we have to have more information before we return. I'll meet you in an hour and a half."

"Okay."

"But don't do anything stupid. Just see what you can learn without getting yourself in trouble." Tyson glanced at the redhead. "And tell your friend that I'm sorry about the interruption."

Carter was late getting back to the shuttle. Tyson had waited in the club as long as he dared and had then walked down to the shuttle bay, where he made the pilot hold while Carter ran across the deck. He leaped up, into the back, and the hatch was closed for an immediate take-off.

On the return trip, they had no chance to discuss what either of them might have learned. Too many others around to hear them, including the shuttle crew. Instead, they talked about the war in general and the redhead in particular.

As soon as they were on the ground and out of earshot of the crew on the shuttle, Tyson asked, "You find out about another fleet?"

"Nothing around as far as I can tell," answered Carter. "Ours is the only fleet overhead."

"Shit!" said Tyson. "That really tears it."

Carter understood exactly what Tyson meant. He grinned weakly and asked, "What do we do now?"

"Just like I said. Find Jefferson and see if we can divert him to a new target."

Jefferson was in his office, cleaning his rifle and wishing that he had opted for one of the heavier weapons. There weren't enough to go around. He looked up when he heard a tapping on the door frame.

"Yeah?"

"Major Jefferson," said Tyson, "we have uncovered some information that might change tonight's target."

Jefferson set his rifle aside and said, "Give it to me."

Tyson closed the door and moved closer to the major. He explained everything that he and Carter had learned while they were up with the fleet. Finally he used an aerial photograph to show Jefferson the shuttle landing site.

"And you think we should hit that base instead?"

"Of course, Major," said Tyson. "It's not that far from the original target and this might give us a few additional answers."

"Show me exactly what you have and then we'll meet with the rest of the staff."

"Yes, sir!"

13

INSIDE THE ADNOLY CITY

—

IT TOOK ALMOST no effort to alter the target for the raid. Although Jefferson had already worked out the compass headings and the distances to the old target, changing them was only a matter of an hour's work. When he briefed the pathfinders, they would get only the revised figures. No extra work for anyone but him.

At dusk, he found that the majority of the battalion was at its staging area. The pathfinders were off in a small group, studying the aerial photos that they had instead of maps. Two of the adnoly stood with them, looking at the photos, but still not understanding what they were.

Jefferson called them over. "Who's in charge here?"

A second lieutenant who looked as if she hadn't finished high school said, "I am, sir."

"Good. I have here a list of your compass headings and the distances, as near as we can figure them. I'm sorry that I can't be more precise, but you've seen the quality of the information and the maps we've been given."

The lieutenant moved forward and took the paper out of his hand. She read through it once, glanced at the aerial photos that went with it, and nodded. "I notice," she said, "that the base is fairly close to the ocean. If we move through the isthmus and stay to the south, we should run into it. Or at least get close.

This bluff, or clearing," she pointed to a large open area, "would be a good rally point."

"I'd thought of that. But we also need a staging area nearer to the enemy. I don't want to use the same location for both."

"Yes, sir," she said. She studied the photos, shifting through them until she found what she wanted. "If I might suggest, and if the location of the enemy camp is correct, it would seem that the best plan would be to stage here, on the far side of the camp, and retreat out, toward our line of escape."

"Let's do it the opposite way. Stage in the closest, sweep through the enemy camp and rally at the far side. Maybe the enemy will be fooled."

"Yes, sir," she said slowly. "Is it a good idea to put the enemy camp between us and our line of escape, if we should fail?"

"If we fail," said Jefferson, "I doubt that a line of escape will help. If, however, we succeed, and the enemy manages to put together a counter force, we might fool them by going in the opposite direction. Any other questions?"

"No, sir."

"Good. Be prepared to move out in ten minutes. Don't let the adnoly know the destination, but don't hesitate to ask them for help. Our point will be a couple of minutes behind you."

"Yes, sir."

"Good luck."

Within thirty minutes the entire battalion, with the exception of the platoons detailed to remain behind to guard the lines of communication, had left the adnoly city. They didn't move out in one mass, but in small groups from various points, in case there were spies nearby. Once they had moved into the jungle, the small units began to form into larger ones, until each company was re-assembled. The line of march was carefully chosen and the points of each company led the rest toward the isthmus.

Near dawn the next morning, they all began to spread out again, taking up defensive positions so that they could rest and pass the day. The pathfinders used the time to explore the immediate countryside so that they would know what to look for during the next night.

All during that time, no one saw anything of the enemy. There were no enemy patrols into the area, there were no civilian adnoly working the land, or traveling between the two continents. There was no evidence of life at all. In fact, they didn't even see any of the strange webs and monkey-like creatures that had killed Joubert several days earlier. Almost no life existed on the isthmus, other than plants and trees and now Jefferson's battalion.

The next night they reached the clearing that Jefferson had wanted to use as a staging area. Under the cover of darkness, the battalion quietly re-assembled, moved in and established a defensive perimeter. Everyone was ordered to remain silent during the day. They were not to explore, they were not to talk. They were to rest and clean their weapons. They were to remain on half alert. At nightfall they would receive the final briefings.

During the day, Jefferson, Torrence, and the young lieutenant from the pathfinders crawled along the edge of the bluff so that they could examine the enemy camp below them. It was spread out on a large plain that sloped gently down to the sea. On the far side was a surfaced runway that looked to have been designed, not for conventional aircraft, but for shuttle flights. Along one side of the runway was a series of large buildings that looked to be warehouses. Beyond them was a stone wall nearly twelve feet high.

Closer to them was a series of smaller buildings that were arranged in a semi-circular pattern that seemed reminiscent of the city where they made their camp. In front of the buildings was a wire fence that looked like it was made of concertina.

Inside the city there was a lot of activity, most of it seemed to be military in nature. Many of the adnoly carried weapons. Not the long, bayonet-tipped primitive rifles that had been in evidence in the first days of the war, but newer, modern assault rifles and laser weapons.

There were also a number of heavy weapons lining the fences and walls. These were supported by lighter machine guns and a few recoilless rifles.

After she had taken it all in, Torrence said, "You really expect us to attack that? We'll be slaughtered before we get close to the fence."

"Of course, we would," snapped Jefferson, "if we tried a

human-wave attack or a frontal assault. We need to use intelligence and fire-and-maneuver."

"You have a plan?"

"Of course. Remember that we are fighting a guerrilla war. We are not interested in taking and holding anything. We are interested in looking inside those warehouses and destroying any military equipment we find. We are interested in inflicting casualties. Once that mission is completed, we exfiltrate to the rally point."

"And we go tonight?" asked Torrence.

"Yeah. We've got too many people in the field to keep from being spotted. We have to go tonight. You want to see anything else?" he asked.

"No, sir," said Torrence.

Turning to his right, he said, "Okay, Lieutenant, let's go on back. Vicky, I'll want to see all the company commanders just as soon as we can get organized."

At the campsite, Jefferson briefed the company commanders on the mission. He explained how he wanted the attack to work. Two companies would hit the wire in four locations at the same time. They would blast their way through, move along the streets, cross the runway and search the warehouses, destroying all military equipment. Once that was done, they would exfiltrate to the rally point.

"Rider, as soon as we break up here, you get with the pathfinders and move out. Your job will be to secure and hold the rally point."

"But, sir, I want . . ."

"No arguments, Lieutenant. You will take and hold the rally point. This must be accomplished by zero one hundred. You will not use your radio. I will assume that you have been successful. We all will count on it."

He turned to the other two company commanders. "Each of you will hold one platoon in reserve. Once you have succeeded in penetrating the wire, and have made contact, you will order them to move up in support. If you run into trouble, they can cover your withdrawal."

He went on detailing all the assignments, where he and Torrence would be, how long they should spend searching the warehouses, and not to worry about destroying the runway because the shuttles could land almost anywhere on the plain without a hard surface anyway. It was to be a classic guerrilla raid and nothing more than that.

When he finished the briefing, he said, "Anyone have any questions?"

Rider said, "Can't one of the others secure the rally point?"

For twenty seconds Jefferson stared at Rider. Finally, in a low voice, he said, "Are there any relevant questions?"

"Do we just blow up the warehouses?"

"I'll leave that to your discretion. You can take anything you can carry off, but the point is to deny the material to the enemy."

"How long do we have?" Sinclair wanted to know.

"Ah," said Jefferson. "I knew there was something I was forgetting. We have to be in and out in ninety minutes. Once we reach the rally point, and everyone is accounted for, we'll move out."

"What do you mean accounted for?" asked Rider.

"This is a hit-and-run mission. We don't have a lot of time to screw around. You have to bring the wounded out with you. If you have to, leave the dead, although it would be nice to pick up everything that would identify us."

"You don't seriously think that we'll fool anyone? The entire planet, the fleet, and anyone else who happens to be around is going to know that we did this."

"But we don't have to make it easy on them," said Jefferson.

"What are you going to do with the adnoly?" asked Torrence.

"I've thought about that a lot," said Jefferson. "Since they can't see that well in the dark, and aren't that familiar with our tactics, I thought the best thing to do was position them with Rider. That way, any adnoly we see in the city will be unfriendly."

Rider pointed at Sinclair. "Is her ankle going to bother her?"

Jefferson looked annoyed at Rider. He was about to jump on him and then realized that Rider only wanted to be included in what he thought was the real fight. He said, "Captain Sinclair is capable of speaking for herself." He turned and asked, "Is your ankle bothering you?"

Sinclair smiled. "No, sir. The break wasn't all that bad and the surgeon gave me a couple of shots that facilitated the

ealing. He said not to jump up and down one-legged, but also
id that it shouldn't cause trouble."

"All right," said Jefferson, realizing that the questions being
ked were of no importance. "Get back to your companies
d be ready to move out by midnight."

Slightly after midnight, as determined by the fleet's clocks,
fferson signalled the beginning of the assault. With one
latoon from Robert Lynn's company, organized into a head-
uarters unit, Jefferson and Torrence headed down a slope and
ut of the jungle. As they left the shelter of the trees, they
egan to crawl toward the wire. In front of them were twelve
en and women who were going to blow the holes in it.

When they were within one hundred yards, where the last of
e cover was, they halted. The sappers advanced beyond that
oint to place their charges. That done, they withdrew a couple
f yards. Moments later there was a series of explosions along
e fence.

As soon as the gaps were blown, the two companies were on
eir feet, running for the holes. No one was firing and there
eemed to be nothing happening inside the city. No lights had
ome on, no sirens had sounded. It was as if the adnoly inside
ere unaware that they were now under attack.

Jefferson and the headquarters platoon hit the wire before
ere was any shooting at all. Jefferson turned to his right,
nning down a street, ignoring the buildings on either side of
im. One-story buildings, wide windows, some that were open
nd some that were covered in plastic.

Jefferson slid to a halt near a corner. He looked behind him
nd saw Torrence was there. Across the street, he could make
ut the shapes of a number of the other people. They took a
ouple of seconds to catch their breaths.

Then, almost as if the enemy had finally figured out what
as happening, shooting erupting all over the city. Near them,
efferson saw or heard nothing. He peeked around the corner
nd saw nothing. He waved an arm, signalling the people
cross the street forward.

As he rounded the corner, he saw one of the adnoly step into
e street. He fired on full automatic, the street around him
ashing bright orange. Jefferson's soldiers returned fire, the

wall behind the adnoly exploding as the rounds hit it. The
creature staggered but didn't fall.

It turned and took several steps toward Jefferson. He
fumbled at the magazine of his rifle, dropping the empty clip
to the ground. As he tried to reload, one of the heavy weapons
began to chug. The adnoly took one of the rounds high on the
chest and went down like his bones had disintegrated. It didn't
move.

Jefferson and his tiny band continued on down the street,
turned another corner, ran along the walls until they came to
the end of it. In front of them was an open field. Jefferson
could see a series of lights had been strung along the runway,
marking its location. He stopped then, staring into the night,
looking for signs of the enemy.

Sinclair was not having the luck that Jefferson was. As she hit
the wire, her company was taken under fire. It was sporadic
and poorly aimed, but it did slow them down. Sinclair,
however, didn't break stride. She kept running until she was at
the edge of the city. She dropped to the ground and rolled
against one of the walls. She sat up, peeked over the wall and
then dropped as the top of it erupted.

The field between the fence and the city was littered with
bodies from her company, but the damage wasn't too great.
Maybe ten, fifteen were down. She turned, and looked into the
city.

Near her she caught the flash of a light machine gun. The
muzzle flash stabbed out nearly five feet long, an orange-
yellow tongue of flame that marked its position. She got to her
knees, pulled the pin on a grenade and tossed it. A moment
later, there was an explosion in front of the machine gun, but
it continued to fire.

On the other side of the street, she saw two of her people.
Together, they took grenades and tossed them at the machine
gun, and when they exploded, both people dove around the
corner, using the cover generated by the flash and the smoke of
the detonation. Again, they failed to knock out the gun, but the
two stormed the emplacement with their lasers flashing. They
leaped the barricade in front of it, disappearing into the dark.
An instant later they reappeared. The machine gun was silent.

Before she entered the city, Sinclair took a final look at the field behind her. She could see no living people on it. She got to her feet, took a deep breath, and then sprinted from cover. She ran down the street, her eyes searching the storefronts and windows. Except for the machine gun, there seemed to be no other resistance. There seemed to be shooting all around her but none of it directed at her.

Torrence came up behind Jefferson and asked, "Where in the hell is everyone? I hear shooting all over the place but I don't see shit."

Jefferson shrugged, "I don't know. Someone has run into something."

"What'll we do?"

Jefferson didn't answer right away. He scanned the runway, but could see nothing out there. About a hundred yards away was one of the warehouses. A single light over the door flickered, but there was no movement anywhere near it.

"All right," said Jefferson, "we'll cross the runway. Keep to the shadows. Let's move it."

Almost as a body they swarmed out from behind the wall. They spread out as they sprinted for the other side of the city. Jefferson led them. He crossed the landing strip, used the butt of his rifle to smash one of the lights, and kept moving. In front of him he saw a short wall that seemed to have been made of sandbags, but was partially and effectively hidden by the moss of the field. He leaped it, stumbled, and fell as the machine gun opened fire.

Jefferson rolled to his back, grabbing one of the grenades in his jacket. He pulled the pin and dropped it. Then, aiming carefully, he threw the grenade. It exploded in the middle of the machine gun nest, but the firing didn't stop. It merely changed direction so that the ground around him began to explode.

Torrence, who had fallen at the edge of the runway, took the respite to leap to her feet. She ran forward, dove for cover and rolled up against the sandbags. She took a grenade, pulled the pin, and let the safety lever fly. She counted quietly to herself and then reached up, letting the grenade drop over the wall and into the machine gun nest.

When the second grenade went off, the enemy soldiers didn't know what was happening to them. They spun again, looking for the new threat. They saw a couple of shadows moving along the runway and opened fire on them.

Jefferson leaped to his feet at that moment, running back at the machine gun nest. He fired into it on full automatic, emptying his weapon. When the bolt locked back, he dropped to the ground to reload.

When the shooting stopped, Torrence poked the barrel of her rifle over the top of the nest, firing it blind. The heavier rounds from her rifle tore up the nest and killed a half dozen of the enemy. The others, wounded, were in no condition to fight back. They dropped their weapons and tried to scramble away, running for safety.

Torrence was on her feet then. She jumped into the nest and fired again, putting more rounds into the enemy dead. She looked at the machine gun and wished that they could take it with them, but it was too heavy for her to move by herself.

She rejoined Jefferson. He pointed to the right and she nodded. Together they ran toward the warehouse. As they approached the door, Jefferson stopped long enough to shoot out the light. He whispered to Torrence, "We don't need to spotlight ourselves."

Near the side of the warehouse, they found a dozen other members from the headquarters platoon. Jefferson asked them, "What the hell is going on here?"

"Waiting for you, sir," said one of the NCOs.

"Okay. Let's take it." He moved around to the door and tried the knob. He wasn't surprised when it didn't turn. He took a lump of explosive from his pack, slammed it against the doorknob, set a fuse and timer, and rushed back, to the side of the building. Seconds later, there was an explosion and the door, along with some of the frame and surrounding wall disappeared.

Without orders, they moved forward. Jefferson dove through the opening, rolled to the right, and came up on one knee. There were some overhead lights spaced around that threw a dim glow around the building. There were no soldiers in the warehouse. Just huge piles of equipment shipped from Earth.

Sinclair, with the majority of her company, were gathered at the edge of the city. They were looking across the runway, at the warehouses, some of which were now burning. In the distance, she saw the brief fight with the machine gun. When it ended, she scanned the field in front of her, but saw no signs of the enemy lying in wait.

Satisfied, she whispered, "Okay, Tailor, you take about six people and form a rear guard. Once we've cleared the runway, we'll cover you."

"Got it."

Without another word, Sinclair left the relative safety of the shadows and ran across the runway in a crouch. Like Jefferson, when she passed one of the runway lights, she used her rifle to smash it. She continued until she came to a shallow depression that might have been a drainage ditch. She dove in, saw a number of others join her, and then waited.

As Tailor and the rear guard cleared the runway, Sinclair waved them on so that they kept going. They reached the edge of the warehouses without taking any fire. Once they had found defensive positions, Sinclair and the rest of the company leapfrogged forward to join them.

When the others reached him, Jefferson had them fan out, over the floor, searching for adnoly. The building was apparently unguarded. As soon as they reached the far wall, they started back, this time examining the piles of supplies.

Before they moved far, Torrence called Jefferson over. "Take a look at this," she said.

In the beam of her flashlight, he could read the label stencilled on the side of a crate. He reached out to touch it, almost as if he didn't believe what he was seeing. Then, to Torrence he said, "Captured?"

For an answer, she flashed the light around. Nearly every crate had the same markings. She said, "Some of it might be captured, but you don't believe that. It was delivered here. Delivered by shuttle."

Jefferson jerked his survival knife from its scabbard and levered it under one of the boards. It popped open, but all he could see inside was the normal high-impact plastic packaging that he was used to. He finished opening the crate, and with Torrence's help, got the plastic container out.

He opened it up and discovered a half dozen of the newest laser pistols. Also included were spare parts and additional power packs. Jefferson slung his rifle, grabbed one of the laser weapons and slammed a power pack home. He sighted on the far wall and squeezed the trigger. The ruby beam stabbed out.

"Let's get these to our people," he said to Torrence. "Then let's set this place on fire." He glanced at his watch. "We've got about seventeen minutes to exfiltrate."

They broke open the closer of the crates, grabbing as many of the laser weapons and power packs as they could carry. When everyone was armed with the advanced weapons, they moved back, to the original hole in the wall. On Jefferson's order, they all tossed a thermate grenade back into the warehouse. An instant later, thermate exploded showering the interior with fire. In seconds the flames were pouring from the roof.

Sinclair ordered her people to spread out, entering as many of the warehouses as they could. She told them to search the supplies first, but to do it quickly. If they found anything they could use, they were to steal it. When they finished the search, they were to destroy the supplies.

With four others, she blew open the door of a warehouse, and dove in. She came up on one knee but saw no movement. The others followed her. She pointed to the right and left and they moved in those directions.

She was about halfway through the warehouse when there was a burst of firing to the left. She leaped for cover, turning toward the sound. She could see almost nothing, except for a nearly invisible cloud of smoke. She continued to stare in that direction.

"Loring bought it," someone shouted.

"You see where the firing came from?" shouted Sinclair, aware that she had just given away her position.

"I've got them located. If you're near the center of the warehouse, you should be in the clear."

Sinclair hoped that the enemy had no one with them who could speak English. She crawled forward, trying to keep the piles of supplies between her and the enemy position. Another burst of firing stopped her, but she quickly realized that it hadn't been directed at her.

She got to her feet, ran forward and halted. She stood up, tried to see over the material, and then began to slowly climb it, as if trying to gain the high ground. Far to the left, she could see the body of Loring. She was lying in a spreading pool of black-looking blood, and looked like she had nearly been torn in half.

Then, not far away, she got a flash of movement. She turned her head and by carefully searching, she found the enemy position. If the dummy hadn't moved, she would have never spotted it.

She backed down the supplies, circled them, and was able to get behind the enemy. She lined up her weapon, using a wooden crate stencilled in English for a base. She changed the magazine to be sure that she had a full one in place and then opened fire.

The rounds slammed through the barrier of boxes raining debris all over the floor. Two of the others joined in, hosing down the area. When they quit firing, there was only the sound of liquid leaking form shattered containers. Sinclair worked her way forward, and found the bodies of two of the adnoly.

"It's clear," she said. "Let's get out of here."

As Jefferson and his people stepped into the night, firing broke out around them. Jefferson saw a couple of people fall. He dropped to one knee and opened fire with a laser pistol. Others followed suit. In a couple of seconds, the enemy had been eliminated. Jefferson got to his feet and ran to the alien bodies. Each had been wearing body armor, but the lasers had punched right through it.

"Let's scram," he called to the others. He hadn't thought about checking to see if any of his people had been wounded. He assumed that they were all dead.

Torrence checked. It turned out that Jefferson had been right. The new weapons being used by the aliens were of such a heavy caliber, with such a muzzle velocity, that even a wound to the hand or foot could be fatal.

They stopped at the wall. Jefferson turned and looked back. All the warehouses were in flames. The airstrip was nearly as bright as it was in the midday sun.

Jefferson stepped away from the wall and turned his laser weapon on it. There was a sputtering as the rock began to glow bright orange and then began to melt and run. Others turned their weapons on it and soon they had burned a gigantic hole in it. He waved them through.

As the last one dove clear, Jefferson turned for a final look at the alien city. He could hear some shooting in the distance and there were tracers lacing through the sky, but the majority of the fighting was over. There were flames shooting hundreds of feet high and there were explosions as the ammunition cooked off. He smiled because he knew that they had nearly destroyed everything that was of military value and probably quite a bit that wasn't.

Jefferson turned away from the scene of the destruction. He leaped past the wall and fell among the members of his platoon. He glanced at his watch and saw that he was out with four minutes to spare. All that was left was to move to the rally point and access the damage to the alien base.

At that moment, another machine gun nest opened fire, pinning them all down, against the stone wall.

14

JUST OUTSIDE THE BURNING REMAINS
OF THE ALIEN'S CAMP

As THE ENEMY machine gun opened fire, the tracers flashing overhead, Jefferson dived to the ground. Rolling away, and then to his belly, he began to shoot back with his laser pistol. Ruby colored beams lancing toward the enemy. It seemed to have no effect. The enemy gunner knew what he was doing. The machine gun probed again, the rounds slashing through the night, trying to draw return fire so that he could identify targets.

"Okay, Major," said Torrence, breathing heavily. "You got us into this. How are you going to get us out?"

Jefferson tried the laser pistol again, but the material of the bunker seemed to absorb the energy. He looked at the weapon and then at Torrence. "I don't believe it. They've got heat tiles. We're going to have to blow it up."

"We have to do something," she agreed.

"I don't need you to remind me of that," snapped Jefferson and was suddenly overwhelmed by a sense of deja vu. He knew that he had been there before. Not, not here. A similar situation. Suddenly, he was crouched behind the dragon teeth on another planet, surrounded not by members of his battalion, but with only Staff Sergeant Mason. Jefferson suddenly had what very few people ever got. A second chance. A chance to earn his medal for real.

181

"I want everyone to open fire in about three minutes."

"I don't think it will do any good," said Torrence. "It's too well protected and we don't have anything to penetrate it."

"Just do it."

"Yes, sir."

Jefferson felt a twisting in the pit of his stomach. He knew what the dialogue was going to be before he heard it. He knew what Torrence would say before she said it. Except that he wasn't hearing her voice. He was hearing Mason's coming from her mouth.

He tried to divert the script by saying, "I'm going to use explosives to destroy it if I can get close enough to it."

Torrence said, "You don't have to do this. You don't have to prove anything. We can knock it out from here."

"It'll be easier my way," said Jefferson. "Get them firing and falling back. We don't want that machine gun to get any of them. Retreat to the wall."

"Please, David, be careful."

Jefferson started forward then, cocked his head as if listening and then whispered, back over his shoulder, "Hey, this will be a piece of cake. I've done it before."

At that moment, the humans began firing. Lasers and automatic rifles shooting rapidly. They were answered by a sustained burst from the machine gun nest that tore up the ground around them, throwing clods of dirt and clouds of dust into the night air. They returned it as best they could.

Without looking back, Jefferson crawled to the right, away from the shooting. Then he angled back toward the nest. He could see the muzzle flashes of the weapons as the enemy hosed down the whole area. He kept moving though, even when it seemed that his legs were turning first to lead, and then to rubber. He found it next to impossible to control his muscles. He was shaking badly, but he kept himself moving. Too many people were counting on him.

For a moment, he was overwhelmed by the sights and sounds around him: the chugging of the enemy weapon and the hammering of his soldier's rifles, flashes of red light from the lasers and the yellow orange flashes from the muzzles of the machine gun. He flattened himself and took a deep breath. He could smell the cordite, the dirt, and the moss-covered ground. Nervous sweat soaked his uniform, turning it clammy.

This is what happened before, he told himself. He had started off bravely enough, but then had stopped until Mason had come out to finish the job. If he didn't move now, it would be Torrence, the only real friend he had in the battalion. She would crawl out and do his job.

With a Herculean effort, he forced his hand forward, grabbed the turf and pulled himself along, ignoring the strobing weapons and the snap of the heavy-caliber bullets. He kept his head down, moving cautiously toward the enemy, driving everything from his mind except the need to keep moving.

Finally, he saw that he was parallel to the nest. In the firelight from the burning city, he could see the outline of the machine gun buried in the armor, heat absorbing plates that protected it. He could see a front that was sloped backward with a dozen firing slits in it. The sides weren't nearly as high as the front, and in the flickering of the fires all around he could see the adnoly moving, firing, and servicing the weapons.

He crawled closer, his face pressed against the soft moss. He slipped the pack from his shoulders and reached inside. The explosive was a neat little ball-shaped charge that had a force of nearly a ton of TNT. Jefferson pulled at the fuse, snapped the glass that separated the chemicals, and then raised up to his knees so that he could throw it. He watched it arc over the wall and land among the enemy and their weapons.

As he released it, the machine gun swiveled, and then fired at him. He dove to the right as the rounds slammed into the ground around him. He felt the impact of the bullets.

An instant later, there was a massive explosion that forced him further into the ground. He felt the heat roll over him and for a second or two, found it nearly impossible to breathe. The air was boiling hot, searing his face and the backs of his hands.

Shaking his head, Jefferson forced himself to his knees. Unsteadily, he scrambled toward the machine gun nest, the laser pistol pointed at it. He dropped down next to what was left of one of the walls, fingered the laser pistol and peeked over the top. There was virtually nothing left in the nest. Twisted metal that had been the heavy machine gun, and bits and pieces of flesh that had been the adnoly gunners. Ripped to shreds by the concussion of the explosion. Cooking meat rolled up and out, making his head spin and his stomach flip flop.

Moments later, Torrence was there, reaching down to lift him to his feet. She whispered to him, "You earned your medal." Then louder, so that the others could hear, she said, "We've got to get to the rally point."

Jefferson looked back, over her shoulder, so that he could see the adnoly city. There were no signs of any organized pursuit. In fact, he couldn't even see any signs of any pursuit. There was sporadic firing, the tracers flashing into the sky, but he couldn't tell who it was. He could only tell that there was some shooting still going on in the city.

"The rally point?" Torrence prompted. "We have to move."

"Yes," Jefferson nodded. "Sorry. Get them moving."

They were among the last to arrive at the rally point. Rider worked his way to them and said, "We're still missing about twenty-five people."

"You mean dead?" asked Jefferson.

"No, sir. I mean missing. Probably dead in the city, but no one knows where they are."

"We go back?" asked Torrence.

"No. No, we can't. We've got to get out of here." To Rider he said, "Make one more count. See if we can identify the missing."

"Yes, sir."

"Are the other two companies back yet? Lynn and Sinclair."

"Both of them," said Rider. "Sinclair came in about fifteen minutes ago. Ran into some stiff resistance but overcame it. Lynn didn't seem to run into much of anything."

Lynn ran up. "You remember Brown? She's the woman who was captured. . . ."

"Yes, what about her?"

"We found her. She was in one of the warehouses. Locked in a small room there. They hadn't done a thing to her. They just carried her off and locked her in a room."

"Okay, good," said Jefferson. He knew that he should feel more, but was too damn tired. Too drained. He turned to Torrence, "I want you to get the battalion organized and get them out of here."

She studied him carefully in the flickering light. His uniform was dirty and torn. There was a large bruise just below his right eye. She wanted to reach out to him, but settled for asking, "You okay?"

"I'm fine. Just fine. I want you to take the battalion back because I'm going to hold here with a platoon to wait for stragglers."

"You don't have to do this. Let someone else do it."

"You just do as you're told," he snapped.

Rider returned then. "We're missing nineteen by the last count. We've got about thirty-two dead in the city that we couldn't recover."

"Get your company ready to move out. Leave one platoon here to secure the point for stragglers."

"Yes, sir. I'll stay to command it."

"You go out with your company. I'll stay."

"But, Major. I didn't get to go into the city. I deserve the chance."

Jefferson was about to snap at him and then realized how he must feel. The young always wanted the opportunity to fight. It was the veteran who kept his mouth shut and did what he was told. To him, Jefferson said, "You did a good job of holding the rally point. You've nothing to be ashamed of."

"But, Major . . ."

"Don't ruin it by arguing now. Get your company formed and prepare to move out. Captain Torrence will be in tactical command."

Three minutes later, the pathfinders were running into the jungle. They were followed by the point of the lead platoon and in under five minutes, the whole battalion had disappeared into the night.

As the rear guard moved out, one of the NCOs left with Jefferson asked, "How long do we stay, sir?"

"I want a squad. We're going to swing back to the city and see if we can find anyone."

"Just a squad?"

"Just a squad. I think that if the unit is small enough, we might be able to make it in and out without being seen."

"Yes sir. I'll go with you and find ten others."

"Let's make it snappy, while they're still confused. We give them the time to figure out what's going on and they'll be waiting for us."

When the NCO returned, Jefferson asked, "What's your name, sergeant?"

"Deane, sir."

"Well, Sergeant Deane, let's go."

They crawled away from the rally point, moving back to the city. Because they wanted to stay low, it took them fifteen minutes to reach the wall. Rather than use one of the holes that had been blasted in it, they scaled an undamaged section.

As they crouched on the city side of the wall, Deane asked, "Now what? We certainly can't search everywhere."

"No, we can't. Let's move to the edge of the warehouses and move along there. Keep our eyes peeled. The vast majority of the losses had to be there."

"Yes sir."

Keeping low and to the shadows, they crossed the open field to the edge of the warehouse area. Some of the buildings had already collapsed into themselves, sending showers of sparks and flaming debris into the night sky. There seemed to be no movement among the buildings and it appeared that the adnoly had no concept of firefighting.

They moved to the south, along the warehouse area, halting occasionally to study the surrounding territory. They saw the bodies of the adnoly and occasionally passed those of humans. They found no wounded humans. There was one group of seven or eight lying together and Jefferson thought he heard someone groan. The voice sounded human, but he couldn't see any wounded soldiers. The only found dead bodies.

They continued running along the burning buildings. A burst of machine gun fire surprised them and two of them fell, wounded. Jefferson dove to one side and came up shooting. He saw an alien soldier charging them. Jefferson aimed his laser pistol and squeezed off a shot. The enemy dropped into the dirt.

Jefferson fell back to the wounded. One of them wasn't hit badly, only grazed by the bullet, but the woman had lost most of one leg. Deane was trying to get a tourniquet on it, but there wasn't enough of a stump left. The belt kept slipping before he could get it tightened. The woman shuddered once and the blood spurted a final time weakly as she died.

"We get out now, Major?" asked Deane.

Jefferson looked at the dead woman and then to the hole in

the wall that was opposite them. He saw that there was very little of the warehouse area left to explore. He nodded and said, "Let's get out."

Almost as one, the squad got up. Deane and one other grabbed the shoulders of the dead woman and began dragging the body. Jefferson held back for one last survey of the damage.

All the warehouses had burned, and the flaming debris had set some of the city on the opposite side of the runway on fire. A hot wind was roaring in to fan the fire and spread the flames. Shadows moved in the distance, but no one was coming at them. There were no adnoly trying to put out the fires, or to come after them, or to organize a defense. Then he realized that he had seen no enemy humans. The whole city had been full of adnoly, and weapons that were obviously of Earth manufacture, but not one human, other than those in his battalion, had been seen. That made almost no sense to him. It was almost as if they had known the attack was coming and had abandoned the city to the attackers.

Jefferson caught the squad at the wall where they had waited for him. "Let's go," he said.

"Wish we could have found all of the missing."

"We have to assume they're dead now," said Jefferson. "If they weren't, they would have gotten to the rally point."

But no one new had made it back to the rally point. Jefferson waited another thirty minutes, listening to the city burn and watching as the flames climbed a hundred feet into the air. Finally he decided that it was time to get out. It would be light in an hour or so, and he wanted the cover of darkness to make the escape.

As the rear guard platoon made its way off the rally point, Jefferson took a final look, shrugged and hurried after the other men and women who were running to catch the rest of the battalion.

It was nearly midday when they found the remainder of the battalion. Torrence had organized them into a defensive perimeter so that they could get some rest. Jefferson had no problem penetrating the perimeter. He found Torrence asleep in the bottom of a shallow foxhole.

"Hey, Victoria, you want to wake up," he said to her.

She opened her eyes slowly and said, "Good thing you're not the enemy, you'd be dead."

"How do you figure that?" he asked as he sat down on the edge of the hole.

She moved her hand slightly and he could see a laser pistol pointed, more or less, in his direction. "I'm a very light sleeper," she said.

"I concede the point. But then, I wouldn't have walked up if we had been at war with each other."

Torrence holstered her weapon. "Now what?"

"I saw no signs of pursuit. We're close to our own territory and I think we should press on back to the battalion area."

"In the daylight?"

"Daylight, night, what difference does it make?"

"Ambush. We could be spotted by . . ."

"By whom?" demanded Jefferson. "The enemy? They already know that we're around. And we're as likely to get ambushed at night as we are in the daylight. We're much too strong to be ambushed easily."

Torrence got to her feet and brushed off her uniform. "I'll get the people ready to move out."

The trip back to the friendly city was without incident. The advance party moved in slowly, cautiously, until contact with the garrison left behind was made. Then, finding everything just as it should have been, the whole battalion entered the city. Jefferson apologized to the men and women who had been left and then asked if they minded one more night of duty. He wanted to give the attack force a whole night of sleep.

As they entered the radio room, the NCO on watch there said, "Glad you made it back, sir. Division has been calling every ten minutes and wants you to talk to them immediately."

Jefferson sat down, pulled out his canteen and took a deep, long drink. He wiped at his face and then poured the remainder of the water over his head. Sighing quietly, he said, "Let's get the show on the road. Get Division on the blower."

As he expected, the response from the fleet was anything but congratulatory. He was surprised that the radio didn't melt. He answered with one-word sentences. He was finally told that a shuttle would be landing in ten minutes to pick him up. He was told that Torrence would accompany him. Jefferson pointed out

hat it wasn't smart to have both the CO and the exec away
from the battalion at once, but was told that orders were orders.

On the ship, they were taken to the general's conference room
and left alone. Jefferson was slightly nervous, feeling that his
military career had just ended. He had figured that a big victory
would cover a multitude of sins. Now he was sure that he was
about to be relieved and that Torrence was going to be given
command as she had suggested she should have been what
seemed like years earlier.

There was a pitcher of water and several glasses sitting in the
middle of the table. Jefferson poured himself a glass and said,
"Here's to you, Vicky. I think you're about to become a
battalion commander."

"What are you talking about?" she asked.

"Oh, hell, Vicky. Will you sit down?"

"I don't want to get anything dirty." She gestured at her
sweat-stained and grime-covered uniform.

"Don't worry about it." He took another drink of the water.
"I think, after the last interview that I had here, they're going
to stomp me. I shouldn't have gone into the city."

Before Torrence could reply, the door flew open and
Prescott, along with a number of other staff officers entered the
room. Prescott put his hand out and said, "Well done, Major.
Well done."

Jefferson got to his feet, bewildered, and put out his hand.
Prescott shook it. He said, "I don't know how you did it,
Major, but you did the one thing that would end this war."
When there was no immediate reaction, he said, "Didn't you
hear me? I said you have effectively ended the war."

Jefferson glanced at Torrence. Her face had gone white and
she had fallen into one of the chairs. Her mouth worked but she
said nothing.

"Over? The war is over?" asked Jefferson.

Prescott waved his staff into the various chairs and said,
"Maybe I should give you a little more detail. It seems that
your raid on the alien base has removed their war-making
capability. Too many of his supplies were destroyed, not to
mention the blow to his morale. Most of the troops fled into the
jungle rather than fight. I understand that the alien capital has
asked to end the hostilities."

"But I . . ." started Jefferson.

"Please, Major, listen. The formal meeting will take place in the next few days. Your battalion is going to be recalled. A caretaker force will be deployed. A few units will go down to finish training the adnoly. Those who want will be integrated into our force, sort of as a ranger outfit or scout outfit. Something like that. But your role is ended."

A thousand questions flashed through Jefferson's mind. There was so many things that he didn't understand about the war, or the things he had seen. He wanted some of them cleared up, but Prescott was on his feet again and moving toward the door.

"Listen, Major, you'll find that your quarters are as you left them. I might suggest that you shuttle over, grab a shower and some clean clothes, and be ready for a party at nineteen hundred tonight. Your battalion is turning its position over to members of the 502nd. They'll all be up here in a few hours."

"Colonel, I would like to know . . ."

Prescott held up a hand. "Why not worry about all that during the debriefing? Today and tonight, just worry about the celebration."

"But my battalion," said Jefferson. "I have people scattered all over."

"Well, according to our records, that's not exactly true," said Prescott. "All the living are in the adnoly city. The shuttle flights rotating the 502nd in have already been scheduled. The graves registration team is working with the enemy capital to recover the dead. So, you see, everything has been taken care of."

With that, Prescott and his staff swept out of the room leaving only a second lieutenant standing near the door. She asked, "Would you like for me to arrange shuttle?"

Jefferson glanced at Torrence and then quietly said, "Yes, please."

As they left the shuttle-docking area in their own ship, Jefferson said, "You going back to your quarters?"

"Well, I did sort of want to clean up. I mean . . ." She stopped, not knowing exactly what she was supposed to say. She knew what she wanted to say, or what she wanted to hear, but she didn't want to put anything into words.

"I have a shower in my room," said Jefferson.

"But I don't have clean clothes in your room," she said.

Jefferson just said, "Oh," and let it drop.

He left her at the corner where the corridor split. He watched her go to her door and then turned so that he could go to his own quarters. He opened the hatch and found that someone had straightened it during his absence. A clean uniform was laid out. Jefferson sat in the chair and pulled off his boots and then his socks. He walked into the tiny bathroom and started the shower, letting it warm, not worrying about the water conservation regulations. He figured that for once he could splurge and no one would say anything.

He stripped the rest of his uniform and dropped it, and his underwear, in the corner. He climbed into the shower and turned his face up so that water would hit him about the level of his hairline and wash down over his body. For a long time, he just stood there, letting it happen, not worrying about all the things that weren't right. He just didn't care that he had been lied to and deceived. He didn't care that the war below him was over. He kept his mind blank, thinking only of the warm water washing over him, loosening the kinks. Nothing mattered.

He jumped when he felt another pair of hands touch him and then he relaxed. He glanced over his shoulder and saw that Torrence had joined him. Momentarily he thought of the young lieutenant who had tried to wash him in the club. Suddenly he understood why he had sent her away. He had wanted to share the experience with Torrence and not with someone he didn't really know. He smiled at her.

"Thought you didn't have any clean clothes here."

"I do now."

"You realize you have just effectively destroyed our working relationship, don't you?"

She took a step back. "It may not be too late to save it."

"I don't believe that was what I had in mind. I just wanted you to know that I don't know how this will affect us. I mean in our working relationship. I think I know what it's going to do to our personal one."

"Don't worry about it now. You spend too much time worrying about how things might be. Just let them happen."

"There is one thing that I am worried about. We're going to

get some leave time now and I don't want to spend it alone. Would you like to spend it with me?"

"Of course," she said, laughing. "But you see, you're worrying about things before it's time to worry about them."

Jefferson turned and pressed himself to her. "Okay, you win."

Later, before they managed to get dressed, Jefferson said, "I hate to bring this up, but I still don't understand what happened."

Torrence smiled and rolled over so that she could look at him. "Well, you sort of asked me to come over here, so I did, but you refused to answer the door. Then you were dirty, so I had to wash you. And I was . . ."

"Okay," he laughed. "Sorry. I was going to say that the defeat of the enemy wasn't that disastrous, but forget it. I don't know why I brought it up."

"I make it a policy never to look a gift horse in the mouth. Division is happy with us. We're off that planet a lot sooner than I thought we would be. And we're both still alive. Let's just take it. For whatever it's worth. Why worry about it?"

"I don't like being manipulated. And we have been. That I do know."

"Manipulated? Hell, you've been manipulated since you got into the army. Everyone manipulates everyone else. The corporals manipulate the privates, the sergeants manipulate the corporals, and so on, right up the chain of command."

"That's not what I mean and you know it." He got up then and walked over to where he had put his clean uniform. He saw that Torrence had brought a uniform with her. "Don't you have any civilian clothes?"

"No." She got up and walked naked toward him.

"Won't do you any good," he said. "I'm still not satisfied. . . ."

"That's what I was hoping you would say," she cooed.

"I mean, with the explanation for the ending of the war. I have some questions that I want answered."

She turned and sat on the bed. "You know, sometimes you're not real smart."

"I'm sorry, Vicky." He touched her breast, massaging it. "You know what I mean."

"Yes, I do. But let it go. It'll do no good to try to figure it
out. They let you get away with everything you wanted to do.
They let you win the war. Even after they told you not to, they
let you win. If you keep asking questions, you'll just hurt
yourself."

Jefferson said, "You're right. You're absolutely right." He
kissed her, figuring that Tyson would have a couple of
answers. But he wouldn't need them until later.

15

ON THE SHIPS OF THE FLEET

THE PARTY WAS already in full swing. The majority of the battalion was there, dancing and drinking, all with the approval of the Division commander. Most of them had no idea why they had been recalled to the fleet and most of them didn't care. Their part in the war had ended.

In a large room away from the party, Jefferson sat with his senior staff officers. They had been told to be there and to wait for a representative of the commanding general. There had been a couple cold beers supplied for them. In a silver ice bucket was a solitary bottle of wine.

Tyson entered after the rest of them. He said, "I've talked to the operations officer. He'll be here in a couple of minutes to debrief us."

"But we don't go back to the planet's surface?" interrupted Norris. She had been told that a dozen times by everyone present, but refused to believe it.

"That's the one thing he assured me," said Tyson. "The only thing he assured me. We are not going back down."

To Tyson, Jefferson said, "I still say that the defeat wasn't that disastrous."

"You still don't get it, do you?" said Tyson. "After all the things you have said and done and all you've seen, you still don't get it. Listen to me carefully. There was no enemy. There never was."

Nearly everyone began talking at once. Some of them shouting questions, while the others were denying that there wasn't any enemy. They had lost friends. They had seen combat. Someone had been throwing lead in their direction. Now Tyson was telling them that it was all for nothing.

He waited until the shouting stopped and said, "Maybe I should say that we are the enemy. Or, to coin a phrase. We have met the enemy and he is us."

"Tyson! Quit talking in riddles!" ordered Jefferson.

There was another round of shouting that only stopped when the door opened and Colonel Prescott entered.

Before he could sit down, Rider shouted at him, "Is it true? Was there no enemy?"

"Just what the hell was going on down there?" demanded Torrence, forgetting what she had told Jefferson only a couple of hours earlier.

"We want some answers, Colonel," said Jefferson.

"Ladies and gentlemen," said Prescott, holding up his hands to ask for silence, "I don't know what you've been told, but I've come here to announce the good news. Tomorrow, at an official ceremony, the commanding general is going to distribute many awards and decorations and hand out some well-deserved promotions. Major Jefferson, your leadership cut through to the real point of the problem. You managed to knock out the shuttle landing site of the enemy and destroy so much of their war material that they have sued for peace. Well done, Colonel Jefferson. That is full Colonel. Not lieutenant colonel."

There was a moment of stunned silence and then a wild burst of cheering. Forgotten for the moment were the things that Tyson had said. Forgotten were all the things that had bothered him. Jefferson wanted to say that it wasn't only him. That a lot of the others had participated in the raid, in the planning, had actually been responsible for conceiving the raid.

Prescott knew what he was doing. He waited for the noise to die and then added, "Major Torrence will take over command of the battalion. Major Tyson will be moved to head the whole of the cultural anthropological unit that will study life on Procyon Two.

"Everyone else in this room will be promoted one grade. The captains are now majors, the lieutenants are captains. The Seven sixty-seventh will be integrated into the new Tenth Interplanetary Infantry which is now commanded by Colonel Jefferson. Major Torrence will assume command of the battalion. Orders will be posted tomorrow morning at zero seven hundred hours."

Now there was quiet in the room. Prescott stepped back, to the door and opened it. A dozen privates in dress uniforms paraded through carrying food and drink. Three of them carried a pile of medals and citations. As Prescott waved them deeper into the room, the video journalist Jason Garvey followed, the camera held up to his eyes so that he could film everything.

"Official presentation will be tomorrow at thirteen hundred hours. These are the preliminaries so that everyone will see what we think of the job that was done. It's incredible. You did the one thing that would stabilize the situation enough that we could pull out the combat troops and send in small teams of technicians and advisors. By the time the enemy is able to mount any kind of operation, the aliens we came to help will be in a position to fight their own battles." He had taken to calling the other side the enemy even though he had told Jefferson in no uncertain words that there were no enemy aliens. Only those the fleet chose not to help.

Prescott stopped talking and smiled at all of them. "Please eat and drink. Tomorrow we'll officially reward you and the day after a several-ship fleet will leave carrying all of you back to Earth for a well-deserved rest and vacation.

"Now, are there any questions?"

No one spoke. Torrence reached out, touched the pile of medals and citations as if to see if they were actually there and then asked, "Is this for real?"

"That's right, Major. All real. Oh, congratulations on your promotion. Congratulations to all of you. Now, I know that the last thing you want is for me to hang around here and spoil your fun." Prescott laughed, as if the celebration was somehow contagious. "Don't get too drunk. You do have a couple of military functions tomorrow."

Prescott waited for just a second and then left. At the door he shot a glance over his shoulder and saw that Rider was pouring himself a beer. Norris had grabbed a sandwich and Torrence was checking the citations.

The discussion they had been having vanished. No one, other than Jefferson and Tyson even thought about it. They were too busy with the things that Prescott had brought to them. Both Jefferson and Tyson stood off to one side, watching. Finally, they noticed one another and gravitated towards each other.

Over the shouting, and the music that was now being piped into the room, Tyson said, "You don't buy this anymore than I do."

Jefferson shook his head. "Let's step out for a moment."

They slipped through the door and into the hallway. Jefferson was afraid that there would be some kind of monitoring devices nearby and suggested they walk. He knew that the whole ship wouldn't be monitored all the time and with luck, they could have their discussion with no one ever seeing or hearing it.

As they walked away, Jefferson said, "What in the hell is going on?"

"I think we've just been bribed."

"Obviously and effectively, I would say," agreed Jefferson. "Do you have any idea of why?"

"Yeah, I think, given everything that we've uncovered in the last few weeks, that I understand it completely. Depending on your point of view, it might be said that everything we've just gone through was for nothing, or it could be called a brilliant masterstroke that worked with only a few lives lost."

"You know, Tyson, I think the thing I like least about you is your ability to talk in riddles." Then Jefferson, caught up in the mood of the moment laughed and said, "Well, there may be other things, but that will do for now. I will say that you're very good at what you do."

"I could say similar things about you, but I won't."

"Okay, then we have a truce. Now, would you like to clarify your riddle?"

Tyson opened a hatch and found an empty office. He entered without turning on the lights. He merely left the hatch open.

"I think," he said, "that any monitoring devices that might be in here will not be functioning with the lights off. To monitor every cabin where there are no lights would be impossible. We can talk in private."

"Fine," said Jefferson sitting in one of the large plastic chairs. He put his feet up on a desk and leaned back. "Now, what the hell is going on?"

"Simple. We've been had. We were used to gain the trust of the adnoly, show them the technology that we have, teach them to use some of it—not just the weapons, but also things like electricity—to become dependent on it, and then leave."

"What?"

"Look, I found a report that talked about the level of technology on this planet. Some of the things we saw in the adnoly city were not developed by the culture that used them. That was why the electrical power was so spotty. That was why only the central castle had electricity. It was a recent arrival. As were firearms, and then lasers, and the primitive body armor. In other words, everything was a gift from us. Their society, their culture can not, will not, support the technology. They are now completely dependent on us for it."

"So what?"

"Don't you get? We own this planet. We engineered the conflict; we supplied one side and then the other, until neither could conduct the war without our aid. We escalated the technology to a level that they didn't understand, but we taught them that the other side would not hesitate to use the new technology. To keep up, they must purchase that technology from us."

Jefferson dropped his feet to the floor and stared at the dim shape of Tyson who was leaning against the desk in the office. Jefferson suddenly understood. The war wasn't being fought to train the adnoly in the art of small-unit tactics, but to teach them how superior the Earth weapons were. Hell, not just the weapons, but the whole Earth technology. If they wanted the Earth weapons, the Earth technology, they would have to buy them from the Earth. And the adnoly didn't have the industry to support repairing and replacing the weapons. Earth would have to do that. To let that technology slip would give the other side the advantage.

"Yes," said Jefferson tiredly, "I do see. We could have accomplished the mission by just sitting back and letting the Division decide that we needed lasers. By supplying the other side first, they forced us into it. And had me up here demanding the use of them."

"Oh, it's all been carefully orchestrated. From the very beginning. Now that we've seen enough here to figure out what has happened, we're all given promotions and medals and a trip to Earth where we can't infect the rest of the Division." He grinned. "I'll wager that your new regiment will be formed and operate independently of the Division."

"You're assuming that no one else has figured it out. We do have some information that isn't readily available to the troops. And Vicky is advocating that we forget it. Be happy that we escaped with our lives. Be happy that we came out of it smelling like a rose."

"She does have a point," said Tyson. "They really had two options here. They could treat everyone like heros, give them medals and promotions, or they could court-martial them."

Jefferson laughed. "From what I've seen lately, I would have thought they would have chosen the court-martial option."

"Oh no," said Tyson. "You court-martial people and you make them mad. They talk to the media. Jason Garvey would love a court-martial. Good video. That could cause the people to demand Congressional investigations. But you give them promotions and medals and they don't make waves. They go home and tell everyone about the glory they found. Garvey files a few uninteresting stories. Actually, it's another very smart move on their part."

"So we tell the story there anyway. Throw the promotions and medals back at them."

"For what reason? This is good for the Earth. We get the raw materials we need. We keep the industries expanding, there is full employment and prosperity. Who's going to listen to a bunch of unhappy soldiers? Not to mention the fact that very few of us have any real knowledge of what happened, or that we have no proof to back it up."

"Okay, smart guy. What do we do?"

"Ideally, we go to Earth and blow the whistle. Humanity rises up and ends the injustice and we become heroes of the world. Realistically? We keep our mouths shut because no one would believe us, reap the fruits of our labors, and try not to get caught in anything like this again."

Jefferson sat in silence, then got to his feet and moved to the hatch where he could see up and down the corridor. No one was in sight. He turned back to Tyson and said finally, "Then let's go party. We have a victory to celebrate."

THE FINEST THE UNIVERSE HAS TO OFFER

__THE OMEGA CAGE Steve Perry and Michael Reaves
0-441-62382-4/$3.50
The Omega Cage—a hi-tech prison for the special enemies of the brutal Confed. No one had ever escaped, but Dain Maro is about to attempt the impossible.

__THE WARLOCK'S COMPANION Christopher Stasheff
0-441-87341-3/$3.95
Fess, the beloved cyborg steed of Rod Gallowglass, has a host of revealing stories he's never shared. Now the Gallowglass children are about to hear the truth...from the horse's mouth.

__THE STAINLESS STEEL RAT Harry Harrison
0-441-77924-7/$3.50
The Stainless Steel Rat was the slickest criminal in the Universe until the police finally caught up with him. Then there was only one thing they could do—they made him a cop.

__DREAM PARK Larry Niven and Steven Barnes
0-441-16730-6/$4.95
Dream Park—the ultimate fantasy world where absolutely everything you ever dreamed of is real—including murder.